McMansion

Books by Justin Scott

Mysteries
Many Happy Returns
Treasure for Treasure
The Widow of Desire
StoneDust
HardScape
FrostLine
McMansion
Mausoleum

Thrillers
The Shipkiller
The Turning
Normandie Triangle
A Pride of Royals
Rampage
The Nine Dragons
The Empty Eye of the Sea (Published in England)
The Auction (Published in England)
Treasure Island: A Modern Novel

As J.S. Blazer
Deal Me Out
Lend a Hand

As Paul Garrison
Fire and Ice
Red Sky at Morning
Buried at Sea
Sea Hunter
The Ripple Effect

McMansion

Justin Scott

Poisoned Pen Press

Poisoned Pen Press
6962 E. First Ave., Ste. 103
Scottsdale, AZ 85251
www.poisonedpenpress.com
info@poisonedpenpress.com

Printed in the United States of America

For Amber Edwards
to celebrate
ten years

Chapter One

Newbury, Connecticut's greediest developer had seen the bull-dozer in time to run.

Billy Tiller had had a moment to hope, too.

His footprints zigzagged, crossed twice by the machine track. His five last steps between the treads stopped at a deep gouge left by the ripper, the rock-tearing steel fang in the back of the machine. It looked to me as if he had somehow slipped behind the blade and thrown himself flat, hugging the mud between the treads as the machine passed over him. Home free, until the murderer impaled him with the ripper.

The tracks the bulldozer had gnawed up the slope were dry. No rain had fallen since the Sunday afternoon he died, and the wind had blown. The ground was rock hard. I probably could have climbed the tread marks without breaking the ribbed crust. But the evidence in this case included the ground; so even though I was the last on the scene, by a long shot, I kept to the side, working my way among clods of earth, stones, and crushed tree branches as I traced the intersecting routes of the hunter and the hunted.

The bulldozer itself was gone, hoisted off the man's body by a powerful crane (which had left its own distinctive tire tracks and outrigger prints) and impounded at the Plainfield barracks. The troopers had escorted it down Main Street, chained to a flatbed like a rogue elephant. The cops were gone, too—both

Newbury's resident state trooper and the Major Case Squad up from Plainfield. The reporters were gone: the network TV crew from Hartford; the cable crew from Bridgeport; the Danbury and Waterbury newspapers. Someone had even retrieved the yellow tape cordoning off the crime scene.

I didn't want to be here, either. I would much rather be showing a colonial to a client hunting for an "antique" house with bee hive ovens, or lunching on Caesar salad and a chilled Gascogne white with my cutie, if I had one. But when I wasn't selling houses I worked as a private investigator, and Northwest Connecticut's number one criminal defense attorney had asked me to check things out.

It looked like a waste of my modest talents. His client had been arrested while sitting on the bulldozer—it was still on top of Billy Tiller's remains—while wearing a backpack filled with cans of spray paint and posters reading, "Power to the People. Long Live The Earth Liberation Front."

Nonetheless, "a job worth doing," in the words of my father, Bertram Abbott, Newbury's revered First Selectman, long in his grave, and my great-aunt Connie Abbott, still lively, "was worth doing right." So I took a bunch of photographs with my cell phone and sketched a diagram. Then I secured the tab of a measuring tape to the ground with an ice pick, walked to a towering white oak to the right, wrote the distance in my note book, reeled in the tape and walked to a wall of ledge to the left and recorded that distance and did a third measurement to a massive hemlock unlikely to be cut down anytime soon.

I could have pinpointed the death spot with the cell's handy little Global Positioning System. Some real estate agents employ GPS to dazzle the clients, but I've always courted the discerning sort of home buyers who expect their broker to locate a property without the help of a satellite. Besides, had I zipped coordinates out of the phone instead of walking the ground I might have missed the fact that Billy's right boot had dug ever so slightly deeper than the left.

He had limped, slightly, for the last year of his life. Maybe it had slowed him down enough to lose the race. That and his big belly. Except that in high school he had been a running back. And even carrying sixty extra pounds Billy had still been a youngish, big, fast man whom I would have thought capable of dodging a machine built more for destruction than speed.

It was time for a bulldozer tutorial. I tried to phone one of my across-the-tracks Chevalley cousins. But no signal reached down in this hollow. I climbed up the back of the property and over a stone wall that marked the boundary of a former wood lot. A deer trail offered a way through the thick growth and I followed it, trusting that the animals had chosen the easiest climb. I continued uphill checking the phone repeatedly. I was nearly at the crest, seeing sky through the treetops and running out of breath, before it rang.

"What?" answered Sherman Chevalley. If anyone knew bulldozers it was cousin Sherman, who was famous in Newbury for having built one himself out of parts he'd found in his barn. And others borrowed from the Department of Transportation garage. Paving the road to Somers Correctional, from which he had recently won early parole.

"It's Ben!"

The signal was fuzzy and Sherman kept shouting, "Who?"

I kept climbing, repeating, "Ben Abbott."

I'm the only child of a mixed marriage, the Abbotts of Main Street and the Chevalleys from the cold, wet north slopes of Frenchtown, which had been the wrong side of the tracks long before the invention of the locomotive. Which makes me welcome in some surprising places, though suspect everywhere.

"Whadaya want?"

"How fast could Billy's D4 go?"

"That son of a bitch owed me nine hundred dollars."

"For what?"

"I drove a front loader for him. Right before I went away? He said he'd pay me when I got out." Sherman erupted in a hoarse laugh that sounded like he was grating Parmesan with his tele-phone. "Man was Billy surprised when I got out so soon."

He wasn't the only one. Whether the warden had been moved by a character reference from Sherman's mother stating, "Sherman isn't a bad person, he just does bad things," or state-budget-crisis layoffs of prison guards, was a topic debated hotly by the bikers who hung out at the White Birch, particularly those on good terms with their mothers.

"Now I get out and the son of a bitch gets killed."

"Tell you the truth, Sherman, I'd rather have your problem than Billy's. I was hoping you could tell me how fast a D4 goes."

Growing old alone, like most Chevalley men, Sherman spent many a night with a six-pack and the History Channel. Before I could stop him, he explained that the bulldozer was invented in the 1920s when some farmers affixed bulldozer blades to their crawler tractors, gas or kerosene powered vehicles that rode on endless chain treads turning on cogged wheels. The farmers had named the entire contraption for the blade, which used to be pushed by mules, Sherman told me. The Caterpillar Corporation that built the D4 called it a track-type tractor.

"Billy's bulldozer, " I prompted. I reached the crest where I could see through the trees down the other side of the hill to a gleam of water far below and tried to catch my breath while Sherman informed me that Billy's D4 Caterpillar was nine feet high at the cab and weighed 17,000 pounds. I told him that I already believed that Billy's last sight on earth had been eight and a half tons of gut-wrenching terror.

He told me that its blade was three feet high and eight feet wide. Wider than the grossest SUV, I noted. Not much, coun-tered Sherman, warming to another area of interest. A "real" civilian Hummer—"not talking any candy-ass H3"—was a full seven feet, two and a half inches wide.

There was no point in yelling at a Chevalley. About the only non-assault way of getting their attention was to keep repeating yourself as you would address a cat weighing the pleasures of in versus out. "How fast can a D4 go?"

"Five-six miles an hour forward."

"That's all? …How about reverse?"

"A hair quicker backing up."

A runner has to do fifteen miles per hour to sprint a four-minute mile. Of course a miler doesn't limp uphill in the mud. I said, "It looks to me like Billy got behind the blade. Could he go over the top, or under?"

"Under," Sherman said. "There isn't enough clearance between the blade and the tractor for a man his size to go over the top. I figure the guy driving lifted the blade pretty high up to crack his skull—I would of—and Billy must of thought real quick and threw himself under the cutting edge."

"The guy was pretty damned quick with the ripper."

"Quicker than Billy."

We said goodbye. I stood there thinking a while and gazing down at the valley.

I recognized the gleam of water. It was a shallow lake that used to be Fred Franklin's best hayfield. Billy Tiller had flooded it by diverting streams from a development for which the Conservation Department had wisely denied permits, until Billy got a court order from a friendly judge down in Stamford who wouldn't have recognized a natural watercourse if it gushed through his chambers.

I climbed back down to the house site. An ochre smear in a foot-deep hollow was all that remained of whatever the medical examiner had scooped off to the morgue. After the bulldozer had caught up with Billy and impaled him with the ripper, the murderer had stood on one pedal and engaged the opposite track to rotate the machine in place like a gigantic disk sander.

"Murder is not a pretty thing," wrote our New England painter Marsden Hartley. He had lost a loved one to the sea, but his bold reds would have served this death site forty miles inland just as well. Had the murderer reduced Billy's body to ground meat in a brutal rage? Or for twisted pleasure? Or to hide evidence that might be discovered on an intact corpse? Or had he simply panicked at the controls?

I walked down to the foot of the driveway. The newly cut road that linked the subdivision to County Road 349 was a long, gloomy alley of skinny second-growth trees that had grown up in the shade. Stripped suddenly naked by the clearing, they had no lower branches.

When the road was finally paved and the lots built out, it would slink between two rows of five-bedroom behemoths known as McMansions. They would all look alike, despite mirrored floor plans and randomly scattered carbuncles of stone veneer. Each would boast a two-story entry. In the upper level of each entry would yawn a Palladian window. And in each of these triumphal arches a chandelier would glitter. If I were selling the monstrosities, I would list them as "In a neighborhood of comparable homes."

On this warm, dry afternoon in late spring, all to be seen of the future neighborhood, other than a nearly completed model, was hardened mud, raw foundations, chipboard stapled to studs, a couple of pre-fabricated, pre-painted two-story entryways poking dull factory colors at the sky, and several parcels of yet-to-be-uprooted forest where the only hint of the destruction to come was a lot number tacked to a tree.

Billy had named the subdivision "Newbury Common" and promptly slapped a Private sign on it, an abuse of the language I found hard to forgive. His advertisements in the weekly *Clarion's* real estate section promised, "Classical Colonial Custom Architecture With European Accents, Marble Baths and Gourmet Granite." Factoring in free public school, they were a lot of house for the money—compared to closer-to-New York, Fairfield, or Westchester County—if Dad was willing to spend three or four hours a day driving to work on ever more crowded roads and Mom didn't mind staring out the windows at an empty cul-de-sac.

To my traditional buy-to-the-horizon Yankee eye, the remote lot up a long driveway where Billy had been killed was the premier site because it was farthest from the others. The homeowners would not have to gaze upon other ugly houses and could actually make love in their front yard without disrupting their neighbor's cookouts. Such seclusion was not the norm in Billy Tiller's developments, where roofs gabled as jaggedly as Patagonian toothfish and two-story marble foyers hailed the street like neon dollar signs.

Total Landscape, Billy's site-prep company, had leveled the two-acre house site to its perimeter. In most cases, unwary buyers might mis-imagine they were buying a house in the woods with a two-acre lawn, only to discover when the bulldozers came back shortly after they moved in that Billy intended to clear two-acre lawns on either side of theirs and erect large buildings that looked suspiciously similar to their exclusive custom-colonial creation. But the land surrounding Billy's death plot was so steep that Planning and Zoning had ruled it off limits.

Billy had sued, ordering his civil engineer/mouthpiece E. Eddie Edwards into Superior Court to convince the judge that what looked very much like a cliff was not really that steep and therefore town regulations had violated Billy's constitutional right to build anything he wanted to anywhere. When the town prevailed, at considerable cost, Billy erected a sign claiming that he had donated the unbuild-able acreage to the Newbury Forest Association as a nature preserve.

Total Landscape had shoved a huge heap of brush, stumps, boulders, and broken trees into the donation. Logging the bigger trees, they had stacked them in twelve-foot lengths near the road. Billy had taken refuge there, temporarily, until the bulldozer had scattered the tree trunks like pickup sticks, and it didn't take a lot of imagination to picture what the man had experienced dodging twelve-foot logs when the machine crashed into the pile. In fact, it was a miracle that he had escaped that alive.

I took a picture of the scattered log pile and had a closer look at the roadbed. The earth had been pounded to dust by lumber trucks, ready-mix trucks, Billy's fleet of dump trucks, and workmen's vehicles. The troopers had impounded his personal truck, a big red diesel pickup, along with the bulldozer, so I could not tell where the machine started chasing him.

If the cops had found any sign of the murderer's vehicle—tire tracks, footprints, eyewitnesses—they weren't talking. Eye witnesses weren't likely. Nobody had worked on the site that rainy Sunday. Nor had the cold and wet weather been the sort to entice strollers to brave a muddy rutted road to admire the wreckage of a wooded hillside. In fact the only reason Oliver Moody, our resident state trooper, found the remains as soon as he did was that an annoyed neighbor across the hill had complained that the bulldozer was working on a Sunday again, even though Billy had repeatedly promised the Planning and Zoning and Building departments that he would not.

The tire tracks rutting the road had been laid down by many deliveries in and dump runs out. And, I suspected, numerous loads of stolen topsoil. It's illegal to strip mine house sites of their topsoil, but builders like Billy Tiller always managed to steal a few hundred yards before some alert citizen called the building inspector.

The many footprints would belong to truck drivers hopping down to roll back a tarp or take a leak, to machine operators, carpenters, immigrant day laborers hired to stack rock, and the building inspector stopping by to cite violations. I though it unlikely that the troopers had plaster castings of a single set of prints guaranteed to send the foolish rich kid they had arrested for the crime away for the rest of his life. Not that they needed them.

When Trooper Moody found him on the machine it was still running and had his fingerprints, in wet paint, on the controls. He had claimed that he panicked when he saw an arm sticking out from under the bulldozer and had tried to move the machine to help the victim.

Trooper Moody had not believed him.

Nor had Connecticut's chief state's attorney, an ambitious fellow who had good reason to hope that a high-profile TV trial would vault the victorious defender of public safety to the head of the pack running for the United States Senate.

Chapter Two

I wasn't the only one who disliked Billy's Newbury Common sign.

Some vandal had spray painted *ELF* on it in big letters. ELF stood for Earth Liberation Front, a secretive, amorphous radical movement that protested the waste and abuse of resources in general—and SUVs and sprawling McMansions in particular—by defacing SUVs and setting fires at McMansion construction sites.

In the same spray hand, *ELF* had been painted on the model house. Someone had also tried to burn it down. But the arsonist had misjudged the force of the weekend rain. The fire had not amounted to much, just some scorch marks, which I duly photographed. Continuing past the model to photograph the sign, I had a sudden, strong feeling I was no longer alone at the construction site.

My so-called sixth sense means one or two of the self-evident five are working overtime. Whether I had heard or seen or smelled something, I knew the direction to look to glimpse motion just inside the tree line behind the model house. I walked quickly toward it, trying to probe the shadows. I thought I saw another flicker. There was a crash of dry leaves and broken branches in the underbrush and I darted forward, running as fast as I could over a hundred yards of bulldozed ground.

When I reached the woods, three deer bounded up the slope, their white tails flashing until they vanished in the tree trunks. I stopped and listened hard. But whatever had crashed through the leaves did not do it again. Another ELF? Or a bear? No deer I'd ever met made that much noise.

I debated searching the woods. But an Earth Liberation radical would have a head start, and I was already winded from my broken field run, while a two-hundred-and-fifty-pound black bear in June would be protecting her cubs. So I retreated back to the road and walked down to Billy's Newbury Common sign. I took a picture of it and the "Private" addendum, about which I and numerous other irritable literalists had already written peevish letters to the *Clarion*, reminding Newburians that the "common" was a custom of sharing land that the colonists brought over from England three hundred and eighty years ago, in which a pasture was used and maintained by all. Newbury, like most Connecticut towns, has one. Ours is called the Ram Pasture and represented an early version of "trickle down" economics in which folk of modest means could hope that when they grazed their sheep a rich man's ram cruising the common would leave in his wake a flock of lambs.

Billy knew perfectly well that a common was supposed to be public. He claimed deep New England roots at Planning and Zoning hearings, boasting that Tillers had settled in Newbury two hundred years ago. Therefore, he argued, no one had a right to limit how many houses he could build on his land. In truth, when Billy's ancestors did finally straggle into town from God knows where, Newbury's original settlers had long since planted crops, dammed the river, erected a sawmill and rousted out the French, the Indians, and the British Army.

But while I could not forgive the abuse of our language, I would not have defaced his sign, nor tried to burn his ugly model. I certainly wouldn't have killed him for it. Or even shot him in the leg. Which someone had done a year before the bulldozer got him.

I had witnessed that assault up close—smack in the middle of town—on our historic Main Street, which is lined with marvelous eighteenth and nineteenth century Colonial, Federal, and Greek Revival houses set far back from the road. I happened to be standing about four feet away from Billy explaining, diplomatically I thought, that in an overdue attempt to improve my character I had taken a vow never to sell ugly oversized houses of the sort he built. Granted I had had a Bloody Mary at lunch. Or two. Late breakfast actually, it being Monday, a slow day in my business because Monday is Newbury's day for my competitors to host open house tours of new construction and the weekenders have gone home.

Billy had taken my remarks personally and got all red in the face, and I had thought, Well now I've provoked a very large angry man. I was trying to figure out where to poke him forcefully enough to make him reconsider his options, if I had to, when suddenly out of nowhere bullets started flying.

It was the first gunfire on Main Street since a mail coach driver urging his team Boston-ward with letters for Abigail from President Adams got into a dispute with an ancestor of mine who had come up with the lucrative idea of blocking the road with a toll gate. (A full century and a half before the Bloody Mary was invented.) As muzzle loaders are no longer the weapon of choice, a lot more bullets were flying this time.

Several scattered the windows in Billy's red pickup like rock candy. One parted the hair of a grandmother who happened to be walking her grandchildren to the General Store for ice cream and smacked into one of Town Hall's marble columns. Another ricocheted off the flagpole, the tallest in the state, and ended up embedded in the sturdy front door of a three-hundred-year-old saltbox. Another pierced my Benjamin Abbott Real Estate sign and one of the panes of glass my father had installed to convert our front sun porch into his and now my office. The last caught Billy in the leg, toppling him onto the broad tree lawn that separates the sidewalk from the street.

By long-standing agreement in our very wealthy state, Connecticut drive-by shootings are supposed to be confined to the city limits of downtrodden urban areas, so the State Police Major Crime Unit was soon breathing down Trooper Moody's thick neck. Everyone in Newbury assumed that Billy had ripped off or pissed off someone sufficiently to shoot him in the leg. But the crime squad didn't get any closer to finding that shooter than Ollie had, and they were still investigating a year later when the bulldozer eliminated their shooting victim.

I had heard a rumor in the White Birch that the shooter had actually telephoned Billy in the hospital to demand, indignantly, why Billy had called 911 from his cell phone while lying bleeding in the street, when they could have worked out their dispute in private. The motorcyclists loved that story and sided, to a man, with the caller. Billy told me, however, that it was total bull. He claimed that he didn't know who had shot him. Which I had thought was total bull, too, but none of my business.

The *Clarion* tried to report the shooting but ran out of steam in the second paragraph as neither Ollie nor the Crime Unit could add anything to the obvious and the only witnesses were people like me who recalled little beyond hugging the ground and praying. Undaunted by a paucity of facts, Scooter MacKay, the *Clarion*'s publisher, editor, photographer, and ace reporter, fleshed out his story with a laundry list of the crimes that the State of Connecticut was investigating Billy for, which pretty much ran the gamut of things that a greedy, unscrupulous developer can do wrong.

I responded with a cranky Letter to the Editor.

Scooter MacKay has a huge, thunderous voice. We've lived next door to each other since we were born, and when he got home from the newspaper office he leaned out his dining room window and boomed at me crawling around in my perennial border, "Do you really want me to publish this?"

"Yes." I could have added that it was easier to get a cranky letter to the editor published in Scooter's weekly than the *New York Times*, but we both knew that already.

"But you don't even like Billy."

"I dislike shoddy newspaper reporting even more than rapacious developers."

"Shoddy?" Scooter bellowed. "Who are you calling shoddy? You write letters complaining about McMansions, I print them. You write letters grumbling that new rich people are driving middle-class citizens out of town, I print them. You write grouching about gas guzzling SUVs, I print it. Did it ever occur to you to buy an ad?"

"You should pay me for filling all that space in your newspaper."

Scooter yelled that I would be better off if I took change in stride. "You're too young to be a curmudgeon. Stop mourning youth passing by. Turn your anger into something productive."

"Anyone with a half a brain should be angry," I bellowed back.

"Lighten up!" Scooter suggested in a voice that echoed to Frenchtown. "The first cave couple lived in the biggest cave they could afford. Soon as they had reason to hope they might nail a mastodon in the near future, they moved to a bigger cave. People like space. You don't live in a small house. Why should they?"

The noise attracted the neighbors, led by my Great Aunt Constance Abbott, who emerged briskly from her front gate and crossed Main Street with the aid of a silver-headed cane. Well into her nineties, Aunt Connie was not as tall as she had once been, while a lifetime of abstemious habits had left her with so little appetite that she had grown too thin. But she still had a crown of thick white hair and she stood Miss-Porter's-School straight as she listened, briefly, to both sides of the argument.

"Change," Connie pronounced, "is the only constant in our lives."

"Yes, but—" Scooter started to agree and I started to dispute.

Connie withered us both with a fiery blue-eyed glance. "Everything changes. For instance, believe it or not I can remember as if it were yesterday a much quieter time in Newbury, before

Main Street was paved, when next-door neighbors could conduct a civilized conversation without raising their voices."

Everyone went home and Scooter, who is an honest man, published my letter.

```
To the Editor,
     I'm trying to understand why, in your
recent article about the state police inves-
tigation of the gunning down of Billy Tiller,
the Clarion provides a list of Connecticut
state agencies currently investigating the
Newbury businessman. I don't understand what
state probes conducted from Hartford have to
do with the subject of Newburians getting
shot on Main Street.
     Or is the Clarion subtly speculating that
the shooters were actually a gang of frus-
trated investigators for the departments of
Revenue Services, Environmental Protection,
Consumer Protection, Motor Vehicles, and
Labor? Perhaps the Clarion's Hartford corre-
spondent spotted them piling into a car and
driving down to Newbury to rake the subject
of their inquiries with large caliber bul-
lets in the interest of saving taxpayers the
expense of a trial?
     Benjamin Abbott III
     Main Street
```

Not so enormous caliber, it turned out. Mere twenty-twos. And not even the hollowtips used for shooting woodchucks, though it did tear up enough muscle to leave Billy Tiller with a limp.

Was the murderer the same person who shot him last year and figured to use a bulldozer this time just to be on the safe side? If so, why had he waited a whole year to try again?

I took a final look around Newbury Common and snapped some more photos of a self-propelled construction hoist used for lifting plywood and drywall to second floors, and a backhoe beside a utility trench, and the pounded roadbed. I did not harbor CSI fantasies that I would unearth some startling piece of crime-scene evidence the state police investigators had overlooked. But I did want to get some idea of their case, intending to bow out on a helpful note.

Chapter Three

"I don't want to do this," I told the ELF kid's defense attorney, when we met that afternoon at his horse farm.

Ira Roth cast a contented eye on his green pastures, which were speckled with thoroughbreds and draped with white fences. The farm was so beautiful, so pristine—so kempt—that you just knew looking at it that a thriving law practice was helping the horses pay for it. Ira was a formidable country lawyer in his late sixties, wise, awesomely intelligent, arrogant, and quite intimidating. He had worked for, and against, my father before I was born.

"Why not, Ben?"

"Too personal. I didn't like Billy. I didn't like him at all. Billy Tiller represented everything I hate about the changes in Newbury. He represented greed and its byproducts, which we'll be paying for in our taxes for the rest of our lives."

"What's new? That was your father's rant back when he was First Selectman. 'They come, have their kids, drive the mill rate up and leave.'"

"Billy's kind of house represented waste of the worst—"

"No one's asking you to love the murder victim," Ira interrupted, again. "Just gather the facts we'll need to defend my client."

"Not liking him will cloud my judgment."

Ira cracked a smile intended to display his good-humored wit. "I'll deal with the judge. You get the facts."

"I mis-spoke, Ira. What I'm trying to say is that disliking Billy will diminish my focus. I don't want the job—Here you go. On the house." I extended an envelope filled with printouts of my photographs, my notes typed up, and a Xerox of my sketch of the death site. I was comfortable with the quality of work the envelope contained. And fairly comfortable with the fact that I had told him the truth, if not the whole truth about why I didn't want the job.

Ira opened the envelope, read my notes line by line the way lawyers do, then looked carefully through the photos, referring repeatedly to the diagram. Ira wasn't telling the whole truth either. He, too, had subtext. At sixty-eight Ira Roth was no less ambitious than he had been at twenty-eight. Rich and famous in our small town—and a titan in the county courthouse—he had always hungered to make it in the Big Apple. His motivation to get the kid off was the contacts in New York City an acquittal would gain him through the kid's powerful father.

"Where are your GPS coordinates?"

"X marks the spot. Between the white oak, the hemlock, and that ledge."

Ira sighed, "You're too young to be a Luddite." Then he said, "But you're forgetting one thing."

"What's that?"

"You owe me."

People say that all the time. Even if they don't say it, they think it. But in this case, Ira was right. I owed him for a horse.

"The deal," he reminded me, "was X number of hours of detective work in exchange for a champion racehorse. This—" He closed the envelope. "—is nowhere near the 'X' we agreed upon."

"And that 'champion racehorse' is nowhere near Sea Biscuit."

He was a big stallion named Redman who had actually won a few races, a decade ago, though not often enough to command a stud fee from any mare's owner who considered consistency an attribute worth breeding for. So Redman was spending his late middle age next door in Scooter's barn, eating.

Ira's smile went out like a vandalized street light. "I'm calling in my marker, Ben. When you needed a horse, I got you a horse. Now I need something in return. More field work. I need interviews with each and every one of the victim's enemies. People mad enough to kill him. I want those interviews conducted by a man with local knowledge, a man who knows everything going on in this town and everyone in it, a man whom people know and respond to—and trust, despite certain elements, shall we say, of your past. Worst case, we'll raise some doubt in the jurors' minds. Best case, we'll spook the State's Attorney into reducing the charges. Best-best case you'll provoke the guilty party into a confession."

I returned a look as dubious as that deserved.

Ira ignored it.

I asked, "Who's in his will? Who inherits?"

"I don't handle his affairs anymore. He switched it all to Total Landscape's attorney. Last I saw it went to his wife, but that was before the divorce."

"Maybe he left it all to a lap dancer married to a homicidal bulldozer operator."

"I'll see if I can find when they're going to read the will. But your job, first thing tomorrow, before the interviews, I need my client's father handled properly. 'Properly' includes convincing the high-powered, impatient gentleman that he has hired the best criminal attorney money can buy to defend his son."

I handed him another envelope.

"What's this?"

"Money for the horse."

He looked genuinely surprised. "Where'd you get it?"

"I'm doing fine."

Ira shrugged. "There's so much money around at the moment, I guess even an orangutan could earn a living selling real estate."

"I've seen several driving Lexuses."

He sighed happily. "I love boom-times money. Those who possess it think it's because they're deserving or intelligent—often both. I've got more work than I can handle defending clients who should have known better. And people are coming out here to buy horses at prices to rival Kobe beef." He nodded at his long, fence-lined driveway and sure enough, up it came a Cadillac Escalade towing a horse trailer. "That fool has no clue that he is towing an announcement that he will meet my price just to take the animal home with him this afternoon. Let these good times roll."

"Yet another reason I don't want this job. I've got tons of work down on the Gold Coast."

"Divorce work?" he asked, nose wrinkling.

"I don't do divorce."

"Why not?"

"I don't feel like videotaping couples who happen to like each other more than they like their spouses."

"The money's in divorce."

"Actually, there's better money in pre-divorce."

"What the hell is pre-divorce?"

"Checking out prospective spouses. Is the guy the 'international executive' he claims he is? Is her Mensa membership genuine? Is his S-Class Mercedes leased, borrowed, or stolen? Is her Jag a gift from Daddy or her lover? Is he still living with his mother?"

"Sounds you should take down your real estate sign."

"The sign's been there a long time, Ira. When the old locals sell, they want an Abbott to handle it."

Pursuing multiple livings was a old tradition in hardscrabble New England. Eighteenth- and nineteenth-century Abbotts had often farmed on the side, while selling or teaching or preaching. When a congregation rebelled or grew bored, there was always the plow. Scooter McKay's great-grandfather kept pigs after he founded the *Clarion*, secure in pork chops if an editorial offended advertisers. So does the second arrow in my quiver allow me the freedom to pick and choose the old-fashioned houses I prefer to sell and investigations I find compelling.

For that matter, Ira knew darned well that his own father had supported the pro bono side of his law practice by lending money and buying land. Although in the old man's case his lending often turned into giving, and he bequeathed most of his acreage to the Land Trust. Ira had not inherited the generosity gene. His attention shifted back to the horse trailer. He stood up and shoved my envelope back at me. "A deal's a deal, Ben."

"I know that a deal is a deal, Ira. All I'm doing is offering to change the terms if you'll agree."

"Keep your money. Detective hours for a horse. Your detective hours."

"Why are you insisting?"

"I want it done right."

"Okay," I said. A deal was a deal.

"You can start by going down to New York, tomorrow, and getting his dad off my back."

⟨⟩⟨⟩⟨⟩

I drove home to Main Street and went out to Scooter's barn, squeezing through the hedge that separates our long, narrow yards to see if the damned animal needed anything. But he was busy, giving a ride around the paddock I had built for that purpose to my young neighbor Alison Mealy.

Alison and her mother lived in the old stable hand's apartment over my barn, which was why the horse resided in Scooter's. Alison's mom cleaned houses for a living and helped out at Main Street dinner parties. Alison, who was twelve, had a missing drunk for a father and me for a friend. She's a skinny little child, but blessed with a superb physicality that put her completely in charge of a horse big enough to kill her if he felt like it. I admired her. I liked watching her flourish. She made me feel useful. Not that I did much. All she needed was a trustworthy adult to take notice of her. I could do that.

"Thank God you're here," Alison called. "Tom's hungry and I've got to stay with Redman 'til he learns this jump."

"Maybe he doesn't feel like learning to jump. He's older than you are."

"He's not old he's just lazy." She patted his head, growled in his ear, "Come on, you misery!" and dug her heels in. Redman obliged with a desultory shamble and actually cleared the hay bale she aimed him at. "Good! You beautiful horse. Good. Good....Ben, Tom really is hungry."

"I'll get right on it. Where is he?"

"In your kitchen."

"Can anyone explain to me why your horse's mascot"—a barn cat that came with Redman because it is supposed to be the calmative stable-mate of a high-strung thoroughbred—"spends so much time in my house?"

"He likes you, Ben."

I squeezed back through the hedge and joined Tom in my kitchen. I put down clean newspaper, opened a can, forked "Mixed Grill" onto an old glass dish, put it down in front of him, and stepped back quickly.

◇◇◇

I had an e-mail from one of the franchise brokers asking to show a house I had an exclusive on and which I knew she only wanted to show to demonstrate to her corporately moved client how much better her just-built modern McMansions were than an "authentic New England Antique." She had a point, if you liked spa-size bathrooms, "gourmet-chef-delight-granite-islanded" kitchens, and a "Costco room" for storing your bargains in bulk more than you liked old gardens, low ceilings, chestnut floors people had polished for three hundred years, and a fireplace in every small room.

Delete.

Then I remembered she was kind of cute, and raising two children on her ill-gotten gains, so I retrieved it from Recently

Deleted and replied, "Be my guest. But please make them take their shoes off because it's still the sellers' home."

I also had several pointless "just touching base" voice mail messages from clients who were afraid to be alone with their cell phones. Delete. Delete. Delete. I had a happy message from a guy who had secured a mortgage for the Barlowe cottage in the Borough that I had showed him. I had an even happier message from a Greenwich couple: their (substantial) check was in the mail for establishing that their daughter's reticent fiancé was neither a fortune hunter nor a child molester, but a wealthy venture capitalist who enjoyed his privacy. And I had a message from Ira's client's father's secretary: lunch at the Yale Club of New York City at one tomorrow.

I went up to the attic, found a suit, a white shirt, and a necktie and hung them on the back porch to air the mothballs. I located a pair of Aldens and buffed them to a quiet sheen and searched out some socks to go with them. I went on line to check the MetroNorth schedule. Wanting a drink, I settled for opening a bottle of rosé and re-heating the second half of last night's osso buco.

In bed I had scary dreams. Huge animals—bulldozer surrogates, of course—chased me in circles until I sprang awake with a pounding heart. I calmed down eventually, but stayed awake, worrying about things. First came money, which I had too much of lately. Last time that had happened I had ended up in trouble; if, as Ira suggested, money confused, huge money confused hugely. I worried about screw-ups I'd precipitated; women I had alienated. I even worried about the future, which used to spring up each morning cheerfully as the sun. Not so much mine, but the world's, or more specifically the town's. Newbury was changing, as was the world, shifting in a crass direction I did not like. I felt myself growing sour and I didn't like that either. I missed seeing the future spring up each morning cheerfully as the sun.

I thought about Billy Tiller's killer and was surprised to feel fear.

I'd certainly known a few killers. More than most people, having served time at Leavenworth—the penalty for a youth misspent on Wall Street—and before that serving my country in the U.S. Navy, where I'd met naturals who had managed to stay out of prison by enlisting as close-combat instructors. I had even bumped into one or two right here in Newbury. But if this guy had really meant to do what he did with the bulldozer, grinding Bill's body to pulp, he presented a picture of a man not so much cold-blooded as no-blooded. Someone who resided in a far beyond where ordinary people were not encouraged to stay or even visit.

But could this be the same guy who shot Billy last year?

Tough call. On one hand, shooters are remote types. On the other, he had sprayed a lot of bullets at Billy and a crowd of innocent bystanders that day. Had he pumped the trigger as frantically as he had erased Billy's body with the bulldozer? Or as coldly?

I voted for cold. How "frantic" could he have been while handling the machine as skillfully as he had? If I guessed right that Billy had scrambled under the cutting edge and hid under the moving machine when it caught up with him, then the act of plunging the ripper into him was the act of a very collected, calm, cool guy. Exactly how difficult—how much skill required—was a question I should have asked Sherman Chevalley.

And why, I wondered, was I so sure the guy was a guy? Mostly because I hadn't met any female bulldozer operators, I supposed, which suggested certain limitations on my part. Male or female, I realized—while the sights I'd photographed in the afternoon bubbled before my eyes—I didn't like this person one bit, feared him or her, and felt repulsed.

I went downstairs for a drink.

On the landing I thought, early day tomorrow. Do I want to go to New York feeling like garbage? I didn't want to go at all. Would a hangover make it feel any better? I could sleep it off on the train. But first I had to drive to the train and I'd be lucky to sleep an hour before it pulled into Grand Central. So

I turned around and climbed the stairs to my bed celebrating a small victory.

<>‹›<>

One way to predict the weather in Newbury, some say the only way, is to schedule a trip away from town. That day is guaranteed to dawn sunny and clear-aired, with low humidity, a crisp northwest breeze, and an intense quality to the light that will thrust those who stay toward their camera, their oil paints, their gardening tools, a ball game, or their hammock. On such a morning I drove down to Purdys, New York, took the first parking spot I found, a mile from the station, and boarded the train to the city where I had enjoyed exciting years after the Navy, and ultimately destroyed my life. Or, at least, changed it.

The train ride south toward Manhattan was like entering a funnel. It started in open land where northern Westchester enjoyed a great spread of blue reservoirs, rushing streams, broad swamps, and the green backsides of private estates. But soon a piece of estate land, marked by grand old trees, had been taken to build a school. Soon after, condos appeared through the trees, creeping closer and closer to the tracks the further south we went. A river bed was captured in a trench beside the rails. Suddenly an auto body shop came in view, a jarring sight surrounded by fenders, bumpers, and crumbling old houses; seconds later a street with new houses and old houses being fixed up. I saw a car dumped in a stream, a factory with fading paint, a warehouse with broken windows, some rusty backhoes, rail yards, and suddenly the shiny office towers at White Plains and an expensive-looking, high-rise glass condo topped with a sign that read, "If you lived here you'd be home now."

Now came the tight little downtowns of old neighborhoods that had once been villages, red brick tenements and apartment buildings, and more factories. A sudden green break marked the New York Botanical Gardens in the Bronx, then walls of old factories converted to storage facilities, factories advertising space, factories offering plastic, leather, iron work, a strip club, then homeless men sorting glass and metal in a recycling dump on the East River. Across a girder bridge and into Manhattan with a brief glimpse of midtown, the Chrysler Building shining. A gridwork of tenements, and just past the 125th Street station the train slipped underground and ran the last eleven minutes in a dark tunnel that ended in Grand Central Terminal.

My consolation for leaving home was that on such a beautiful day New York was gorgeous, too, and as I walked across Vanderbilt to the Yale Club I hoped that my host would choose an outdoor terrace table at the restaurant on the roof.

Mr. Kimball was waiting in the restaurant, I was told by the hall porter, who directed me to the elevator. I shared it with a quartet of lovely Ivy League lawyers who I gathered from their conversation were heading upstairs to celebrate trouncing the U.S. Attorney in court that morning. They were younger than I thought lawyers should be and far more attractive than I thought lawyers could be, and I found myself wondering where my life would be now if I had met them back when. Except that back then they'd still have been at Yale. Or in high school.

I worked up a good smile as I entered the restaurant, and scanned the room while I waited for the lawyers to be seated. Before the maitre d' returned, I knew I'd be eating indoors. Mr. Kimball had to be the tight-lipped, full-of-himself businessman seated with his back to the wall like a gunfighter. The maitre d' walked me straight to him. He did not stand up when I introduced myself. That made him a peasant in my book, and I did not offer my hand. But I kept smiling because if I was going to do right by Ira Roth, I had better look confident.

"What do you think of the kid?" he asked without preamble.

"I've not met your son."

"You haven't met him? What the hell are you doing here?"

"I'm here at your invitation."

Mr. Kimball gave me an unpleasant look. "I would have thought you'd make the effort to visit the kid in jail. Get his side of the story."

A wise shrink, who had helped me when I needed it, once told me that hotshot business types share essential personality traits with psychopaths. She explained that a high opinion of one's own magnificence, manipulation in the service of greed, and an inability to care about, much less notice, fellow members of the human race will not derail a career. Only when expressed physically are such character flaws judged criminal.

No longer smiling, though still confident, I said, "I decided that it would be more helpful to your son if I got the cops' side first."

He didn't like that, but finally got smart enough to say, "I don't see any profit in telling you how to do your job."

"Soon, I will interview your son—which of course Attorney Roth has already done."

"What do you think of his story?"

"Until I discover otherwise, I'm assuming he's telling the truth."

He said, "At first, I couldn't believe how stupid he was to get caught sitting on the machine. But when I went out there to the site I saw how isolated it was. I tried to put myself in his position. All alone, coming upon such a horrible sight, wanting to help, panicking...."

"You went there?" I asked.

"I had to see it."

"Why?"

"Listen, Abbott. All that you and Roth have to do is create doubt. Reasonable doubt that the kid didn't kill that man. That's all we need."

Clearly, he thought his kid did the crime. If it troubled him to regard his son as a murderer, he didn't show it. And what he said next indicated that as far as he was concerned the trial was nothing more or less than a contest to be won.

"I hired Roth because he's got a winning track record. What I want you to do is comb the entire goddamned county up there for doubts. They've got no witnesses to the actual crime. Find somebody else who might have done the crime. Find somebody else who wanted to do the crime. Doubt! All we need is doubt."

"Attorney Roth has already given me those instructions."

"Well I'm giving you them too. And I'll pay a bonus for every seed of doubt you find. Fair enough?"

"Ira's already paying me."

"Well I'm going to pay you to try harder."

"I appreciate your concern for your son. But I don't do things halfway. You don't have to pay me to serve Ira any better than I would without your paying me."

"Mr. Abbott, stop being high and mighty! And stop pretending to be dense. If I have to fire Roth, I don't want to start from scratch with a new investigator. I want copies of all your reports to him."

"If it's all right with Ira, you're welcome to them. If not, then you're not."

"In that case, I'll fire him this instant and hire you on the spot."

I stood up. "That would put your son at terrible risk. You won't find a better defense lawyer in Connecticut than Ira Roth, as you already figured out. And if you bring in New York lawyers, the judge will roast them alive. Slowly."

He surprised me with a brisk smile. "Where are you going? You haven't had lunch. Come on, sit down. I'm just mouthing off. I'm wired about this mess. Fucking kid."

I sat. He reached for the order chit and picked up the pencil. "What would you like?"

"I'll have one of your club's famous martinis. Vodka. Twist. Straight up."

He said, "I'd join you, except I've got to go back to work."

I figured I had already done a very good day's work. And it wasn't even one thirty.

He transformed into a thoughtful host, ordering a plate of dim sum to accompany my martini. We both decided upon Cobb salad for lunch and chatted amiably until the drink came. "Cheers—I say 'fucking kid,' but he's had a tough time. The divorce—just at the wrong age. And then all those years living with his mother, who is a piece of work."

He gazed longingly at my delicious drink. "It was not a friendly divorce. Knock down, drag out. And I came out of it the villain in the kid's eyes. Are you married, Ben?"

"No."

"Ever been?"

"Never."

He looked at me a moment, wondering why. With two more martinis in me, and a couple in him, I might have admitted that I regretted having foolishly blown not one, but two splendid opportunities.

"I gotta tell you, it's been nine years since I split and there hasn't been a morning yet I don't wake up smiling, Free at last, free at last, thank God almighty free at last."

I offered the requisite rueful head shake.

Kimball said, "But the kid paid the price of my escape."

Three sips down, I felt sufficiently magnanimous to say, "Well, we all get through this stuff in the end."

He said, "The kid's big problem is that I became pretty well off after the settlement....Wealthy, I mean. I was paying big alimony and big child support. They're comfortable enough. But after the settlement, a project I'd been involved in hit big and I went from a guy who was doing better every year to…well, a rich guy. Only way to put it. I mean, I was a scholarship student, working summers in construction, and now I've got a penthouse and a house in the islands, and a country estate in Fairfield County. I bought there—Newtown?"

"Yes, I know it."

"—thinking I'd be nearer the kid, but he never comes. Bought him his own Jeep. When I was his age all my old man ever gave me was a piece of free advice: put the beer can between your legs when you're driving through a toll booth."

That seemed sensible, as far as it went.

"Ira Roth mentioned you were in the music business." Along with being a big political donor with friends in New York.

"We've morphed into fashion. Getting tough to make money in music, but there's a fortune in street clothes."

"What kind of music?"

"Hip hop."

Which would not have been my first guess. He was white—pale, blue-eyed white—not black, ethnic, nor even vaguely exotic. No ponytail. No unshaven grizzled cheek. No earring. His dark suit would have made an accountant yawn. And while he was wearing an interesting necktie, I was willing to bet it had been chosen by a young girlfriend in an attempt to keep her friends from giggling.

"What I'm saying, Ben, is this—the kid may be troubled, he may be a slacker, he may be a college dropout, but he is not a killer."

"Trooper Moody, our state trooper, apparently told the state's attorney that there was bad blood between your son and Billy Tiller."

"That came as news to me." Kimball closed his fist and pressed it hard on the tablecloth, reminding me of yet another quality often shared by successful businessmen and psychopaths: charm as readily conjured as it was superficial. The gloves were off, again. We had returned to the purpose of my summons to New York. "Doubt, Abbott. Doubt. You will create doubt."

Chapter Four

"Where'd you learn to drive bulldozers?" I asked, after they locked us in the interview room.

Jeffrey Kimball was a skinny twenty-one-year-old, lost in an oversize jailhouse running suit. He wore glasses and a hangdog expression that suited his circumstances. Actually, he looked less hang dog than equal parts resigned and relieved. Common emotions for many prisoners, relieved of having to act and make decisions.

He had a soft voice. I could barely hear the answer to my question. "I was studying landscape design and I wanted to earn money? So Dad got me into the union."

A bright idea shot down. But he just didn't look like a bulldozer operator, so it had seemed reasonable to ask. I thought of something else reasonable to ask. "Were you good at it?"

"The teacher told me I was pretty hot."

Wonderful, I thought. "How well did you know Billy Tiller?"

A jaw that up until now had appeared a little weak hardened perceptibly. He reached inside his orange top to scratch an itch. I was surprised by a glimpse of the ropey muscles of a mountain climber. Not as skinny as he first appeared.

"How well did you know Billy?"

"I only met him once."

"Trooper Moody told the prosecutor that you had some sort of a set-to five or six years ago."

"Yeah. I took a swing at him."

I sat up straighter. Ropey mountain climber muscles or not, Billy must have outweighed Jeff by a hundred and fifty pounds. It would be like me taking a swing at my cousin Pinkerton Chevalley, who occasionally entertained his friends at the White Birch by bench pressing a Harley Davidson.

"I'm surprised you're still among the living."

He shrugged.

"What happened?"

"I don't want to talk about it."

"How old were you then?"

"Fifteen."

"How did Trooper Moody find out?"

"My mother filed a complaint."

I was curious why I hadn't heard about this. It was the kind of story that got around. Although, of all of Billy's well-deserved legal troubles, no one ever mentioned any kind of assault charges. Despite his size he was the classic nonviolent con man.

"Jeff, it could help us both if you would tell me what happened."

"Why?"

"I would like to know how the prosecutor might use it against you."

"They can't."

"Why not."

"Juvenile court. Sealed records."

"How did it get into juvenile court?"

"When my mother filed a complaint Billy Tiller and Eddie Edwards pressed charges."

"For what?"

"Assault."

"One fifteen-year-old against two grown men?"

"They said I attacked them with an ax."

I looked at him. "Did you?"

"No!" He shook his head vigorously. "But they said I did…. Their word against mine."

"But you said you took a swing at him. What kind of swing?"

"I only tried to punch him."

"Why?"

"I was really bummed," he said with a single-minded sense of black-and-white reality that I would have associated with a younger kid. Before I asked why he was bummed, I said, "I'm having trouble picturing a fifteen-year-old boy throwing a punch at two grown men."

"It wasn't two men."

"I thought you said there were two."

That earned me a look that asked, are you too stupid to talk and breathe at the same time? "Mr. Edwards wasn't there."

"You just said—

"Mr. Edwards wasn't there. They only said that later when they lied about the axe."

"Mr. Edwards wasn't there? Why did he say he was? He have something against you?"

"He worked for Billy. Who do you think paid him?"

"Billy Tiller was not Eddie Edwards' only client."

"I don't know about that. All I know is he worked for Billy and he lied. It was just Billy and me out in the woods. Or what used to be woods."

"What woods?"

"Behind my mother's place."

The only "woods" I knew behind Jeff's mother's house was a mind-numbingly ugly subdivision named Tiller Woods. Billy had built it on an overgrown farm he had inherited from a bachelor uncle. It had been his first development and it was everything you could hate about a subdivision, tiny lots crowded with big houses, vinyl siding, oversize garages facing the street, and every tree on the property laid waste. (I had actually entered it in the Connecticut Board of Realtors' Ugliest-Neighborhood-in-the-State contest, an informal, unpublicized event held in the basement bar of the Yankee Drover. It lost, narrowly, to a New Milford neighborhood that boasted a defunct paper mill.)

But for Billy, at least, it was beautiful. His uncle's bequest had vaulted him out of a career that had ranged from assistant septic tank cleaner to automotive repair shop manager famous for "changing" his customers' oil with other customers' oil, thus saving the expense of buying new oil and disposing of the old. Tiller Woods had made him rich because even a wolverine could make a ton of money building houses on free land.

"Are you talking about Tiller Woods?"

Jeff's jaw set again and he got a fiery gleam in his eye. For the first time I saw him as his father's son. Not necessarily the sociopath-businessman, but a kid who would mature into a man tough enough to take what he wanted.

"I grew up in those woods," he said. "I could run out the back door and disappear. I used to camp in there. Sometimes I'd just go out and watch the animals come to the pond. Once a big weasel came down a silver birch to drink and he didn't see me until he was this close, like you and me. And he stopped and he looked me in the eye, stared, like he was saying, 'If you want to fight, we'll fight. Unless you'd rather sit there quietly. Either way, fine with me.' He was absolutely fearless…Sometimes I'd build a fire and cook a burger—you know, like wrapped in tinfoil and you throw it in the coals? Old Mr. Tiller, he didn't mind. He didn't farm anymore and it was all overgrown, thick. I never went near his house or anything. And then he died and all of sudden fat Billy Tiller and Mr. Edwards were stomping around and then the surveyors came and there were plastic tapes blowing in the wind. Fucking blue and red tapes. The color of destruction. And then one day, my birthday, Billy drove in on a big D-10 and just tore it apart."

Tears welled up in the kid's eyes and trickled down his sunken cheeks.

I looked away to give him some privacy. Then I asked, "Was that when you got interested in the Earth Liberation Front?"

"I already knew about ELF. In school, we had checked out their website, found chat rooms. I mean I didn't need Billy Tiller to prove to me that this whole damn country treats the environment like an ATM machine. Rip it off and you get free money. But I gotta say, it was one thing reading ELF postings, but a lot worse seeing the enemy in action right behind my own house." And then, just in case Jeff Kimball had not admitted enough motive to give the state's attorney anecdotes to dine out on at the next lethal-injection seminar, he said, swiping fresh tears from his eyes, "I hated that fat bastard so much."

"So why did you climb on the machine?"

"I told my father's lawyer. I told the cops." He was tired. He just wanted to go back to his cell.

"Could you tell me, please?"

"I saw his arm. Like his mackinaw? No blood or anything. Just a arm in a coat, like your arm or my arm. So I jumped on to drive it off him. It was still running. But the second I got her in gear I thought, wait a minute, which way?"

"Which way?"

"Which way do I go? So I don't hurt him." His voice got stronger. More adult. "And then reality set in. It was horrible. Blood was seeping out of the sleeve. And my brain goes, whoa, I've got to find some way to lift it off him. We need machines. We need a heavy-lift crane. I was just turning on my cell phone to call 911 when Trooper Moody came up the drive."

"Did you actually dial 911?"

"No, I was still waiting for a signal. Why?"

"The cellular server should have a record that you dialed."

"Trooper Moody came before I got a signal."

"Wait a minute. You said you were waiting for the signal. Did you actually turn the phone on?"

"Well, yeah. How do you think I knew there was no signal?"

I didn't answer that it seemed like an easy story to make up. But I wondered would the cellular company have a record of Jeffrey simply turning his phone on. It just might help as circumstantial evidence that the kid was trying to call for help. I asked him what cell phone service he used. Mine hadn't reached down there, but his might.

And then, as I was leaving and the guard was taking his arm, I flashed on an image of Billy's mackinaw-clad arm sticking out from under the machine. "Jeff? How'd you know it was Billy under the machine?"

"I didn't."

"What would you have done if you had?"

"What do you mean?"

"Would you have tried to save him anyhow?"

"Well, yeah. I mean wouldn't you?"

I asked the guard, "Could we have another minute alone, please?"

"Time's up."

"Judge Laver is right across the street. He and my dad went to school together. It'll take me ten minutes to get an order for more time. Why don't you save us both the trouble?"

The guard weighed the likelihood of my story against the long-term side effects of pissing off a grandee of the court system. He backed out and closed the door. I stood close to Jeff and said, "You still haven't told me how you survived when Billy swung back."

"He didn't really swing. He just shoved me out of the way."

"Then why'd your mother press charges?"

"It was just a kind of a slap," he explained, with no rancor. "But my face was red and it made her mad."

"I saw your dad, yesterday. He hadn't known about that."

"Yeah, well my mom was mad at him that year."

"Do you mind me asking why you never told him."

"I didn't like his girlfriend."

"You know, your father came up here to look at the site. Where it happened."

"He did?"

I said, "I wondered about your father. He didn't seem the type to be a hip hop mogul."

"He's not, but he thinks he is. You should see his latest girl-friend. He buys her fur coats and a Hummer that gets ten miles to the gallon."

"Still, it must be kind of cool having a father in the music business."

"He's just an investor," Jeff said scornfully.

"For what it's worth, he's on your side."

That jaw hardened again. "Yeah, well it's a little late for that."

"Too late to help get you off? Or too late to make up for past wrongs."

"Both."

"Did he visit you here?"

"I wouldn't see him."

I drove back to Newbury thinking about all the kids of divorced parents I had met while showing houses being sold for the settlement. Even though they knew I had come to sell their home out from under them, they would tour me so eagerly room to room, noting a million details. They always knew so much more about houses than their parents did.

Brave kid, taking on Billy at fifteen. Or just mad enough to kill?

But to wait six years?

‹›‹›‹›

"Jeff Kimball tried to call for help on a Verizon cell phone," I reported to Ira. "My call record lady can't find a connection." I kept a corporate account at one of the on-line data brokers and I'd used them enough so it had gotten personal, which usually sped things up. "I'm wondering if you know somebody there who could check it out whether they registered his signal."

The attorney was not impressed. "I got just off the phone with the state's attorney. The cops already checked with Verizon. They have no record that Jeffrey turned on his cell phone, much less dialed 911."

I sat in his client chair and stared at my boots. "I was afraid of that. I couldn't get a signal when I was out there. But each service is different. Maybe his worked there, but the signal hadn't locked in yet."

"The prosecutor put it more succinctly."

"What did he say?"

"'Your client is lying.'"

"They can't prove that."

Ira sighed.

"What?" I asked.

"The curse of getting older is having to explain the world to the young—They don't have to prove that Jeffrey didn't dial 911. There's no record. Nothing to say the kid isn't lying. Find Billy Tiller's enemies, Ben. It's the only way."

‹›‹›‹›

The town has grown so much that I didn't recognize all the names in the *Clarion* "Police Reports" to which I turned for a refresher course on Billy's misdeeds and offenses. I pulled them off several years of the newspaper's website archives—*Clarion*-Online, offering a Newbury version of Google, supplemented by publisher-editor-reporter Scooter MacKay's availability next door to fill in blanks from memory. Then, long list in hand, I went calling on people who were mad at Billy Tiller.

Chapter Five

Landslides are almost unheard of in New England, where granite ledge crops out of the ground like pond frogs emerging for a wary peep. What farmers and gardeners laughingly call "earth" is actually a threadbare blanket of soil and stones stretched over solid rock, which is anchored to the core of the planet. (The occasional boulder that breaks loose is moved by frost and gravity into the next hole a person tries to dig.) So our hills are sturdy and you would have to go way out of your way to cause a landslide.

Billy Tiller had managed one that almost made the Richter scale.

Ralph and Sheila Gordon had the misfortune of living next to a slope Billy had been "developing" into a crush of McMansions he had named Newbury Walls. From what I could see from their driveway, all the Queen's horses and most of her men had fallen into their backyard.

They were an elderly couple of modest means, retired teachers living on Social Security and private school pensions. Mr. Gordon (he would always be Mr. Gordon to me, as she would be Mrs.) had taught me history at Newbury Prep. Mrs. Gordon had done her best to acquaint me with mathematics.

Had they been the sort to sue, they could have taken L.L. Bean to court for plagiarizing their lifestyle. Mr. Gordon wore corduroys and a vest over a flannel shirt and sturdy hiking boots. Mrs. Gordon had on cotton trousers and a sweater she had probably knitted herself. A black Lab slept at his feet. A cat sat on her lap. They offered me tea and they looked as gentle, and genteel, as a minister and his wife.

I broached the subject of Billy Tiller.

"I'm glad that son of a bitch is dead," said Mrs. Gordon.

"And we pray he roasts in Hell," her husband added.

Of the three kinds of gardeners in Newbury—crawlers, pointers, and checkbookers—checkbookers write a check to a landscape designer and go on a cruise; pointers instruct hired help what to dig, plant, weed, mulch, and prune; and crawlers spend most of their time on their knees, digging, planting, mulching, weeding, while occasionally standing to prune something overhead or turn their compost heap. The Gordons were crawlers.

They had devoted the happiest years of their lives to a patch of ground that had been one of the high spots on the annual Conservancy tour. They showed me glossy gardening magazines that had done four-color photo essays on their place. Then they led me to the window. Half a year after Billy Tiller's Total Landscape company started work next door, it looked like a Bolivian shanty town smacked by a hurricane.

"That used to be the pond," Mr. Gordon said, pointing at a gray slick. "Over there, where you see the splintered crab apple, we had a small lawn."

His wife smiled, wistfully. "The lawn shrank, annually, as we added new beds and borders."

"We called it 'border creep.'"

"Did Billy pay for the damage?"

"No. He said to sue him. We couldn't afford that."

"Barely afford our property taxes the way they've been going up."

Of their beds and borders, perennials, bulbs, bushes, corms, and rhizomes there was no sign, and I asked the million dollar question, hoping fervently that Mr. Gordon answered in the negative. Because, as much as I wanted to get poor Jeff Kimball off if it turned out that he didn't kill Billy Tiller, I certainly hoped that this nice couple had no more suffering on the horizon. "Did you do the machine work yourself?"

"Machine?" They laughed, in chorus. "Wheelbarrow."

"I guess a wheelbarrow is easier to drive than a bulldozer."

"I wouldn't say that," said Mr. Gordon. "I was a Seabee in the Navy. Let me tell you a bulldozer is a lot easier to handle than a wheelbarrow. Especially by the end of the day. Thank God for Aleve."

"And Old Fashioneds," said Mrs. Gordon.

"I guess that was a long time ago."

"When?"

"When you drove bulldozers in the Navy."

"Forty years. What am I saying? Forty-two. Funny, how you never lose the knack. My unit had a reunion down in New Jersey last summer. We all went out to the Operating Engineers training site. Ever see it out on the Turnpike?"

I had, in fact, driving an elderly friend down to Camden to visit the battleship New Jersey museum. "Like a giant erector set."

"We had a ball, driving machines. Old ones, antiques, new ones. Every kind of bulldozer you ever saw. Man they're a kick. You ever drive one, Ben?"

I shook my head, and looked down at his hiking boots, which were the kind L.L. Bean would advertise as offering firm support for climbing hills like the one behind the house lot where Billy died.

"You float across the ground. You feel like a lumbering god."

His wife interrupted. "They didn't float for just anybody. Jim was the best. He made it dance." Then she got an Ohmigod! look on her face. "Ben! You're not suggesting that—"

I assured her I wasn't and left after a decent interval of tea and small talk. But I had the strongest feeling I would not be invited back and felt more than a little ashamed of myself.

<>‹›‹›

Doubt.

I climbed up the outside stairs of the General Store to see Tim Hall, who was my friend and lawyer of choice—Tim being a lot less expensive than Ira Roth. "Remember the guy who sued Billy Tiller for cutting down his trees?"

Tim's big open face clouded over. "Yes."

"How did that work out?"

"We won. Eventually. Billy and Eddie Edwards blitzed the court with lawyers and experts and every brand of bull you could think of. Cost my poor client fifteen grand in legal fees and he still hasn't collected the judgment."

"But you had a good case?"

"Ultimately, it proved impossible for Billy to deny that my client's two acres of trees had arrived at Pawloski's lumber mill on Billy's trucks. Pawloski was really pissed because it made him look a crook, too, which he most certainly is not. He was happy to testify against Billy."

"So why didn't your guy press charges?"

"We couldn't shake Billy's story that he thought the trees were on his land. Not enough to get a criminal conviction. Best we could do was reparations to plant new trees. It was a joke. The judge had just been transferred up from Stamford, temporarily filling in—Remember Judge Clarke, that jerk who got the Conservation Department off Billy's back?—He didn't know a tree from a self-storage unit. You could see he had a picture that my client could just buy some eighty-foot-tall, hundred-year-old trees from Agway and stick 'em in the ground. Outside the courthouse, Billy laughed in my client's face."

"Your client pissed?"

"Not at me. He saw how it went down. Paid my bill and even sent some work my way. Why?"

"I want to see where he stood with Billy."

Tim gave a big-shouldered shrug and said, "He struck me as a guy who would rather just move on."

"Meaning?"

"Meaning that even if Ira's client didn't murder Billy, this guy would still not be a legitimate suspect."

"You mind if I tell him we talked?"

Tim shot me the kind of look you can only shoot at an old friend. "If you were going to talk to him anyhow why didn't you just drive out there instead of bothering me?"

"Because he put up a huge iron gate and I can't see the house from the road and he's got an unlisted telephone number."

Tim shook his head and said softly, "Goddamned Billy. He had no idea how he hurt the guy."

"What do you mean?" I asked. It wasn't the first time I had found Tim to be a touch more complicated than his open face would suggest.

"Sorry, Ben. I've said more than enough."

"Okay. I appreciate what you did say. And I won't tell him we talked. Later."

"By the way, Vicky keeps saying we should invite you to dinner."

"I never turn down a free meal." Vicky McLachlan—Newbury's First Selectman and a good prospect for governor of Connecticut one day—could not cook worth a damn. But in her company, food was the last thing that came to mind.

<>‹>‹>

Tim's client whose trees Billy Tiller had stolen was named Andrew Sammis. He was new in town, an apparently wealthy man who had bought one of the old estates that had been another rich man's country house for the past sixty years. Unlike many newcomers, he had kept it intact. It was quite private, the house nearly a quarter mile from the road and no other houses in sight, a small, handsome, well-kept Greek Revival with white pillars that was dwarfed by a bloated Cadillac pickup parked in front.

When I finally got through to him by trailing his cleaning lady, Marie Butler, through his gate and up his driveway, I was confronted in the parking area by a man a little bigger than me and several years younger who had recently erected an enormous gate and surrounded his property with ten-foot chain link fence and was now accusing me of trespassing, even as I stuck out my hand to introduce myself.

Marie Butler—the town's primary gossip—a big, loud woman who was never that anxious to get busy cleaning, shoved between us with introductions of her own. "This is Ben Abbott. I've told you all about him, Mr. Sammis. You know, from the Main Street Abbotts. His father married a Chevalley—and boy I bet he never heard the end of that from his parents. They were a pair of tight old Yankees." She paused to gulp breath and it occurred to me that Marie did not think there was anything wrong with gossip. No way a person could be that good at it if she felt guilty. "He's the real estate agent. The one who went to—"

"Thank you, Marie," I interrupted.

"—jail for—"

"Thank you, Marie."

"—fraud."

God knows what Sammis thought at that moment, but at least Marie calmed him down and got him off the trespassing subject. I pressed the small advantage she had gained for me by saying to Sammis, "I wouldn't want you to get the wrong idea. It wasn't exactly fraud. It had nothing to do with real estate. It wasn't in Connecticut. And it was a long time ago." He didn't bite. I went on, "Wall Street. It was insider trading. According to the government."

"What did they give you?"

"Three years."

Marie felt obliged to add, "In Leavenworth Penitentiary."

Sammis finally looked interested. "How'd they manage hard time on insider trading?"

"There was a dispute about testifying against—" I started to say "a friend," which wasn't quite accurate, and settled for, "people I knew."

Sammis nodded and the guard inside him stood down and I knew quite surely that he too had served time, somewhere, for something. Which ought to make talking to him a bit easier.

"Come on down to the barn," he said. "Marie, you get started. I'll stay out of the house until you're finished."

"Don't you want to talk to Ben in the house?"

Sammis ignored her and we walked briskly to the barn where, in a woodworking shop equipped with both a table and radial saw, he was building bookshelves. "So why'd you sneak in here? The place isn't for sale."

I decided to play it absolutely straight. If he had done time he probably still possessed a bullshit detector. I said, "I've got an occasional sideline. Sort of a half-assed private investigator for some of the local lawyers."

"Detective?"

"Keeps me out of trouble and fills in the slow spots in the real estate."

"How did you get a PI license if you were convicted of a felony?"

"Actually, I avoided getting a license for a long time, on the theory that if I had no license no one could threaten to take it away."

"That doesn't answer my question."

I saw that I had no choice but to answer his before I could persuade him to answer mine.

"I got my private detective license the same way I got my real estate license. I applied for—and was granted—what's called 'Relief of Civil Disability.'"

I did not mention that my Aunt Connie had expedited the matter by calling in a favor, as she had, years earlier, for my Congressional appointment to the Naval Academy. Nor did I reveal that I had got a permit to keep my father's gun collection the same way, and a license to carry, though the guns stay home in a safe in the cellar. The detective license actually turned out to be worth the trouble and expense—twelve hundred bucks up front, five hundred renewal every two years—as people respond favorably to labels.

Sammis would not let it go. "How did a former stock salesman meet the work-experience requirement?"

"You know more about Connecticut licensing law than most people," I said. "Are you a lawyer?"

"That doesn't answer my question."

Still hoping he was going to answer mine, I said, civilly, "I gained my work experience in the Office of Naval Intelligence when I was in the service. A long, long time ago," I added with a smile.

"All right. What are you investigating?"

"I'm working for Ira Roth. He's a top-gun defense lawyer up here. He's got a client—a kid, charged with murder."

"The kid who bulldozed Billy Tiller?"

"It's possible he didn't."

"What I read in the *Clarion* sounded open-shut—I mean him sitting on the bulldozer which was sitting on Billy Tiller. Is that not what happened?"

"The order in which they stacked up is in question."

"Well, that's what they pay lawyers for. I hope the kid is rich."

"His father is."

"Good."

"I gather you had a run in with Billy."

Sammis gave me a quick look. "Where'd you hear that?"

"Read it in the *Clarion*. Do you mind me asking what happened?"

"Let's just say that Mr. Tiller presented quite a challenge to my anger-management sessions."

"I heard he laughed about those trees."

"Yeah, he laughed. But I was going to get the last laugh. Would have, if your client hadn't ended up on top of him."

"How?"

"I had a plan."

"For revenge?"

"Yeah, for revenge. What the hell do you think I'm talking about?"

"Mind me asking how?"

"Moot point, now."

He picked up a board, sighted down it, penciled an X on the crooked end, measured six feet, drew a cut line with a square and went to his radial saw and looked surprised that I was still standing there. "Goodbye, Mr. Abbott."

"Do you know how to drive a bulldozer?"

"What kind?"

"How about a Caterpillar D4?"

"Goodbye, Mr. Abbott." He put on eye protectors and ear protectors and turned on his saw, which made a remarkably loud and piercing noise.

We had here a classic meeting of two alpha dogs, only one of whom could become alpha-alpha. The trouble with being alpha is you don't always think that straight. Or think at all. Which can be a great advantage. Or a terrible mistake. Maybe it was because he reminded me of prison, but the blood suddenly storming through my mind told me that I could not survive if I backed down.

I yanked the power cord from the wall.

Sammis was remarkably quick. Moving as fluidly as a skater, he snatched up a battery-powered circular saw and held the long-toothed rip blade inches from my face. I looked at his index finger curled around the trigger switch.

Chapter Six

I tried to gauge his eyes through the safety glasses. They were glazed like marble with a mad dog stare. Again I looked at his index finger on the trigger and said, "You don't have the balls, dude. You've been out too long and you don't want to go back."

Sammis shocked me. I really didn't believe he would trigger the saw. But he jerked the switch with all his might.

I was right about one thing. He had been out of prison too long. He had not lost his anger, nor his desire to survive. But he had lost his edge. He had gotten so heated up that he forgot to press the saw's safety switch with his thumb. And, thanks to the federal rules that were supposed to protect do-it-yourself handy men and women, the saw did not start. That surprised him long enough for me to pick up a whippy length of quarter inch steel rod he was building something with, point it at his face and announce, semi-truthfully, "I fenced for the Naval Academy. Why don't we stop the rough stuff before you lose an eye?"

He glared at me, glared at the steel rod, and glared at his saw, saw where his thumb had missed the safety, and threw it down on the bench. He looked angrier than scared, but he sounded weary when he said, "Get the fuck out of here and don't come back."

Sensible again, I backed out the door, went home and Googled him, which I should have done earlier. It took a lot of scrolling, but I found that Andrew Sammis had indeed done time. In Maine. Not for assault with bulldozer, but close. He'd been convicted of running over his wife with a pickup truck, which he had denied vehemently but unconvincingly. After a year in prison, his conviction had been overturned by an appeals court. Which not only freed him, but permitted him to inherit his wife's considerable estate and collect her life insurance.

I found it hard to believe that he would risk throwing away his new-found freedom and fortune to avenge some stolen trees. Still, I'd seen his anger in action, so I wrote an asterisk beside his name and continued down my list.

I spoke with a homeowner who went red in the face about Billy's trucks roaring through his neighborhood on Sundays. I found the president of a community group that had formed to try to stop Billy from scamming a grandfather-clause loophole in the zoning regulations to force single-acre housing into a two-acre neighborhood. I found people who blamed him for crowded roads, noisy leaf blowers, and bad-mannered newcomers with too much money. Everyone damned him for rising school taxes.

"Welfare!" one apoplectic geezer sputtered. "It's like we pay welfare to Billy Tiller. Our taxes go up to educate the kids who move into his houses. He keeps the profit."

None of them admitted knowing how to drive a bulldozer.

More promising was a guy who had been suing Billy for shoddy construction work on his nine-hundred-and-fifty-thousand-dollar McMansion. It didn't sound like a thing that would go to bulldozers, but when I learned that the homeowner had rented a backhoe to excavate a pond in a wet spot in the back of his property—a wet spot that had already been a pond before Total Landscape filled it in one dark night to preempt a wetlands-protection challenge to that particular development—I figured I better talk to him.

Billy had named the development Equestrian Ridge.

The houses were wedged in a dark hollow and nine hundred and fifty thousand hadn't bought much space. The big guy who opened his front door and stepped back to let me enter tripped on the curving staircase Billy had pried into the two-story entryway. I helped him to his feet. Something loud began to roar somewhere in the house and we both looked at the ceiling.

A crystal chandelier shook musically.

"My wife's in the Jacuzzi," he explained.

I was tempted to ask with whom? Framed posters were shifting on their moorings. The floor vibrated underfoot.

"I grew up in apartments. I never owned a house before. Is this supposed to happen?"

I backed out from under the chandelier. "Depends on your builder. Not if he's a craftsman like Ed Soares or John Blomberg. Or even Louie Minalgo," I added, naming a cantankerous Yankee who did superb work if it wasn't trout, deer, or turkey season. "Guys like them still build a solid house. Your wife could teach line dancing upstairs and we wouldn't feel a thing."

"That's what I kept telling my idiot lawyer. Billy Tiller was a chiseling shoddy crook."

"How was your lawsuit going?"

His face fell. "The lawyer told me she thought we'd lose. I was feeling pretty bad, before that kid killed him."

"I heard you dug a pond."

"I tried. I figured a backhoe was like driving a car. But it sunk in the mud. I finally had to bring in a pro. Dave Charney."

"The best."

He walked me out onto a scruffy lawn, the hallmark of a building lot scraped clean of natural topsoil, and showed me his pond. I told him it would look wonderful in a few years. Which it would, if the plants he had bought at the nursery to replace the mountain laurel flattened by Total Landscape matured before the deer ate them.

Back indoors, his wife came down all flushed and pretty in a terry bathrobe. She complained to her husband, obviously not for the first time, that their Jacuzzi had consumed all their hot water, and insisted that I stay for coffee. On the way to the kitchen, we passed a living room which was empty but for a baby grand piano with the lid wide open and dust thick on the strings. She noticed that I noticed and said, "They told us to close it, but it looks so pretty open."

"Who plays?"

"We're going to get lessons for the kids."

The kitchen, the usual lineup of granite, stainless steel, cherry, tile, big screen TV, and marble bar leading to the family room, reeked faintly of bacon grease as a Billy Tiller "gourmet chef delight" was designed more for unwrapping takeout than actual cooking with a real exhaust fan that vented outdoors. Over excellent coffee, they both talked about how lonely they felt moving to Connecticut. I told them that Yankees warm slowly, and recommended volunteering at the high school or joining the community theater. Pitching in was always welcome. I did not mention that new people living in expensive houses on quiet cul-de-sacs often took the heat for the developers.

"We'll settle in," the woman said. "We'll make it home." Then she smiled, "I always dreamed of living in a new house. With fresh paint and lots of room."

◇◇◇

Ira Roth was wearing his wireless headset. He motioned me to sit while he wrapped up his call: "I know he's a psycho. But he's our psycho."

"Another client?" I asked when he rang off.

"Another private investigator. What do you have for me?"

I told him about Sammis and his wife's insurance.

"Nice work if you can get it." He had a habit of keeping his headset on with the microphone stalk blocking his mouth, which gave the impression that he saved the good stuff for people on the other end of the line. "But a man who took Billy to court has demonstrated a certain willingness to stay within the law, which won't much help our young gentleman. Find more people mad at Billy—mad enough to flatten him with a bulldozer."

"I don't know, Ira. I've talked to a bunch. An amazing number of people know how to drive bulldozers, but—"

"They don't all have to know how. I'll take some who were mad enough to hire someone to flatten Billy with a bulldozer."

"How many ordinary people would kill over trees or floods?"

"All we need are people who seem like they could have killed the son of a bitch. Andrew Sammis and Mr. Gordon are a start, but I need at least a half dozen victims of Billy."

"I look forward to seeing you maul Sammis, but I can't seeing dragging people like old Mr. and Mrs. Gordon onto the witness stand."

"Lamentable, but better than our client jailed for life—what do you have against Andrew Sammis?"

"This doubt strategy is like throwing sand in the face of a charging bull. It might blind him, but he's not going to stop. Is this your idea or Jeff's father's?"

Ira owned an attorney's poker face, but he was not able to hide the cold anger that radiated from his body like wind from a frozen lake. He took the headset off and dropped it on his desk. "Ben. I've been winning criminal cases since you were in diapers."

Maybe so, but I had met him shortly after that and I had never seen him so angry. Sounded to me as if—uncharacteristically too eager to please—Ira had allowed Jeff's father to call the shots.

<>< ><>

I knew of two more incidents that might bolster the case Ira was making for Jeff Kimball. I had been holding off on both because Billy had really put the poor devils through the mill.

I started with the more recent victimization. Jimmy Butler, a hard-working, decent, easily led little guy, got into trouble driving a 1972 ten-yard Mack dump truck he had been led to believe belonged to Billy Tiller. The Mack was hauling a flatbed trailer bearing a Link-Belt excavator which Jimmy said Billy had assured him was only eleven feet high, which turned out not to be true, but extremely germane. Clearance under the railroad trestle was eleven foot six inches.

One could make a case—and the authorities did—that the driver should have measured his load himself, but Jimmy was in a rush because he was working several jobs to make payments on a brand-new yellow school bus he had contracted to drive for the high school. Being in a rush, he was going pretty fast.

While railroad engineers prepared to test just how precariously the railroad trestle was dangling, Trooper Moody ticketed Jimmy for violating all the state laws that pertained to low clearance bridges. Then he ticketed Jimmy for driving without a fire extinguisher, for driving without a medical card, for driving without a state fuel stamp, for driving a truck that had not had its annual federal inspection, for driving with unsafe tires, for driving with defective brake lines, and for towing an unregistered trailer and for driving a commercial vehicle without a commercial vehicle driver's license.

Trooper Moody knew that Jimmy had a commercial license. He had left it in his school bus, not intending to drive a truck that day. But by then Ollie was in a vicious mood: traffic was backed up for a quarter mile and a hydraulic oil spill from the Link-Belt excavator resulted in numerous motorists skidding in a soup of powdered concrete and viscous fluids into each other and nearby ditches. Ollie cited each for making a restricted turn, and several people new to town for failure to update an address on a drivers license.

The *Clarion*'s front-page photograph of four cranes returning a locomotive to the tracks was captioned, "Railroad crews tested the strength of the damaged bridge by running a locomotive over it." Inflamed, the owners of the railroad were even madder than Ollie.

I drove down to Frenchtown to get Jimmy Butler's side of the story.

His driveway was blocked by an enormous wrecker whose beefy driver was attaching a hook to Jimmy's yellow school bus, which was parked beside his house, a low ranch in need of a paint job. While the wrecker might by some stretch of the imagination be hooking onto Jimmy's bus to tow it in for repairs, the company name stenciled on the wrecker's boom and the beefy driver's pec-stretched shirt—Now Repo!—suggested something more ominous than a transmission job.

Jimmy was watching from his front door and he looked very unhappy. I parked in the driveway of the empty house next door, walked up the scattered flagstones that made his front walk, and asked, "Is this as bad as it looks?"

"Son of a bitching bank."

"How many months are you behind?"

"Only six."

"I'm sorry, Jimmy."

"Goddamned Billy Tiller. It's like he's grabbing my balls from the grave."

"I thought they gave you back your license."

"The railroad told the DMV they'd sue the governor if they didn't take me off the road."

"I thought Tim Hall helped you with that."

"Tim tried. But a bunch of parents said they'd sue the school board if they let me drive their kids. I have the whole goddamned state of Connecticut after me, and half the parents in Newbury. Just for doing a guy a favor."

"Weren't you working for Billy?"

"No! I quit soon as I saved up the down payment for the bus. I was ready to roll."

"Why were you driving his truck?"

"He asked me would I run a rig back to Frenchtown. How was I supposed to know the cops were looking for it?"

"Did Billy know?"

"Why do you think he conned me into driving it?"

"What are you saying? He was setting you up for a fall?"

"No, no, no. Jesus, Ben. No, Billy didn't have anything against me. He probably figured that if I could get it across town and under cover he was home free."

"That doesn't make sense. Why would a guy making the bucks he was bother stealing a truck?"

Jimmy looked at me like I was fifth grader who had just lost his lunch in the back seat. "You didn't understand Billy. Nobody did. He didn't deliberately steal the truck. It somehow fell in his hands. When he found out it was hot he figured if he could just hide it long enough to strip it he'd make a few bucks and keep some parts."

"The truck was a hunk of junk."

"Haulin' a fine machine on the trailer."

"But he already owned a bunch of fine machines."

"Don't you get it?"

"No, I don't get it. Why would a rich builder steal a truck?"

"Billy didn't think he was rich. In his head he was still getting six bucks an hour driving a honey wagon for Old Man Hopkins."

"Come on, everything he touched turned to gold."

"Builders are gamblers. He knew he could lose it all in one week if the economy went bad just when he finished a bunch of spec houses."

Jimmy had a point, there. If prices went down because interest rates went up, he could be sitting on houses he had to sell, but couldn't, with the banks calling in their loans. Development had been so hot so long it was easy to forget the bad times when the banks shut everybody down and then the Feds shut the banks down. There were years—a long way back—when there was not a single pickup truck at the General Store buying coffee in the morning.

The repo man crawled out from under the front of the bus and moved a lever on the side of his truck. The boom groaned and the front of the bus began to rise from the driveway.

"Besides, Billy knew you people on Main Street still looked down on him, no matter how much money he made." Jimmy's matter-of-fact observation of the tattered remnants of the old social order before the population doubled was delivered without rancor.

"So what did he have against you?"

"Nothing. I was handy. If somebody else was standing nearer he'd have asked him."

"What did the cops say when you said you were driving it for Billy?"

"They asked did I work for him. I said I used to. Not any more. So why would you be driving a truck for him? they asked. I said, ask Billy. They went to Billy and Billy and Eddie Edwards told them I asked if I could park the truck in Billy's barn."

"Their word against yours?"

"I couldn't prove I didn't. The cops couldn't prove I had actually stolen the truck, thank God. But the railroad and the parents were on my case, so they settled for taking away my license."

"So everyone went home happy."

"Except me. No license. I couldn't drive the baseball teams last spring. Couldn't drive for summer school. I couldn't drive anything to make my payments."

"Did you confront Billy?"

"Sure."

"What happened?"

"He laughed at me."

"That must have pissed you off."

Jimmy watched his bus disappear around the corner. "When I heard that kid got him with the bulldozer I said to myself, 'Why didn't I think of that?'"

I looked at him closely. "That was a pretty fancy job of bulldozer driving from what I saw."

"I could have done it easy. I've been running machines my whole life....All I can say is I hope the kid gets off." He stared, blinking mournfully at the empty space in his driveway. "Couldn't they get him time off for public service?"

"I'll suggest that to his lawyer."

Jimmy manufactured a smile.

"So what are you going to do?" I asked him.

"See if I can find a job. Before they take my house."

"You behind?"

"Only five months."

"Maybe you can work something out."

"Are you kidding? The mortgage company wants this house for a tear down. They already foreclosed on my neighbor." It finally registered on me that the empty house next door had no For Sale sign. "With all the building going on the land's worth more than the houses. They'll tear both down, make one big lot and stick a McMansion on it."

◇◇◇

It looked like date night at Home Depot.

Couples were streaming in for a do-it-yourself evening out, sparkling with hope. The women wore makeup and had done their hair. Their guys hadn't gone to quite as much trouble in the looks department, but most had showered, recently, and slapped some mousse on their hair or covered it with a clean cap. Walking in alone and feeling suddenly out of it, I recalled a time when I was a kid before guys rubbed "hair product" in their hair, before they invented Home Depot—back when lumber yards existed for the express purposes of humiliating men who weren't contractors and offering women an opportunity to be leered at indoors.

Many women appeared to be test driving new guys. The guys looked happy to buy into Home Depot's I-can-do-it-myself promise—build that deck, tile that bathroom, install that Jacuzzi, lay that parquet, expand that kitchen. They puffed up around the tool department. But the women were leading the way toward Bath and Kitchens and while they let the guys stop, briefly, like dogs at hydrants, they were unfolding sheets of paper with measurements written down.

I was hunting a bankrupt contractor named Georgie Stefano-poulos, who used to specialize in decks, pool houses, and the surrounding landscape. We had played ball together when we were kids. By the time I returned to Newbury from my excursion into the wider world, Georgie owned a very large landscaping outfit. Last time I was here buying pressure-treated posts for

Redman's corral, I had spotted him wearing a name tag that said "George" and an orange apron that read, "I Can Help In Any Department."

I found him in Lumber, surrounded by flocks of customers, and trailed him as he answered questions on an orbit from Hardware to Plumbing to Electrical, outside to Gardening and back through Kitchen, Bath, Floors, Paint and Mill Work and back to Lumber, where I was finally able to make myself useful helping George help a carpenter on crutches who was buying three-quarter-inch birch-veneer plywood. We were breathing hard by the time we trundled the carpenter and his wood through checkout and loaded his pickup. I stood with George while he had a cigarette in the parking lot.

He hadn't put on a pound since high school, still a tightly wound little guy, with arms and legs as taut and strong as aircraft cable, the woven stainless steel wire rope that will not stretch.

"How you doing with the probation?" I asked. Management was on his case, he had told me last time, for flaring up at a customer who had annoyed him.

"Where'd you hear about that?"

"You mentioned it last time I saw you."

"I did?" He laughed, dryly. "I was spilling my guts, like the rage counselor said to. Yeah, it's okay, now. I'm off."

"Congratulations."

"Freakin' stupid thing to be congratulated for. Freakin' idiot customer endangers his life and everyone in the aisle by climbing a wood rack and I'm the one who gets in trouble. They had a guy killed in the wood rack couple of years ago. It's like a factory floor in there but people treat it like they're buying cotton balls in the drug store. I had no idea how stupid people were 'til I got into retail."

"I'll bet you miss construction," I said, unsubtly. He looked mad as hell and that's exactly the frame of mind I wanted him to discuss his nemesis Billy Tiller.

He said, "I miss the money. I miss being my own boss. I miss my garage full of machines. I don't miss the headaches." Then he launched into more philosophy than he would have back then. "Freakin' customers, come to you thinking they want a pool or a deck or a—a…"

"Patio?"

"Doesn't matter if it's a patio or pool or freakin' pool house. They want the same thing. They want a dream realized."

This was a conversation that would have made more sense in a bar, on the third round. I blamed his sessions on channeling rage.

"But since they are incapable of expressing their dream in any concrete manner, they expect you the contractor to express it for them so that the job looks exactly like what they dreamed—note I say dreamed, not imagined, as they don't have any freakin' imagination to speak of, only a checkbook and a desire to own something perfect they can show off to their freakin' friends."

"I wanted to ask you about Billy Tiller."

"Billy? That scumbag. Funny coincidence."

"What do you mean?"

"We're talking about dreaming, here, right? That's what Billy sold. From the get go. From the time he got out of high school."

"I don't follow you."

"Billy was a con man."

"He started a con man. But he became a developer."

"He was a con man."

"Originally," I said. "But he became—"

"Remember the oil change scam?" he laughed. "There were cars in Newbury that shared the same oil for three years running. God knows how many turbos he burned up."

George was surprising me. He sounded almost admiring of a man I had assumed he hated. "My favorite," he said, "was the car rental scam."

"I missed that one."

"Don't you remember, when he had the garage, Billy got a car rental franchise?"

"Right. Pink mentioned that. So Billy's repair customers had to rent a loaner instead of getting it free. That's not exactly a con."

"He didn't do it for the customers. He did it for the parts."

"What parts?"

"Batteries, tires, transmissions. Entire engines. Which he would swap out of the rentals and replace with the guts of clunkers."

"You're kidding."

"The man was a genius."

"But are you saying he was con man as developer, too? I thought he had kind of moved up a rung."

George shook his head. "It's not a big jump from cheap con man to developer. They're both into risk. They're both opportunistic. Both amoral, if not immoral. And they're both naturally entrepreneurial."

"Not every developer is a crook."

Georgie looked off into the middle distance, as if somewhere between the Home Depot, Stew Leonard's, and a discount liquor warehouse, he might glimpse one who wasn't. "Maybe not," he conceded at last. "But these are people who get stuff done. Which means getting your way over other people. You gotta hand it to them. They're self-starters. Say what you will about Billy, he was a self-starter. And a darned smart one, too."

"Do you think Billy was really smart?"

"You better believe he was smart. Listen, I was in business a long time. He was one of the smartest guys around. Smart businessman. Smart con artist. All he needed was a break. When he got it—when his uncle left him the farm—he went from a small time grifter to a big time developer. How? Simple. It's the same head. And don't forget, you make your profit by cutting corners, which can include not paying your freakin' bills to suckers like me."

"If you knew that, why did you get involved with him?"

George tossed his butt under a Volvo. "I was your classic con victim. I wanted to believe. I needed to believe. I needed the work. I was suddenly in trouble. Got overextended. He offered a deal that could have saved me. Hell, it would have if he had kept his word and paid me what he owed me. Instead I'm bankrupt and working for fifteen bucks an hour. At this rate I'll have my debts cleared up in 2030." He said it in a bantering tone, but his eyes were bleak.

"Couldn't you earn more driving a machine?"

George looked at me, hard. The tendons in his neck went taut. "I won't drive another man's machine. I tried. Couldn't stand it."

"What did you think when he got killed?"

George laughed. "Not what I would have predicted."

"What would you have predicted?"

"That I'd be glad. I actually opened a beer and started to toast the kid who got him. Couldn't." He looked across the lot at the couples streaming into the big store. "I don't know what happens. You get older or what, I don't know. But it just didn't seem right to laugh about a dead guy. I mean, if anyone deserved to get killed it was Billy. But it's not funny. He was killed. Think about his last moments. You want to be that scared? You want to *make* somebody that scared? Even somebody you hate? I mean, would you really do that to somebody?"

He looked at me, demanding an answer. I said, "No."

"Neither would I.…I know what you were thinking, Ben. Sorry to disappoint you."

Chapter Seven

Jeff Kimball's mother looked like she had been drawn with sharp pencils and a straight edge. Her hair fell in a direct line to her shoulders, her cheek bones were high and strained her skin, her chin was pointed. She had a surprisingly full mouth, turned down at the corners. There was anger in her face, but she was not severe, not with the despair that clouded it like a bruise.

"What can I tell you?" she asked, meaning she had nothing to say. Maybe not, but I was running out of options.

We were standing at the front door of her once-pretty clapboard farmhouse. The paint was fading and newer homes were crowding the property. On one side, a road opened into the heart-stoppingly ugly mansions of Tiller Woods—Billy's first project. On the other side were a raised ranch that dated back to the mid 1990s and a late 1990s McMansion. Trees had been cleared and a foundation poured for a third house, which would be even bigger than the McMansion. Even if I hadn't already checked the records at Town Hall, it would be obvious that Jeff's mother had been reducing her tax bill, or making ends meet, by selling bits and pieces of her land.

Having already introduced myself, I asked, again, "May I come in?"

"Why?" she asked. "You're working for the lawyer Jeff's father hired. I have no say in all of this."

"I am trying to do everything I can to help your son beat a very serious charge. The more I know, the more I can help."

"Did you talk to his father?"

"Yes."

"And?"

"And I want the boy's mother's take, too."

"He's not a boy. Not any more."

"Well, frankly, ma'am, from what I've seen, he's not a grown man either. He's a kid caught somewhere in between and I'm not sure he's even able to fully comprehend how much trouble he's in."

She said nothing.

I said, "His lawyer just learned this morning that the state's attorney is going for first-degree murder. Premeditated."

"Premeditated?" she said loudly. "Based on what? They can't unseal those court records. He was a juvenile."

"The ELF fliers in Jeff's backpack apparently have the state's attorney believing he doesn't need to unseal those records. Though don't think he won't try. He thinks he can beat a self-defense plea. If he does, it won't be manslaughter. Jeff could get life in prison. Or lethal injection."

"Oh, God," she said, but still didn't move from the front door.

"The clock is ticking," I said. "I don't know if you're familiar with Connecticut judges, but this is not California and these are not TV courts. Connecticut judges demand a clean, quick, disciplined trial. As good as Attorney Roth is, he fears Jeff will be facing a jury very, very soon. Can you help me?"

She gave an angry sigh. "Jesus Christ. All right, talk. Come in. Do what you want."

Her furniture, rugs, and draperies were worn and beaten down and on no surface or any object did I see the sheen of hands laid regularly, appreciatively, or lovingly. The windows were dirty. She led me to the kitchen. It was fairly clean, but not at all cheerful, despite the sun pouring in. An older television sat on the counter. "Look out for the wires," she said and

I stepped over the cable and electrical connection. "What do you want me to do?"

"Talk to me. Tell me anything about Jeff that might help me help his attorney defend him. Could we start with when he drove away that morning?"

"He had no car."

"I thought his father bought him a Jeep."

"He gave it away."

"To whom?"

"Somebody out west."

"Okay, so that morning, did you drive him somewhere?"

"He wasn't staying here."

"Where was he staying?"

"I don't know. He had been gone for two weeks."

"Where?"

She shrugged. "Probably on one of his 'expeditions.'"

"What do you mean? ELF?"

"What do you think I mean? When they announced those indictments out in Oregon, I thought, oh God, he got caught at last."

"He told me he didn't know that bunch."

"They always say they don't know each other," she cut me off angrily. "They're like Alcoholics Anonymous." Her face twisted with a bitter expression. "I thanked God it wasn't him. Now I wish it been him. He wouldn't be in this mess."

Suddenly, tears trembled in her eyes. They ran down her face. She lowered her head and wrapped her arms around her chest. I moved back, not sure what to do. Her shoulders heaved, violently. It was wracking her whole body and I knew I had to do something. I stepped slowly closer, laid my hand on her shoulder, then my arm, and gradually drew her into both arms.

"Oh God," she gasped. "I'm sorry. I'm sorry. I'll stop."

But she was crying like someone who had put it off a very long time and she could not stop. She cried and cried and cried. She began shaking so hard I started to fear for her life. She was having trouble breathing. I held her even tighter and patted her head like you would comfort a kid or a dog, which didn't help at all. I tried to edge her toward the sink to pour her a glass of water, but small as she was, I couldn't move her.

She tried to speak, several times. But all that came out was something that sounded like, "He," as in Jeff, and she could not form a sentence. She started hiccupping uncontrollably, and for some reason that started her laughing. I thought, Oh my God now we're exploding into complete hysteria, but it was not hysteria. It was just the laugh of someone finally blessed with the ability to see some small, unexpected relief from her misery.

"Water?"

She reached blindly. I filled a glass and closed her hand around it. She took a sip. It slipped from her hand. I was almost quick enough to catch it, but it slipped from me, too, and shattered at our feet, which proved to be a godsend. Suddenly we had a job to do mopping up broken glass. By the time we had wiped gingerly with paper towels, then mopped the water with more towels, then found the vacuum cleaner and vacuumed for shards, she had returned to something like normal.

She splashed cold water on her face and I handed her the last towel from the roll.

"Oh my God. I'm sorry, Mr. Abbott. I just—I don't know what hit me." Her face, reddened, clouded. Her voice grew dull. "I guess it all hit me. Whew." She sat the kitchen table, staring at the back of the TV.

"Why don't I make you coffee," I said.

"Thanks."

I found some coffee in a can and a cafetiere that hadn't been used in a long time and boiled water while she sat in silence, dabbing her face with the paper towel. After it had brewed and I pressed it and poured, she said, "Jeff is very brave."

"I suspected that," I said.

"There is something in him that won't let him turn his back on what is wrong. And it is a terrible thing that he will be locked up for the rest of his life for being brave."

"He's not locked up, yet, in that sense. He's awaiting trial. He's got the best lawyer in Connecticut."

"His father always demanded the best. Even when he couldn't afford it." She sipped the coffee, then looked up at me. "Where does a child develop passion?"

"Home?"

"Not in this home."

"Are you sure of that?"

"Deathly sure. Before Jeff went away, when he was younger, he used to ask, 'Why did Dad leave?' What was I supposed to tell my child? Your father left us to become rich and famous which he couldn't do when he was tied to us? In this home all he found was anger."

"The set to he had with Billy Tiller. Was that when his father left?"

She didn't hear me. "My anger scorched this house. I used to love this house. It was my parents' country house when I was growing up. But my husband poisoned it for me. I only stayed because Jeff wanted to. Then when Tiller destroyed the woods, he was heartbroken. His anger—against his father for leaving, against me for letting it happen, or making it happen, God knows—all came out at Tiller. Tiller became everything that went wrong in Jeff's life. He couldn't help it."

I looked away to hide my face. She thinks Jeff killed him, I thought. Same as his father. They both think he did it.

"I tried to find a boyfriend to find Jeff a father. But I couldn't pull it off. And by then, he didn't even want a father. He found an enemy that took the place."

Chapter Eight

Although I routinely scanned the tour reports published on the MLS website for Newbury's brokers' and agents' open houses, I never expected much. The places I show either come exclusively to me or, if they haven't, from listing agents who figure I have a lock on weird clients.

Speaking of weird, here was a listing so weird that I read it out loud: "Builder's own manor."

It took me a moment to recognize the latest twist on the old "Builder's own home" mystique, where the customer was encouraged to hope that a builder's personal residence had to be superior to those he built for the average slob. Ignoring the reality that he was only living in it until he could sell the turkey.

Fred Gleason was showing it, which surprised me because Fred had never been the sort to allow comically pretentious language in his ads. On the other hand, he had just sold his agency to a national franchise. I read on, to see which builder was unloading the turkey Fred had dubbed a manor.

"Jesus H! That was fast."

Fred was selling Billy Tiller's house less than two weeks after he was killed.

⟨⟩⟨⟩⟨⟩

Ten o'clock in the morning, I was the first to knock on the ugly front door.

The only car in the driveway was Fred's, a magnificent silver Phaeton.

From the outside, this house was so awful that I had taken to driving out of my way not to look at it. Spurning New England materials like stone, wood shingles, or clapboard, Billy had located a railcar full of glazed yellow brick somewhere, and put it in charge of a Florida architect who had apprenticed on self-storage units.

"Fred," I said, when he answered the door, an amalgam of wood, steel, and stained glass. "I do not envy you."

Fred, a jolly fifty-year-old optimist in a checked jacket and sprightly yellow bowtie, said, "All I need is one tasteless fool with a checkbook."

I pretended to admire the entryway, from which one could see wide-screen TVs in three directions and a living room fireplace made out of what looked like burnt sauce pans, but which Fred assured me was an "art material."

"How did this come on so fast? What about probate? Did he have a will?" As I had suggested to Ira Roth, it would be interesting to learn what heir gained from Billy's untimely demise.

"First thing I asked. Turns out Billy didn't own it. Total Land Rape—Scape—owns it. Apparently he didn't keep private accounts."

Nobody gained? Nobody inherited? "Do you mean the company owned Billy's own house? Who owns the company?"

"Partners, I guess. Or investors. Or Billy's estate."

"How can they liquidate assets if they haven't read the will?"

"The company doesn't need permission to sell company assets. The powder room is solid nickel. Want to see it?"

My old friend was pumping himself to excite his visitors, so I said, "But of course," even as I wondered who was getting the money. We admired it and moved on to the kitchen, which Fred's handout described as "A showcase of timeless beauty."

"Who hired you?"

"Total's lawyer. With promises."

"Of what?"

"The condos. If they get it approved."

"Condos in Newbury?"

"There's a need. Older people want to unload the big old place, but stay in town. Total Landscape might pull off a zoning change."

"Somebody should shoot those sons of bitches."

Fred shrugged. "Everybody's got to make a living somehow."

The doorbell rang and the door opened and a pack of women agents came in calling, "Yoo hoo. Fred. Are you here?"

"Look around, Ben. I've gotta—"

"Go. Go. I'm fine." He hurried to the door. I waved to the women, all of whom I knew, and wandered into what Fred's handout called "A master suite fit for Kings and Queens." God knew what Kings and Queens went for these days, but Billy had gone first and foremost for size. There were his and hers dressing rooms, of course, a bathroom big enough to play half-court basketball, and a workout room fitted with a some very serious machines. One whole wall was curtain, and I found a switch to make it magically pull open and saw immediately why Fred had closed it. It covered a glass wall that looked onto a courtyard garden overgrown by several seasons of weeds—tall ones brown from last year, fresh green ones shooting for the sky.

The phrase "poor lonely bastard" skipped through my mind. It looked like the kind of project a guy living alone would get an idea to do, only to get overwhelmed by it. I was surprised that Total Landscape employees hadn't been drafted to keep it up. One of the pleasures of owning a construction company had to be the free labor standing by. But did he actually own it? I had to run this by Ira.

"Hey, Ben."

"Sherry!"

We hugged. Sherry Carter was married to my childhood friend Bill Carter, a one-house-at-a-time builder. She sold real estate, when she wasn't helping Bill, and was one of my favorite competitors. She looked like a gazelle, a very attractive gazelle, a very attractive flirtatious gazelle. A mutually ego pleasing (brief) grope at a beer picnic a while back had cemented our friendship.

"What is that?"

"Used to be a garden."

"Pull the drapes before you knock fifty thousand off the price."

As they slid shut again Sherry said, "Billy should have put the pool in there instead of those weeds. It would be really cool all walled in like that. Instead of where he put it. You could swim naked and no one could see."

"Maybe he was designing for exhibitionists."

Sherry, who was one, and knew it, grinned, rose up on her toes and stretched her long arms so we could both imagine her morning dive.

"I'm surprised to see you here," she said.

"I try to keep up with the latest and hottest."

"But you don't know anybody who wants a house like this."

"Not offhand."

"Somebody'll love it. How much is Fred asking?"

I consulted the handout. She rested a pleasant hand on my shoulder as she leaned close to look at the price.

"Jesus H," I said.

"Oh, Fred'll get it— So how've you been, Ben?"

"Ummmm. Okay. I'm tangled up in the Billy bulldozer thing."

"That horrible ELF kid."

"He's not a bad kid. Or at least he doesn't seem like one."

"Not a bad kid? He killed Billy Tiller, not my favorite person, but—"

"Except maybe he didn't kill him."

"If they're going after builders any of us could be next."

"They?"

"The ELF nuts."

"Nuts they are, but they don't kill people."

"I heard you were kind of obsessed about this."

"From whom?"

"I don't know. People were saying you're obsessing on the kid who did it."

"Because I don't think he did it."

"Ben." She took my hands and looked in my eyes.

"What?"

"Maybe you ought to take a little time to re-think what you're doing?"

"I'm not hurting anybody, I'm just helping his lawyer establish his defense."

"What if you're hurting yourself? Come on, if you saw me doing something like what you're doing, wouldn't you say, 'Hey, Sherry, what's going on? What's wrong.' You know?"

"No, I don't know."

She grabbed both my hands in hers. "I'm talking to you like a friend, Ben."

I said, "I'm touched by how sincere you sound. And how much you care."

"Don't be touched. Just listen."

One of our competitors, a woman new to town who had arrived with the national that bought Fred Gleason, walked in, saw us holding hands and said, "Oh, excuse me."

Sherry released me with a final squeeze. Then, smiling very little, she said to the woman, "If I hear a silly rumor I'll know where it started."

Quietly, I said to Sherry, "Thank you. I know what you're saying. I appreciate you saying it. I'm just going to run this whole thing through my head a couple of more times and that's it."

"Good. Thank you. Come to dinner Saturday."

"What can I bring?"

"A smile."

She gave me a very nice kiss and sashayed out to the living room, where I heard her saying, "Great house, Fred. I've got a couple of clients who will love it."

<>‹›‹›

Homeowners huddled on metal folding chairs in a low-ceiling room in the basement of Town Hall, waiting for the bi-monthly Planning and Zoning hearing to begin. Some clutched papers; others, notes for speeches; Penelope Collins, horse breeder, set up an easel and spread out a colorful hand-drawn map of her neighborhood that depicted density, traffic patterns, watercourses. Most sat in gloomy silence; a few gathered in quiet conference with neighbors drawn into alliance against development of woods and fields they had cherished all their lives. One group even had a lawyer, Tim Hall. But whether they were upset, indignant, angry, determined, or frightened, all looked as unhopeful as cows trudging up a ramp into a dark building marked Beef.

The P&Z commissioners met on first and third Tuesdays to hear builders explain how their proposed developments adhered to Newbury's building and zoning regulations or, if they didn't, why the regulations should be modified in their case. People whose property would be affected by the proposed developments were invited to speak in support or against the projects, which pitted homeowners against builders. Nearly everyone was against the builders. But those against were hoeing a tough row. The ninety-nine percent of the population not trained in public speaking were further flummoxed by a P&Z hearing rule that allowed the presenter for the builder to rebut the protestor, while the protestor's sole means of rebuttal was to look aggrieved.

Among the one percent of the population who did know how to hold an audience or sway the P&Z commissioners, all were employed by the builders. Of that elite, the best was E. Eddie Edwards, who coupled an engineer's precision logic to a lawyer's dislike of facts that did not advance his cause.

He was nicknamed "Evil Engineer" Edwards by the hardworking volunteers of the Newbury Open Space Conservancy. Rumor had it he was a drunk. But I never saw him drunk and he didn't look drunk tonight. Tall, broad-shouldered, reasonably good looking, and well-dressed in a natty tweed jacket that said, "I'm not a lawyer, just a simple engineer," he soon was wrapping the commissioners around his practiced finger and smoothly puncturing the complaints of the homeowners who rose trembling to speak in public for the first time since they failed Show and Tell in fourth grade.

I attended P&Z hearings religiously. It behooved my business to keep up with the latest projects. And it behooved my spirit, if not my soul, to voice complaint when I thought a project begged to be complained about. Tonight I had a third reason: I wanted a close look at the dead Billy's colleague. I'd seen Evil Engineer in action before, of course, but only from the perspective of a townsman obliged to protest pillage that masqueraded as homebuilding. Tonight I was hoping to learn something about their relationship that might prove useful to Ira Roth's doubt campaign.

Edwards was defending a project that everyone had hoped had died with Billy Tiller. But, as Fred Gleason had hinted this morning, the corporate entity Total Landscape—nicknamed Total Land Rape by the Conservancy wits—was moving ahead with it, Edwards reported. I recalled Jimmy Butler complaining that Billy was grabbing his balls from the grave.

Chairman Rick Bowland—a volunteer, like all the board members, who gave up a ton of free time for the dubious pleasure of refereeing cat fights—inquired, "Who's running Total Landscape now that Billy's gone?"

A lawyer recently moved to town introduced himself as Owen Woodward and said that he had been engaged to represent the company which was re-organizing management.

Was the company financially capable of posting the road-building and fire-fighting tanks performance bonds the town required, Ted Barrett, a commissioner, asked.

No problem, said Attorney Woodward. They had plenty of cash on hand, excellent credit, and "Mr. Tiller" had smoothed the transition with astute, even perspicacious estate planning. The lawyer bowed his head as if suggesting a moment of mournful appreciation, which no one seemed inclined to join.

With those distractions out of the way, Evil Engineer Edwards resumed pitching Billy's plan to build condo apartments in a neighborhood zoned for houses on two acres. It was a typical Billy Tiller move against a neighborhood of mostly smaller, older houses, inhabited by people who couldn't afford a fight. (A similar proposal in one of Newbury's estate sections would have pitted Total Landscape against litigators awaiting presidential nomination to the Supreme Court.)

A good but not excellent case could be made defending the town's half-century precedent of two-, three-, and four-acre zoning regulations—which my grandfather had written when he was first selectman. Not excellent because Billy's people were proposing that some of the condos be reserved for the elderly, and some for low-income people, and some courts had ruled that towns had to support a variety of housing stock for a variety of types of people. So while the density question was one way to resist the intrusion, the best-case argument against Tiller Town Estate Houses was flooding.

Fred Franklin, whose hayfield had been turned into a lake by Tiller Heights, a development contiguous to the proposed Tiller Town Estates Houses, asked about flood effects. E. Eddie Edwards claimed that wasn't germane to this separate application. Fred Franklin, turning red in the face, said that it was seeing as how he had lost a tractor in quicksand while attempting to mow his fields, which had been high and dry before "some big city judge from Stamford" allowed Tiller Heights to flood him out. The Chairman asked Engineer Edwards to give assurances that diverting the same streams, again, wouldn't cause more flooding. Eddie Edwards replied that he could not recall the circumstances without going back to his office to review his files.

I stood up to say, "It's only two years since you promised that project could survive a hundred-year flood. You built it last spring. Last summer joggers running past Fred's hayfield had an opportunity to cross-train for the swim segment of a triathlon race. And now you're submitting site plans to build right next to it. How much reviewing do you need?"

"Good question," growled Fred.

Total Land Rape's Attorney Woodward said, "The chair has not recognized Mr. Abbott."

I said, "The project that Engineer Edwards designed flooded just last August, normally a dry month. It can't be that far from his memory, Mr. Chairman. Especially if he's proposing to overturn existing zoning to cram a condo development right next to it."

E.E.E. cast a plaintive look at Chairman Bowland, who said, "Ben, I have not recognized you. Please sit down."

I said, "If a student at the middle school made excuses like Engineer Edwards for not doing his homework, that kid would be sent home with a note to its parents."

Chairman Bowland banged his gavel. "Ben—"

I said, "Where he intends to send his next flood is certainly germane to this proposed adjacent development. Unless he's offering to buy kayaks for the neighbors."

"Ben, either come to order or leave."

I left.

Or tried to. But I was still storming up the aisle to a gratifying smattering of applause when the fire siren atop Town Hall snarled a bone-shaking bass note that soared to a soprano scream.

Chapter Nine

Four men and three women dropped notes, flood-plain drawings, and traffic-pattern maps and barreled out the door, down the hall, and across the parking lot, where the Newbury Volunteer Hook and Ladder Company One duty watch was raising the tall firehouse doors and cranking up the engines.

Rick Bowland banged his gavel again. "Meeting adjourned until two weeks from tonight." Those homeowners who hadn't run off to fight the fire gathered up their papers, moving slowly as if unsure whether something good or bad had happened. Edwards and his new lawyer looked annoyed, and as Edwards caught up with me on the steps, he said, "You're like the Dutch boy with his finger in the dike."

"Didn't the Dutch Boy end up the hero?"

Edwards looked at me. Or, rather, he looked through me, like an SUV driver pretending he doesn't see the car that has the right of way. "As I understand it, the Dutch Boy developed gangrene in that finger. They didn't amputate in time and he eventually lost his whole hand and died in the poor house."

He brushed past. Before I got to the sidewalk, Total Landscape's new lawyer took my arm. "I want to talk to you."

"About what?"

"About going around town raking up unpleasantness from the past that harms my clients' business."

"What do you mean?" I asked innocently, while firmly removing his hand.

"You know exactly what I mean, Mr. Abbott. You are harassing people about past encounters with Mr. Tiller."

I said, "First of all, I'm not harassing, I'm asking. Second, I'm working for the accused's lawyer. Let's keep in mind that the kid has a right to a defense."

"Might it not be wise to let the trial take its course without slinging mud?"

"Wise?"

"Wise," he shot back. "Good for you."

"Are you threatening me?" I asked, stupidly. I was too surprised to react any other way.

Woodward stepped closer and spoke in a low voice. "I'm telling you that there will be development in this town, like it or not. But if you work with us, rather than fighting us, we will work with you to help preserve space and minimize impact. And I am warning you that we will not work with someone who treats us like an enemy."

Maybe I was getting soft. But I actually paused to weigh the consequences of punching out an attorney in front of witnesses on Town Hall steps.

He took my hesitation the wrong way and pressed what he seemed to think was an advantage. "Also, you ought to consider the consequences to your business were you to lose your real estate license as a result of actionable complaints to the many, various, and appropriate authorities in Hartford."

I looked at him in utter disbelief. It wasn't as nasty as Andrew Sammis attempting to saw my face off. But it could sting. If they really went after me I would have to waste time and energy driving to Hartford to defend myself, and probably spend money on lawyers, too.

"Or," he said, "we might exercise our right to sue you. Have you ever been sued? By someone with deep pockets who keeps attorneys on retainer? It is a stomach-churning, sleep-destroying experience. It gets so you dread the mailbox and the telephone."

I stepped closer. "I am about to churn your stomach with a short left, which no one will see because my fist will travel only six inches to ram your gut into your spine."

He tried to back away. Friendly as a Rotarian, I encircled him in my right arm. "You must be new in town. Among our old Yankee customs, we do not threaten independent Realtors unless we're prepared to duke it out with them."

"I should warn you that I am a retired Marine officer."

"Glad to hear it. I would not want it getting around town that I brutalized a man who couldn't defend himself."

Woodward was cool enough to manufacture an expression that resembled a grin. "Hey, lighten up, Mr. Abbott."

"Call me Ben. And now, if you will excuse me, there's a fire I want to attend."

I ran into the street and flagged down Scooter MacKay, who was chasing the fire engines with a blue light strobing in his Range Rover's windshield. I buckled in as he floored it, reached over, and freed his dinner napkin from his belt.

"Where is it?"

Scooter keeps scanners on his desk, sideboard, night table, lawn mower, and dashboard eavesdropping 24-7 on police and fire radios. "Harry's Olds."

We knew, of course, that General Motors' Oldsmobile division was out of business and that Harry Greenan had retired and sold the dealership to Dave Goldsmith, a refugee from the crowded Southern Fairfield County I-95 Gold Coast corridor who had arrived just in time for the boom in Chevy and Cadillac SUVs and Hummers. It was just that Harry had started selling Oldsmobiles there four decades before Scooter and I were born and the name stuck in our minds.

"You know this new lawyer, Woodward?"

"Met him at the Lions. He's handling Billy's stuff."

"What do you think of him?"

"More city than country, lawyer-wise. And now that you ask, more business guy than lawyer, though he mentioned he was affiliated with a big New York firm. Why?"

"I saw him at the P&Z. Pushing Billy's condo scam."

I found it hard to believe that Attorney Woodward and Total Landscape feared that Billy's past threatened their future. So I chalked it up to the lawyerly instinct to head off any conceivable trouble before conception.

Half a mile out of town, Scooter said, "Wow!"

Wow, indeed. The fire cast an orange beacon brilliant as a lighthouse.

Most Newbury fires are brush fires and quickly extinguished. House fires are rarer and tend to be clothes drier lint fires. While spreading horrific smoke damage when the homeowner's laundry chute functions as a chimney between laundry room and bedroom, they aren't that much fun to watch. And with development gobbling up the dairy farms, neither of us had seen a good barn fire since we were in high school. But Goldsmith's Cadillac and Chevrolet looked well on its way to a highly enjoyable event, as tonight it was unlikely anybody was trapped inside. Just a good, rip-roaring fire any amateur pyromaniac would be stopping the car for.

Trooper Moody was there ahead of us, stopping traffic to make way for the fire engines. Scooter parked on the shoulder and we walked quickly toward the flames. Trooper Moody was waving people off, but he let us pass—Scooter because he was Press, me because Ollie would not have minded at all if his least favorite real estate agent contracted second-degree burns.

But immediately inside the fire department's Day-Glo orange diamond warning signs and parking cones both of us were stopped by Jay Meadows, first assistant chief of Newbury Hook and Ladder, who was acting as incident commander. Jay greeted Scooter and me with a cheerful, "Stay back, you idiots."

"I gotta get pictures!" Scooter protested, waving his camera.

Jay informed us that a burning car might blow up so maybe it would be a good idea to stop here now. And while we were at it, would we please get out of the way of the pumper that was backing away before an explosion forced a new round of bake sales to buy a replacement. Not to mention that they couldn't spare any firefighters. For the first time ever, there was a shortage of volunteers as the town grew larger and more people worked far away. Nobody was panicking yet, though they had placed a modest sign in front of the firehouse—*Volunteer Wanted. We Need One Good Man or Woman.*

I always felt vaguely unimportant at fires. The firefighters look double-wide in their rubber boots and fireproof garments, and Paul Bunyan tall. While wearing helmets, dragging hose, and carrying pike poles and portable extinguishers, they clearly deserved to be here, having devoted time and energy training for this.

Scooter snapped a bunch of pictures and scribbled some notes. We couldn't see exactly what was burning, but the flames were approaching a closely parked rank of Chevy Trackers, Blazers, Tahoes, Suburbans, and Avalanches. I said, "Write down Battleship Row."

"What for?"

"They're lined up like the battleships at Pearl Harbor. If one of them catches fire they'll all blow up like the Japanese had bombed them."

Scooter stopped writing and gave me a pitying look. "My only readers who remember Pearl Harbor are on life support."

"What about the history teacher?"

Heavy machinery, shouting, and radios blaring drowned out whatever he answered. Flames lit the night, flickering shadows all the way to the tops of tall trees. More sirens descended as the Frenchtown unit responded. Jay Meadows switched on his bull horn. In a voice now sounding more anxious than cheerful he ordered his men and woman to fall back.

Not a moment too soon. Flame raced up the hood of a Chevy Suburban, danced across its roof, and tumbled down its square backside like a waterfall. Two seconds later the SUV's gas tank exploded with an earsplitting crack that threw fire and burning metal onto the Trackers, Blazers, Tahoes, Suburbans, and Avalanches lined up in a long, neat row.

It looked for a moment like the high-end half of the business would escape, as Harry's inheritor had parked the Cadillacs at a distance to denote exclusivity. But when the last Blazer blew up the explosion ignited the spare tire hanging off the back rack and sent it soaring across the divide and through the windshield of a Platinum Edition ESV Escalade. The ESV Escalade, burning fiercely, exploded a nearby SRX, and an EXT Cadillac pickup truck caught fire. And then the whole row ignited, one vehicle after another, like a luxurious Roman candle. Last to detonate were the Hummers, and soon it looked as if their prospective owners had, in a burst of vicarious patriotism, off-roaded to Iraq.

Averaging seventy thousand bucks a pop, the explosions were not going to make the insurance underwriters happy. The good news was that fewer gas guzzlers would clog Newbury's roads in the coming months. In fact, it was a wonderful fire for someone who hated gas guzzlers, too-bright lights in their rearview mirrors, and fat vehicles hogging the passing lane. An environmentalist's dream—tarnished, to be sure, by a soupy black smoke of incinerated tires, paint, plastic, and insulation spewing into the night sky.

Poor Dave Goldsmith looked stricken. Gas prices had gone down, recently; a temporary blip or not, no one knew, but there were plenty of people around with more money than brains and the damned things were selling again, which meant that General Motors was not likely to allocate hard-to-find vehicles to dealers who had been so careless as to let their stock catch on fire. I offered my condolences and he told me that he had borrowed way too much to expand his showroom on the basis of imminent sales of vehicles now up in smoke.

Dave was so upset that he started wandering toward the fire. I'd sold him a huge old house and he had a slew of brothers, sisters, and in-laws planning to move to the area, too, so he was not the kind of customer I could afford to lose. Just in time, I grabbed his arm and jogged him firmly away. Another explosion boomed. A fender whizzed close overhead like a helicopter blade. The serious sound of such a large object parting the air and nearly scorching our hair sobered Dave quickly. "Geez-zus! Thanks, Ben."

"You okay?"

"Sort of." He gazed across the road at the smoldering wreckage that had been his livelihood. "Could have been a lot worse. If this happened during the day, somebody would have gotten killed."

I didn't state the obvious, that if someone were around they'd have noticed the first car burning in time to put it out. Nor did I ask him whether in his experience as car dealer he had ever seen such a fire. He had enough on his mind. So I asked again if he was okay and when he assured me he wasn't going to run back into the flames, I went looking for Jay Meadows and found him huddled with his lieutenants. I waited until he had sent them back to hose down the remains, and then asked, "How'd it start?"

"Accelerant."

"Arson?"

"It looks like an accelerant to me."

"Like gasoline?"

"We'll ask the fire marshal," Jay replied.

"Cars are full of gasoline," I noted.

"In their tanks." Jay looked really pissed off. "Whoever did it could have killed my people. It's not like some lamebrain starting a brush fire."

"If it was arson."

"See you later, Ben. I'm busy."

I wandered away. Scooter was busy interviewing firemen. Ollie was busy directing traffic. First Selectman Vicky McLachlan drove up with Tim and jumped out, chestnut curls flying. She didn't see me as she hurried over to get a report from Jay Meadows. I debated walking home. But I really didn't want to meet a driver with failing night vision on a dark road while I was wearing a dark jacket and trousers, so I waited at the edge of things to catch a ride with Scooter.

"Mr. Abbott?"

A woman's tentative voice from above and behind. I turned and looked up, up, up into the very intense face of a very tall woman who asked, again, "Are you Mr. Abbott?"

She was quite young and startlingly attractive with sharp cheeks, bright eyes, and a steep, stark slash of black hair that looked more radical than stylish. I had the strange, strong feeling that I had met a turning point in my life. I had heard older friends joke how a guy discovers his age the first time his hair thins enough to get a sunburned scalp. My hair was doing fine, thank you—still thick as a wolf's—but I had just discovered for the very first time an interesting woman who I knew in my gut was way too young for me. Which did not stop me from extending my hand and smiling warmly, "Ben Abbott. I don't think we've met."

She took my hand in a strong, dry grip, using only her long fingers, and stepped closer. So close, in fact, that I suspected I was talking to someone who wanted something from me. Close enough to command my attention. Close enough to smell her perfume if she had been wearing perfume. Close enough to let me breathe in the aroma of unadulterated woman if she wasn't wearing perfume. But if she did emit the fragrance of unadulterated woman, I couldn't smell it over the raw, prickly stink of gasoline.

Chapter Ten

"I'm Jennifer."

Maybe Jennifer had ignored the Don't-Top-Off warning at the self-service pump. Or maybe she'd just been gassing up her chainsaw. Or maybe she had stood downwind of the fire. But I saw no chainsaw. Nor did I smell smoke on her clothes.

She said, "I have to speak to you."

"About what?"

"Jeffrey told me you could help."

"Jeffrey?"

She looked alarmed and even younger. "Jeffrey! You talked to him. In jail?"

"Oh—I'm sorry. Jeff Kimball. Totally out of context….Of course. You're friends?" Of course. Jennifer and the spray-painting elf were about the same young age.

"Could we talk?"

"Do you have a car?"

"My van's back there." She pointed way down the road through the storm of apparatus, people, and cars. A yellow VW microbus was parked on the shoulder at the end of the gawkers' row of cars and trucks.

"Well, if you'd like, drive me back to town and we'll have a drink at the Yankee Drover. Or a Coke."

Her VW bus was old and looked as quaint as a sepia print of oxcarts on Main Street. The yellow paint had been brushed on by hand, and the entire vehicle was ringed with scenes of animals scampering in rain forests under the loving gaze of long-haired, half-naked hippies. Many of the slogans pasted in the windows and affixed to the bumpers were as up-to-date as "Solar Power" and "Real Men Don't Hit Women"; others were older, all the way back to a faded "Make Love Not War."

"Borrowed from your grandfather?" I asked, and ran my fingers around her gas cap.

"No," she answered seriously. "I bought it in Indiana."

My fingers came away from her gas cap dry as a bone. And whatever they smelled of did not include gasoline. I stood in the road and held up my hand for traffic while Jennifer backed and filled until she got it turned around. We clattered back to Newbury and parked in front of the Yankee Drover. Jennifer asked for white wine. Anne Marie carded her—casting me a pitying look—and returned her drivers license, which was from Michigan, saying, "Happy birthday."

Jennifer answered with a steeliness beyond her years, "Last month," and said to me, "could we sit at a table?"

I found a quiet, empty one in the corner, tilted my Pellegrino at Jennifer, and said, "Is it Jeff you want to talk about?"

"Yes."

"Is he your boyfriend?" Nice thing about talking to a twenty-one-year-old, you can be direct like a scary professor or a brave parent.

"No."

"Just a friend?"

"We met at Seattle."

She said "at," not "in." I matched my grammatical observation to the slogans on her van, her sober gaze, and Jeff's penchant for spray-painting Earth Liberation slogans and asked, "At the demonstration?"

"Yes."

"What was that, about three years ago?"

"Six."

"They sort of tore the town up, didn't they?"

She finally smiled. "We sure did." And as quickly unsmiled. "Do you have a problem with that?"

"Hey, I'm as anti-suburban sprawl, contra-globalization as the next guy. But I'm also adverse to throwing bricks and setting fire to SUVs. Although if I were to change my mind about setting fires it would probably be to an SUV."

"Jeff said you understood."

"You and Jeff must have been pretty young back in Seattle. When did you see him next?"

"What are you going to do for him?" Nice thing about being twenty-one, no one insists you beat around the bush.

"Strictly speaking, I'm not doing anything for Jeff. I'm working for his lawyer. His lawyer is who you should ask. I'm just helping out."

"But Jeff said you were cool."

I drew back in my best (stiffest) Main Street, Newbury, Connecticut, New England stance. "Cool, maybe, but not stupid."

It went right over her head. "No, he didn't say you were stupid."

"Two compliments in as many seconds."

That went over her head, too. Which I'm sure didn't bother her one whit because she said, "Jeff is innocent."

"Good. I am so glad to hear that."

"You are?"

"Do you have any evidence that might help his case? Like you were at the movies with him that afternoon and it was just somebody who looked like him that was sitting on the bulldozer on top of the murder victim?"

"You're joking about something that is not funny."

"I know it's not funny. But it's not fantasy, either."

She blinked.

I said, "You're his friend. Tell me something, anything, that will help him."

"He wouldn't hurt a fly."

"I spent three years incarcerated in Leavenworth Penitentiary. Most of my fellow prisoners had used that same line as their defense. Some even got their mothers to testify they wouldn't hurt a fly."

"You were in jail?"

"Jail is temporary. When they've got you for good it's called prison."

She stared at me.

I said, "So please don't tell me that I'm joking about something that is not funny. I know what's not funny. And your friend is looking at prison for life if I can't find a way out for him."

"What if he did it?"

"Then prison is where he belongs."

"I didn't mean that. I mean he didn't do it."

"I hope you're right."

"If you only hope, why are you helping?"

I didn't tell her about Alison's horse. I didn't have to. I didn't tell her about disliking Billy and his McMansions, either. I didn't remind her that in her recent high school years they must have taught her that in America you were innocent until proven guilty. Instead, I said, "Here's what troubles me about the open and shut case against Jeff Kimball. Prosecutors prosecute. It's what they do. I've got a cat who lives in my barn who kills mice, squirrels, possums, and weasels. That's what he does, stalks and kills. What my cat does not do is entertain second thoughts. Which makes him very dangerous to mice, squirrels, possums, and weasels. Prosecutors, in common with my cat, do not entertain second thoughts, either, which makes them very dangerous to the innocent."

I was speaking partly from the heart, partly to soften her up for a big question.

"Their goal is to convict. They will take any conviction over no conviction. When they win a conviction, they don't look back. They go looking for another. So I'm helping because in a case as open and shut as their case against your friend Jeff, the prosecutors are not entertaining second thoughts or any other possibilities."

"Possibilities. You mean other suspects?"

"They don't want other suspects."

"What if the killer had help?"

"They've already got the killer—" I raised my hand to quell protest. "They think they do. They are sure they do. They are positive they do. They don't want to muddy the water. The only way they will accept another killer is if the guy they've already got fingers his accomplice. Which would give them two convictions. But they're not going to go around to every friend of Jeff's and ask, 'Where were you last Sunday afternoon?'"

"But don't they want to catch the real killer?"

"In their minds they have. Where were you last Sunday afternoon—"

"Me?"

"—is a question they don't want to ask. But since we're on the subject, where were you? Last Sunday afternoon."

"I don't have to tell you that."

"I thought you want to help Jeff."

"I do. But I don't want to tell you where I was."

"Then don't."

"I wasn't in Connecticut."

"I am not relieved to hear that."

"Why not?"

"I was hoping you would tell me that you were with Jeff until moments before he was arrested and that you could testify to his state of mind which was not the state of mind of a man about to kill another man."

"Well, I can't. I was in Pennsylvania."

"Did anyone see you there?"

"I don't know. I mean I was just driving through."

"Fortunately, you're not a suspect," I said cheerfully. "In Billy Tiller's murder. Are you a member of ELF also?"

"What do you mean?"

"Are you allied with the Earth Liberation Front."

"I wouldn't tell you if I was."

"But are you?"

"People who serve ELF do not undercut their ability to serve by turning themselves in to the cops."

"Jeff's quite open about it. Of course he's already gotten caught spray-painting 'E. L. F.' Which is why the prosecutor is not going around asking such questions of other people. Even people like you driving around without an alibi."

"That's ridiculous. I don't need an alibi."

"For now, at least. They like the easy way. Which is why they're always trying to gut the Constitution." And now for the question. "May I ask you something?"

"What?"

"Something personal."

She turned from me. Away she was quite beautiful. Facing me she threw up so many masks that her beauty was lost. "Not if you're going to hit on me."

"You're too young to hit on."

"Everybody hits on me."

"Would you rather no one noticed you?"

"Yes."

"Would you give me your hand for a moment?"

"You are hitting on me."

"Just for a moment. I'll give it right back. I promise."

Reluctantly, she extended her hand, then stiffened as I drew it to my face.

I said, "May I ask?"

"What?"

"Why do you smell of gasoline?"

Chapter Eleven

Jennifer stood up so quickly she knocked over her glass. I caught it, saving the glass, if not the wine. She shoved past me and banged out the door. Anne Marie hurried over with a towel. "Did the girl come to her senses?"

"No. I did."

Sort of. Truly sensible, I suppose I would have telephoned 911. I mean wouldn't anyone who smelled gasoline right after an arson fire? I told myself I definitely would have if anyone had been killed or injured. As it was, Dave Goldsmith's financial troubles notwithstanding, I guess I felt a certain empathy for an arsonist who targeted SUVs. Hardly civilized. Hardly even civic minded, depending on your definition of "civic minded," which in my book—the OED on my hard drive, when I walked home from the Drover to look it up—means "public spirited."

The editors quoted a music critic named Neville Cardus on the subject: "He was not civic-minded and could never be trusted at a garden party."

If there was one place I could be trusted it was at a garden party. Most of the time.

While I was at it I looked up "bulldozer" to see if Sherman knew what he was talking about. Not completely it turned out. The name came from an old American South construct of "bull dose," original meaning an extra heavy dose of "medicine" as in flogging a slave to death or dragging someone out of his house while holding a large pistol to his head.

Already at the computer, I went on line to TireRack and read a bunch of consumers reviews and professional evaluations of automobile tires—four of which my ancient, lovingly maintained Oldsmobile would be needing in a few thousand miles. Tires were nothing I skimped on because the old car was drastically overpowered. It had started out life as my father's staid sedan in the long-ago days when no self-respecting Newbury Realtor would be caught dead in a Mercedes. When I inherited it, my cousin Renny Chevalley, who was a gifted mechanic, had swapped out the silly original motor for a bored and stroked Caddy he had pulled from a wreck.

Renny had been my childhood best friend and I loved the car. After Renny was killed—murdered—Pink had taken over the garage and maintained the Olds like a shrine to his little brother. When called upon it still could, in Pink's parlance, eat Corvettes and BMWs for breakfast. So it needed and deserved great tires. To my surprise, when it came to precise handling and adhering to the road in the rain, TireRack's surveys all concluded that the new Goodyear Triple-Tred outperformed the classy favorites Michelin and Pirelli. I was dubious about a rubber company's inability to spell the word tread. But I took a chance and I ordered four tires for the amount of money that Pink would cheerfully charge for two and arranged to ship them directly to Chevalley Enterprises Garage to mount and balance them at a price to be negotiated.

Before signing off, I checked the local banks' mortgage rates, which had been yo-yo-ing almost daily. I saw that despite the Fed's darnedest efforts, the markets would continue to allow home buyers to spend money they shouldn't. I was pouring a celebratory malt whisky when I heard a knock at the front door. Not a door usually knocked upon. Kitchen door for friends, side door to the glassed-in sunroom real estate office for business.

I opened and looked straight into the eyes of Jennifer, who was standing on a lower step. "I'm sorry," she said.

"For what?"

"For running away. But you frightened me. I travel a lot. I always feel I'm a stranger. In small towns I'm always afraid of being stopped by the police."

"Now you smell of soap," I said. "The kind you find in the Frenchtown Diner wash room."

"I washed my hands. Could I come in, please?"

"Sure."

She stepped inside, looked around, partially smiled. "I love old-smelling houses like this."

"The mold or the furniture polish?"

"Both. I was like a relo child? My parents were always moving. They had to buy tract houses, 'cause they're easy to sell when you get transferred again? But I always tried to make friends with somebody at school who lived in a house like this. If you thought that I started that fire why didn't you call the police?"

"Because I didn't smell gas inside your bus, so I told myself that you hadn't carried a can of it in the bus."

"I can't tell when you're telling the truth."

That made two of us. I said, "Let's talk about Jeff. You met rioting in Seattle. When did you hook up again?"

"We didn't 'hook up' that way."

Another reminder that I was talking to a younger person. I meant "meet." She meant something more entwining.

"When did you next meet?"

"Iowa."

Time and place seemed one with her. As if she lived in events, event by event.

"Where else did you meet?"

"Michigan, last time. Oregon. He came out to Montana, after New Hampshire."

"Let me guess, you were Deanies."

"We were trying to take our country back."

"What I liked most about your candidate," I told Jennifer, "was that he made it seem stupid and lazy to be a cynic."

I was preaching to the choir, of course and when I got the smile I expected I said, "So what do you want to do for Jeff?"

"Can we get him out on bail?"

"No. They don't give bail to murder suspects. Particularly to murder suspects who travel as much as Jeff did."

Jennifer said, "Wouldn't it be helpful if you were able to discover who really killed that disgusting developer?"

"Well, that's kind of what I've been trying to do. Without a lot of success. I mean I've found plenty of people with motivation. And a few with the means—if you can call the ability to drive a bulldozer the means. But I don't see any of them as doing it."

"I want to help him."

"Well, in a way you already have."

"How."

"You've nudged my thinking in a new direction."

"What direction?"

"Let me sleep on it. There's some people I want to talk to in the morning."

I stood up. Jennifer didn't.

I moved toward the front door.

Jennifer said, "Can you recommend a place to stay tonight? That's not very expensive."

Anne Marie had started renting B&B rooms upstairs at the Drover. Each room had a name. The Pumpkin Room, the color. The Hills had a view. The Organza Suite, famous for clouds of cloth billowing about a king-size four poster, had been re-dubbed by Newburians drinking downstairs the Orgasm Suite. Organza, however, did not come cheap and the only place "not very expensive" was a ratty motel ten miles down Route Seven. I said, "It's kind of late to go looking. You can stay in my guest room, tonight." I emphasized "tonight" as in "tonight only."

She said, "My job starts tomorrow."

Surprised, I asked, "Doing what?" She didn't seem the job type.

"I'm in the Northwest Connecticut Landfill Reclamation project."

"That's a great project. The Audubon Society got behind that."

It was north of Newbury, up in the woods. I knew it as the Jervis Dump, a swamp that generations of the close-knit, inbred Jervis clan—who traded guns, ecstasy, high-test marijuana, and untaxed booze and cigarettes with their Canadian cousins—had found convenient to make inconvenient things disappear. Audubon would unearth fewer surprises reclaiming the La Brea Tar Pits. "What will you be doing there?"

She became animated. "I'm in a work study program. From school? I'm studying environmental engineering."

"Where?"

"Montana Tech."

"How'd you get to Connecticut from Butte?"

"I applied for the site characterization study. So we'll know what we'll find and how it will influence the economics. Will there be methane? Can we reclaim it? Will there be subsidence when we excavate? How will the contents affect the equipment? Reclaimed waste is abrasive. How much will that abrasiveness shorten the life of excavation equipment?"

Maybe she *was* the job type. She suddenly sounded more like an academic than a barn burner. Maybe she hadn't torched forty SUVs after all. I got her settled and showed her the shower and found her a terry robe. Then I went to my own room and lay awake for quite a while.

I wondered why couldn't I answer what was it about Jeff Kimball that made me doubt he had killed Billy Tiller. As for the unlovable, unlamented Billy, I found myself marveling at his meteoric rise. While Billy was not the only ne'er do well in Newbury to inherit a valuable chunk of free land—there was too much in-breeding to prevent that—none I could think of had ever made such a success of it.

Jennifer had raised an interesting question about the killer having help. Two killers? Maybe his victims had formed a committee. But on the subject of two, was I seeking the wrong sort of "other suspect" for the wrong motivation? Had I gotten stuck in the able-to-drive-a-bulldozer approach, while I should have been asking who—who could drive or hire a bulldozer—who was also capable of spraying Main Street with bullets? Put another way, was Billy Tiller really so thoroughly awful that not one, but two separate individuals would risk a murder conviction for the pleasure of killing him?

Chapter Twelve

Trooper Moody telephoned at dawn, sounding uncharacteristically polite. "Ben, I gotta tell you, your Aunt Connie is canning again. You want me to—"

"I'll do it, thank you. Thanks for calling."

"Half a mile down Seven," he said and hung up. I jumped off the bed into pants, shirt, and shoes, wasting no time on socks and underwear.

Ordinarily, a report that one's elderly great aunt was canning would not raise eyebrows in New England, where many old aunts and grandmothers still put up fruits and vegetables for the long winter, as our ancestors had before the invention of freezers and microwaves. Sadly, this bridge to our past was the not case with Aunt Connie.

Trooper Moody's call was the third such in seven and a half months.

I shot out of my driveway onto Main Street. There were lights in her windows across the street. Not surprising, as she had always been an early riser. When I used to walk to school on dark winter mornings I would often stop in her kitchen for a moment, fill her in on whatever homework I'd done, and maybe ask her a question. I've shared afternoon tea with Connie Abbott most of the Tuesday afternoons of my life, including this week.

Half a mile down Route Seven, I spotted her walking tentatively along the shoulder. There was no mistaking her frail figure.

She wore a calf-length dress under a raincoat too light for the morning chill, and steadied herself with her cane. In her free hand she held a black plastic garbage bag. Suddenly she stopped, bent slowly to the ground, and straightened triumphantly with a beer can, which she plopped into the bag.

I parked the car at a distance and hurried after her.

"Good morning, Connie."

To my great relief, she recognized me instantly. The first time she hadn't had torn my heart out. But those memory lapses were rare and this morning she acted as if she knew exactly who I was and why I was there.

"Good morning, Ben. You're out early."

"So are you," I said. "How are you?"

"Lovely morning, isn't it?"

I agreed that it was a lovely morning, and that the day promised to be a little warmer and dry.

"About time," she observed. "This weather has been just ghastly."

That was an accurate appraisal, which further relieved me. I decided upon directness, which had always been her way. "Trooper Moody said you were out on the road."

"Oh, I saw him. I must say the town gets its money's worth. Oliver Moody is always on duty."

"He was a little concerned, Connie. Worried about you out on the road here."

"I'm perfectly fine. Just picking up a little extra money."

I looked at her.

She said, "Deposits."

I asked, "Do you really need them?"

Connie was sole heir to the affluent branch of the Abbotts, which had been raking it in since pirate days and investing shrewdly in whale ships, canals, railroads, insurance, and land. But try and tell her that a wealthy woman—with foundations and charities in place to disperse every penny of her fortune the day she died—did not need beer can deposits.

"It astonishes me," she said, "how people will just throw money out the window. Not to mention litter."

"Why don't we go home and get cup of coffee?"

"Oh, Ben. I just got started." She shook the bag, which rattled. "Only four."

"Four's a good start."

"It's a good enough start, but hardly a morning's work."

"I need your help with something."

"Well, can't it wait?"

"No. I'm under the gun."

She sighed. "I really wish you could learn to plan ahead. All right. All right. Your place or mine?"

I thought of the under-age giraffe in my guest room and said, "Yours."

I got her belted into the car, turned around, and drove home. As we pulled into her drive she craned her head to stare across the street at my house.

"Ben, there's very young person stepping out your door."

"A one-night guest."

"Well, shouldn't you offer her breakfast?"

"She's rushing off to a new job. She'll find breakfast on the way." I hoped Jennifer had enough cash for a take-out coffee. But I wasn't going to leave Connie to run after her.

I got Connie out of the car and in her back door into the kitchen. She insisted on brewing the coffee herself. All the while she kept glancing at the mud room where we had deposited the clanking bag of cans, and I could see her thinking hard on what exactly she had been doing.

While I reflected on the relationship between eccentricity and dementia. I was hoping, I suppose, for a promising connection between them. I told myself that she was the last of a generation with a bred in the bone hatred of waste. Wastefulness had been the worst Puritan sin in harsh New England. I clung to the comforting thought that when Connie Abbott did go round the bend she did not stray far from who she was. She had always been frugal.

A red watering can stood by the sink, into which she poured the left over half glass anyone else would have dumped down the drain. As a boy I had asked why. She had explained that every glass of water drawn from the faucet required electricity to run the pump that pushed it up from the well, and oil to generate the electricity, while reducing the reserves in the underground aquifer. At the same time, every drop poured down the sink put the septic field to unnecessary use. Maybe that was why I disliked the McMansions so much. Their defenders maintained that every generation builds bigger houses, and that they create employment, but all I saw waste of materials, waste of land, waste of scarce resources.

Connie had always been precise, organized, measured, and intensely civic minded. So how strange was it to wander the highway picking up the cans and bottles slobs threw from their cars? You see people in the cities do it all the time, plodding and bending with huge Santa Claus plastic sacks. People with no home who need the money.

"I suppose I've had another spell," she said suddenly.

"Just a brief one."

"Ben, I hate this."

I'm not as brave as she is. I couldn't face it directly and I heard myself mouthing platitudes. "It was just a moment. They come and go. Day by day, right?"

She cast me a look less than grateful and said, "Try not to treat me like a fool when I'm not having a spell."

Early last winter she had suffered a series of mini-strokes. Transient ischemic attacks, they're called. TIA. Doctor Greenan sent her down to Yale and they ran the tests. If there was good news, it was that TIA appeared not to be harbingers of larger strokes. Instead, they worked their way slowly through the brain in tiny bites, like hungry little mice.

That we knew it was not Alzheimer's offered some scant solace. One of the Yale doctors, a shrink, sat me down privately to pass on the slightly comforting information that the sort of dementia that stemmed from transient ischemic attack did not usually cause the sorts of personality deterioration suffered by Alzheimer's patients. "She'll remain mostly who she is," he said by way of explanation. "As fastidious, as polite, even as lively, for a while at least. Unless she is a person who hid a personality disorder behind a screen of superior intelligence—I do note that your great-aunt is unusually intelligent." He waited for my response, which was one of relief.

"She's too brave to hide anything. She would deal with it."

"I thought so," he said. "But down the road, remember, memory will continue to fail. Confusion will increase. And confusion breeds fear."

Connie was glaring across the kitchen table. I said, "Sorry. It's upsetting."

"I know it's upsetting. It's happening to me. You said something about wanting help. Or was that just a ploy to lure the old fool indoors?"

"You're not an old fool."

"But I am old. Thank you for coming after me, Ben."

"Thank Trooper Moody."

"I will write him a note. You said you need help?"

"Yes. I do. What can you tell me about E. Eddie Edwards?"

"Well I knew his great-grandmother, of course."

"Great-grandmother? I didn't realize they were around here that long."

"Before they came here they were down in Easton and Stratford."

"I've never thought of them as a Newbury family."

"Good Lord, Ben, the Edwards are more Yankee than we are. Our people may have come up from Stratford to found Newbury, but that was only after the Edwards founded Stratford. If you want to get technical about it, we're rather Johnny Come Lately. By comparison. Not that they ever accepted the responsibilities such families should. You'll not find the Edwards serving anything but themselves. And if you think I'm eccentric, Samantha was an absolute nut case."

"Samantha?"

"E. Eddie's great-grandmother. She owned half of Easton, though you'd never know it, seeing her dressed like a Polish peasant, right down to the boots. And she had a trick she used. She…she…"

"What?"

Connie's gaze drifted toward the mud room again. Her mouth worked.

"Boots, you were saying?" I asked.

She took a deep breath. "Air guitar."

"Beg pardon? Did you say, 'air guitar'?"

"It just popped in my head. I was trying to remember what I was going to say about her boots and the only word that came to me was air guitar. Phrase, actually, isn't it?"

Her jaw set and she waved the missing thought aside like a deer fly. "It will come to me. Or it won't."

I was overwhelmed with admiration. And gratitude. She had banished fear from the room. "You were saying Polish peasant?"

"I don't remember. But she was a very clever woman."

"But what about E. Eddie?"

"Just as clever from what I've seen. It's appalling the developments he's managed to get approved in Newbury. He plays P&Z like a bass fiddle."

"He always strikes me as more lawyer than engineer."

"That's his best trick," said Connie. "And why the builders love him so. He thinks on his feet like a lawyer, but he commands the respect the commissioners give an engineer."

"He's a pretty lousy engineer considering the floods he's caused."

"He engineers the rules, not the hills. He goes by the book— the book that allows him to build the most houses. Don't get me started on this, Ben. It just appalls me. Why are you asking about Eddie Edwards?"

"I've heard two stories about him lying to protect Billy Tiller."

"Oh, the bulldozer. How did you get involved in that?"

"Ira."

"I should have guessed." She was not a big fan of Ira Roth, whom she considered to be a pale, crass shadow of the civic-minded citizen his father had been.

"I owe him for Alison's horse."

"I could have told you that would come back to haunt you. Still, Redman is a decent animal, despite his appetite and dubious bloodlines, and Alison's happy."

It was suddenly almost as if the morning hadn't started with her picking beer cans off the road. She was her usual quick, sharp self. Except when she stole a look toward the mud room where that black plastic bag lay on the floor. But she filled me in a bit more on E. Eddie and Billy, naming a couple of land deals even I hadn't heard about. She owns quite a bit herself, and the grandees do tend to eye each other.

"How was your trip to New York?" she asked.

"A little depressing. I watched the land beside the tracks in a way I never saw it before. I mean places where the river runs in a ditch and you don't see a single tree or patch of earth not cemented over. It kind of shook me to think that at one time that ground looked just like Newbury."

"A very long ago one time."

"But isn't it fragile?"

"I just remembered about—shoot, there it goes again. Oh, I'm sorry, Ben, I'm getting hopeless."

"It will come to you."

"Or it won't…"

"Anyway, I—"

"I was reading a mulch bag the other day."

Oh dear God, I thought. Here we go again. That had landed out of nowhere, like a silent mortar round. "How," I asked, "did you happen to be reading a mulch bag?"

"Have you noticed how the new houses have such mulched borders?"

My wary "Yes" occupied three or four syllables.

"Their beds and borders are so neat and crisp."

"Yes."

"But there aren't any plants."

"Gary at the nursery told me it's because the people are so overextended buying their house all they have left is twenty bucks for an arborvitae at Home Depot."

"Of course," Connie said briskly. "They are buying as much house as they can afford, which people have always done and is actually quite sensible. Values always rise, in the long run."

"What if the bubble bursts in the short run?"

"Not every gambler wins. But I was wondering why they mulch empty beds where they have no flowers. When I was a girl the gardener used shredded leaves and straw from the stable. These people don't have stables and precious few leaves with all the trees the builders knock down. So they go and buy all that mulch. At any rate, the explanation is right there on the bag. The mulch manufacturer tells them they should make neat borders even if they have no flowers."

"Ah," I said with great relief. "That's why you were reading a mulch bag."

"Why," asked the old lady staving off dementia, "do these people believe the mulch manufacturer?"

<>◇<>

I drove down to Frenchtown to the Chevalley garage looking for Cousin Pinkerton. Betty, my cousin Renny's widow, told me that Pink had said he had to see a guy about something, which meant he was most likely hoisting an early eye-opener at the White Birch.

There's a six-hour drinking window after which you don't really want to be in the same bar with Pinkerton Chevalley, and I hoped that this morning's visit to the White Birch marked the beginning of a party, not the end. I asked if he had looked like he had been to bed last night.

Betty said it was always hard to tell and asked me to send him back if I found him.

I drove quickly to the White Birch. The parking lot was mostly empty so early on a weekday morning. I didn't see Pink's bike or any of his cars or trucks, but he could have been saving gas "test driving" one of his customer's vehicles, so I went in.

There was more tension in the stale beery air than would be expected at eleven a.m. with only two customers in the place. Wide Greg, the owner, was pretending to read his morning newspapers, but he had one cold eye on those customers, my cousins Pinkerton and Sherman Chevalley, who were seated several bar stools apart, hunched over bottles of a discount brand brewed somewhere in Rhode Island. Pink was asking Sherman as I walked in, "What did you say to me?"

Pink was a very, very large man. The largest Chevalley currently alive. His father had been larger, some said, but he had met an early end before Pink was full grown, so no one knew for sure. He tended to be quiet. When he did speak, people listened. But apparently Sherman was not listening.

"I said it clear a minute ago," he replied. "I ain't repeating myself."

Wide Greg edged closer to the PVC pipe he had nailed under the bar to hold his baseball bat. I said, in a big, cheery voice, "Good morning, cousins."

"What the fuck do you want?" asked Pink. I guessed he had not been to bed.

He and I get on well, as a rule. Renny and I had hung tight as boys. Pink had looked after him, and me too, and what others considered flaws in my character, the willfully unevolved Pinkerton admired. Occasionally, when an investigation requires me to ask what might be construed as offensive questions, he comes along as backup and I feel as secure as a diplomat with a satellite link to a submarine full of cruise missiles.

"Answers," I went on cheerily. "Answers. I have questions for both of you."

Now Sherman was staring, too, unpleasantly. Chevalley men fall into two general body types. Huge and incredibly huge, like Pinkerton, form the larger group. A few are skinny. Sherman was of the latter, quite tall and remarkably strong, though thin as a snake. A snake with a deep, gravelly voice. "What kind of questions?"

"First I have a question for Greg," I said, turning to Wide Greg. "Good morning, Greg."

Greg nodded. Experienced at keeping order among the disorderly, he knew that I was trying to distract them from killing each other. He appeared mildly curious whether it would work.

"Greg, my question for you is, could you bring another round for me and my family?"

Sherman smiled a little. Pink looked suspicious.

Silently, Greg opened three bottles, placed one each in front of Pink and Sherman, and brought me mine. I was still on my feet, standing at the end of the bar, very near the door. I placed a twenty-dollar bill on the bar and told Wide Greg, "I'll need a receipt. It's on the client."

Greg returned a dark look. The business had gone cash-only after Visa and MasterCard installed detectives in the parking lot with direct lines to their Lost and Stolen Card Divisions. I tipped my bottle in the direction of the boys down bar. "Cheers, guys."

This was the crucial moment. Like the moment the rodeo clown climbs out of his barrel to draw away the bull—in this case bulls—bent on goring the rider. "Pink," I said, "remember when they shot Billy Tiller on Main Street?"

"Yeah?"

"Remember that rumor you told me?"

"Which one?"

"That it was a setup."

"Yeah?"

"Was it?"

"Was it what?"

"A setup," interrupted Sherman Chevalley. "You deaf or something? He's asking you was it a setup?"

Pink turned on him. "No, I'm not deaf or something. Are you stupid or something? Or are you just tired of looking at your face in the mirror because if you are I can change that for you."

"Out!" said Wide Greg, indicating the door with his baseball bat.

Pink's massive jaw dropped like a cinder block. "What did I do?" he protested, aggrieved as an eighth grader wrongly accused of lobbing a spitball. "Hey, come on, Greg."

Greg stood still as a ledge of granite.

"I didn't do nothing."

"Out. One week!"

There was a powerful dynamic operating. Surely, Pink felt no fear even though Wide Greg was aptly named and close inspection of his baseball bat might reveal bone splinters. But the White Birch was home. A permanent banning would leave a man with nowhere to go ever again but his car repair business during the day and his mother's double-wide house trailer at night. A full week would be hell enough.

"Out," Wide Greg repeated, almost gently. "Don't force me to make it two." He turn his attention to Sherman, who was gloating. "One word and you are gone for three."

Sherman turned his attention to the interior of his beer bottle. Pink hulked to his feet, threw a wad of money on the bar, and shambled past me out the door. I followed and found him climbing mournfully into a borrowed car.

"Here. Finish this." I thrust my bottle in his huge paw.

"I didn't do nothing."

"Nobody ever said life was fair."

"You can say that again."

"Listen, Pink, that setup rumor, how did that go?"

"It was bullshit."

"That's what I thought at the time. But you insisted."

"Maybe I was wrong."

"You said you heard the shooter called him in the hospital. Said he was pissed because Billy called 911."

"It was bullshit."

"That's what Billy told me."

"Billy knew what really happened."

"What was that?"

"Ben, you don't know a damned thing about anything, do you?"

"Hey, I'm just a spoiled brat from Main Street. But tell me this. Somebody was warning him off. Weren't they?"

"Looked that way."

"They had probably warned him off a couple times. But he kept doing it, right."

"Billy always kept doing it."

"Doing what?"

"Fuck knows."

"A land deal, maybe?"

Pink shrugged, shaking the borrowed car. "Maybe."

"Maybe destroying something somebody cared about."

"Billy nuked a lot of stuff."

"Maybe he ripped off a supplier?"

"Wouldn't be the first time."

"Maybe he didn't pay somebody what he owed him?"

"Maybe."

"Pink, I'm not learning a lot from you."

"You're not asking me anything I know."

"Or even heard a rumor about?"

"No."

"Tell me this. What really happened? Who was the shooter?"

Pink drained the beer I had given him. Slowly. Silently.

"Was he alone? Did he have a driver?"

"Driver? Are you fucking crazy?"

"I'm only asking because he was shooting .22 longs, which was probably a rifle and how the hell do you fire a rifle repeatedly while you're driving. For that matter, if he wanted to get Billy why didn't he use a shotgun?"

"You are so out of it."

"Come on, Pink. Give me a break. Stop telling me I'm out of it. Help me here."

"There was no car."

"What are you talking about? Everybody saw a car."

"Did the cops ever find a car?"

"No."

"Did they get a marker plate?"

"No."

"You were there, Ben. Did you see a car?"

"I saw a car go by fast."

"Did you describe it to the cops?"

"I didn't pay any attention to it. Then the shooting started."

Pink started his borrowed car and raced the engine, listening carefully. Then he pressed down hard and got ready to pop the clutch. "The way I hear it," he yelled over the roar of the engine, "the shooter waited for a car to go by fast. Then he opened up. With a rifle."

"From where?" I shouted.

"Meeting House belfry, I heard. I also heard he was in the clock cupola on Town Hall."

"That was a lot of shooting. Funny the cops never found any shell casings."

"Maybe they did and didn't say. Maybe the shooter picked them up. Maybe he put a bag over the ejection port. Maybe it's all bullshit. It doesn't matter. He got him in the end."

"What do you mean?"

"He got him with the bulldozer."

"Who?"

"I'd start with the kid sitting on the bulldozer."

Pink popped the clutch and tore away, laying down just enough rubber in Wide Greg's parking lot to show that while he understood Greg's need to keep things quiet and peaceful in a bar the town fathers dreamed of shutting down, a man still had a right to be hurt, angry, and deeply disappointed in Greg's inability to distinguish the innocent from the guilty.

I went back inside and asked Cousin Sherman how skilled an operator had to be to impale a crawling man with the ripper. Sherman answered at length over the next beer I bought him. The short version was, very skilled, or damned lucky.

"For all we know the dude took four or five shots at Billy before he nailed him. You know: Pow! Pow! Pow! Pow! Pow! while Billy's squirming around trying to get away."

"I only saw one deep gouge."

"The way that machine was spinning around? Nobody knows how many shots he took with the ripper. Pow! Pow! Pow! Pow!"

"So, skilled or lucky?"

"Or both." Sherman peered into his empty bottle like he was mourning a dead friend. I bought him another, brushing aside his thanks with a casual, "It's on Attorney Roth."

"No it ain't. It's on Jeff."

"Who?"

"Little Jeff Kimball, that Ollie arrested."

"Well, in actual fact the beer is on his dad and he can afford it."

"The least he can do," Sherman mumbled, running a dirty hand through stringy gray hair. His eye rose to the silent TV, which had a morning gun show on. A man dressed like a Marine was demonstrating how a .50 caliber rifle could shoot holes in steel.

"What do you mean, the least he can do?"

"That poor little guy. I never saw a little bastard so needing his old man."

"You know him?"

"Know him? Who do you think taught Jeff Kimball how to drive a bulldozer?"

"You taught Jeff to drive a bulldozer?"

"What about it?"

"Why didn't you tell me before?"

"You didn't ask."

He was right about that. I paused a moment to consider whether I was truly stupid. Or just not paying attention. "How did you happen to teach him?"

"He paid me. His old man. The kid handed me the dough. But it was the old man's check."

"Was this when his father got him the union job?"

Sherman snorted. "Rich people aren't as smart as they're cracked up to be. The old man gets the kid a union job with Federal pay driving a machine—instead of some guy trying to make a living—and suddenly, 'Whoa! How do you run a machine?'"

"How'd they pick you to be the teacher?"

"You know how they do the career day at the high school?"

"Yeah?"

"They roped me into showing the little bastards bulldozers. I brought my machine up there. Somebody remembered."

His attention shifted to the TV again, where the man dressed like a Marine was shooting holes in a concrete wall. "Hey, Greg? Remember that guy selling those .50 caliber rifles?"

"No," said Wide Greg, without looking up from his morning papers. Police reports in the Waterbury *Republican,* Danbury *News-Times,* and Bridgeport's *Connecticut Post* offered a reasonably accurate headcount of out-of-town regulars free to drop by the White Birch tonight.

"Come on Greg, you remember, he had a whole bunch of cool stuff. Bayonets, flash grenades."

"I don't remember," said Wide Greg.

"And the conversion kit for your semi-automatic?"

"No."

"What the hell was his name? Funny name. Angel! Latino dude from Waterbury. He calls himself Angel. Yeah. That's it. Angel. Next time you see Angel, this Latino dude from Waterbury, tell him I—" Sherman hesitated, as if he had suddenly recalled the terms of his parole. "Tell Angel—tell him I know a guy who might want to buy one of those fifties."

Greg put down his paper and said with finality, "There won't be a next time as there wasn't a first time."

I nudged my cousin back on line. "Sherman, do you like teaching?"

He nodded. "I figured out the trick to it. First you look real careful at the guy learning. Then you say, 'Okay you're good at this. And that. And this. Let's work on this, at which you suck.'"

"How good was Jeff?"

"Good. Damned good."

"Good enough to kill Billy with the ripper?"

Sherman said, "The funeral's tomorrow."

"Billy's? Are you sure?"

"Damn sure."

"It wasn't in the *Clarion*." Billy's five-line obituary had not listed burial plans or where to send donations in lieu of flowers.

"I helped Donny Butler dig the hole. His machine was down."

"I didn't think they'd release the body so soon."

Sherman shrugged. "They'll be burying more coffin than body."

"So how good was Jeff?"

"The kid is a natural."

"Goddamn it," I said.

"What's wrong, Ben?"

"I'm goddamned disappointed to hear that. I was pretty much convinced he didn't kill him."

"Jeff? He didn't kill Billy."

"What?"

"Jeff didn't kill him."

"You just said he was a natural."

"Yeah, but there was no way Jeff Kimball could have killed Billy Tiller."

"What makes you so sure?"

"When the dude who did him ran the meat grinder on Billy, he rotated the machine right. Right?"

"Sherman, I don't understand what you're talking about."

"Jeff always rotated left."

Was I hearing the best news I had since Ira Roth called me? "Explain," I said. "What do you mean?"

"I mean Jeff stomped the left brake every time, locking the left tread, so the right tread, which keeps turning, spins her left."

"Every time?"

"I tried to break him of the habit. I told him, 'You're going to get hurt one day when you have to go the other way all of a sudden and don't have time to stop and think about it and then it will be too late and you'll end up under the machine when it rolls over on your fucking head.' But he wouldn't change. Or he couldn't. I mean everybody's got some dumb thing they hang on to, don't they, Ben?"

Chapter Thirteen

When I ran into Ira's office saying, "You have got to hear this," the lawyer was explaining the world to someone on the other end of his telephone headset. He waved me to a chair, continuing affably, "You raise an excellent point sir and indeed I too often marvel at that fine line between the expense of documentation, the cost of due diligence, the price of disclosure versus the danger, shall we say, of standing less than fully prepared before the court."

Ira was not a fat man, despite the vest, but in his arsenal of effects he kept a fat man's laugh, which he loosed, when his client stopped talking, in an eruption of merry wit and world-weary worldliness. "Quite right, sir. It is the client's money. Not to mention the client's liberty."

He motioned, again, for me to sit down—I was pacing—ran the poor devil through his goodbyes, and hung up with a satisfied sigh.

"So Ben, where are we?"

"The man who taught Jeff how to run a bulldozer told me that Jeff could not have killed Billy Tiller because the murderer rotated the machine on top of him in a right-hand pivot and Jeff always rotated left."

"Why did Jeff always rotate left?"

"Kind of a mental tic. Always left. Billy's murderer pivoted right."

Ira thought on it for a moment. "Interesting."

"Interesting in one way—I mean it's good for us to know he could not have killed Billy, but—"

"My client killed no one," Ira interrupted.

"But I am not convinced that the gentleman who told me will be an asset on the witness stand."

"Why not? Teachers make excellent witnesses. Forthright, articulate, accustomed to speaking in public, thereby commanding both court's and jury's respect."

"It's my cousin Sherman."

"Ah," said Ira. He looked out his office window, seemed to wish it was the window that overlooked his racehorses instead of the clapboard side of Newbury Savings and Loan, and observed, "You bring me a convicted felon to strengthen our case."

"At least strengthen our resolve."

"I understand Sherman won parole," Ira mused, hopefully. He shook his head. "Cancel that thought. By the time Jeff's trial starts Sherman will likely be locked up for something else. Well, looking at, or at least for, a bright side, you are right about resolve. Your resolve. You can believe even more surely that Jeff is innocent. Despite appearances. Perhaps this knowledge will inspire you to more heroic efforts. Perhaps locate a witness less likely to be served with an arrest warrant as he mounts the stand."

"I'll keep looking. By the way, Total Landscape's lawyer tried to lean on me last night. Told me to back off. Stop besmirching the reputation of the company's revered founder."

"You're kidding." Ira looked as surprised as I had felt. "Really?"

"I came close to punching him out."

"That would have secured your reputation. Did he say why?"

"Bad for business."

"Did he threaten you?"

"Nothing I could file a complaint for."

"Of course not. He's an attorney. So how did he lean on you?"

"First he suggested that we could work hand in hand to preserve open space if I, quote, let the trial take its course. Then he threatened to report me to various agencies in Hartford."

"That's bullshit."

"Then he said they would drive me crazy with lawsuits, clearly implying that they could afford lawyers I couldn't."

"I wish I had that in an e-mail," Ira said grimly. "Did anyone hear?"

"No. He was careful."

"Was Eddie Edwards there?"

"Not in earshot."

"Strange—Well, I'll tell you, Ben. It's very corporate, actually. You get these guys who convince themselves that the company is sacred. Occasionally they get so over excited they'll say something really stupid. What's his name?"

"Woodward. Owen Woodward."

"I saw him at the Lions. Up from Stamford, I think. I'll check him out. You've made me curious. Okay, what else?"

"Fred Gleason is selling Billy's house. It wasn't owned by Billy. It's owned by the company."

"Not when I was his attorney."

"Why would he put the house in the company's name?"

"God knows. Tax scam. Or to keep it from the next wife. People do remarkably silly things to dodge Uncle Sam. Not to mention creditors."

"Would you telephone Plainfield jail? Tell them you're sending me over first thing in the morning to interview your client and you don't want to hear any nonsense about time limits."

Ira started to touch his speed dial. He paused. "One rationale behind this 'doubt' strategy you were questioning?"

"Yes?"

"Best-worst case—if we have to plea down—we get Jeff second-degree murder and out in fifteen years. Which could be a pretty good deal."

"Great deal. Unless he didn't do it."

Ira's gaze drifted to the clapboard wall. "I did not say Jeff did it. But if the state's attorney gets past us and has his way, a jury will say he did do it. So, in the best-worst case, we will influence the jury's take on the nature of what they say he did—the degree of murder, as it were. And the nature of the sentence."

"Fifteen years is a very long time, Ira."

"The heart and soul of a young man's life," Ira agreed. "Yet not as long as worst-worst case."

Chapter Fourteen

I ran home to catch up on messages.

Alison was waiting in my office curled up in the cracked-leather armchair that, in concert with faded wallpaper and musty damp, is supposed to appeal to house hunters seeking authenticity. She had brought in the mail and put it on my desk.

"Have you been expelled from school?"

"It's June, silly. I had a final this morning. I came home to study." She curled up tighter, stared at her book, and said, "Guess what?"

"What?"

"I think Mom met somebody."

"That's nice," I said, fully aware that Alison's mother, who had run away from a drunken father to marry a drunk, could not be expected to possess a clear eye for Mr. Right. "How do you feel about that?"

"I don't know. I mean I hate that she's lonely, but…"

"But what?"

"I wouldn't want to leave here."

I felt my stomach drop.

"Well, that's sort of getting ahead of things, if she's just started seeing someone."

"But she's so excited."

"Well…"

"Well what?"

"Well, we'll see what happens."

She returned a worried glance. I asked, "Are you going to ride Redman when you finish studying?"

"I finished."

"So are you going to ride?"

"Maybe later."

We locked eyes, miserably. I said, "Listen, I've got to drive out to meet somebody at the Richardson place. I'll only be there a minute. Want to come along?"

"Okay."

◇◇◇

"Walk me through Sunday afternoon, Jeff."

He looked hangdog this morning, scared, lonely, and thoroughly miserable. He was scratching his cheeks and tugging his chin. His left eye was swelling like he'd caught a punch.

"Starting when?"

"Wherever you think is the place to start, ending with Trooper Moody finding you on the bulldozer."

"I told all this to the cops. And I told it to Mr. Roth."

"Please tell me."

"Are you trying to trap me into some kind of mistake? 'Cause you're wasting your time."

"Jeff, I don't want to shake your story. I want to believe it."

"It's not a story. It's what happened."

"Tell me what happened."

"What's the point?"

If Jeff was innocent, he could give me a picture of the crime scene before the murder. In that picture I might see some clue as to who else might have been driving that machine. If he was guilty, he could give me a picture that would serve him.

He proceeded to tell me, verbatim, what I had read in Ira's transcript of their first conversation. Verbatim. As in word for word. "It was raining, drizzling, and when I heard the machine, I hid inside the cellar of the second house, the one that had the first floor built. I was scared. I had thought I was alone. But I didn't hear any workmen. Didn't see any trucks. I had been about to start spraying the front of the second house and I thought the machine meant I'd get caught. But it didn't come my way, the sound faded when it headed up the road they had cut through the woods. But I knew I couldn't keep spraying if people were around. So stashed my paint in my pack and headed back over the hill. I was just into the woods when I heard a scream."

"A woman?"

"No. It was man, but he screamed. Not a yell. A scream. Like total pain. I stopped and listened. But nothing happened. I could still hear the machine working. Then after a while it stopped. So I edged over that way, along the woods, to look down on the lots. I could hear it idling. Then I saw it, just sitting there. Nobody on it. Then I saw the arm. I thought it was somebody's coat. But something didn't seem right. I kind of snuck lower down the slope. Then I see it really was a person. I ran up and jumped on to get it off the guy. Then I thought, Oh God, which way? Then I knew I needed help. I got my phone out of my pack and I was just turning it on when all of sudden Trooper Moody was coming up the slope, with his gun in his hand."

He stopped talking. I asked, "What did you think?"

"I was scared."

"Because the gun was pointed at you?"

"No. He didn't point it. It was hanging at his side. None of that aiming and pointing stuff with two hands. Like you see on TV? Just swinging from his side."

I nodded. As a resident state trooper, Oliver Moody patrolled alone, ruling the many square miles of his Connecticut turf by instilling fear in the fearsome. He was a powerful man who regarded a firearm primarily as a club—when a fist or his five-cell Maglite wouldn't do.

"Where did the bulldozer start from?"

"I don't know. I didn't see it down where I was. Must have been parked farther up the road."

"Did you hear it start?"

"Yeah."

"But the man's scream came later?"

"Sure, after the machine was running," he mumbled. "Why do you think he screamed?"

"Jeff," I said with a lot of exasperation, "I'm beginning to suspect you've been sniffing your spray paint."

"I don't get high that way."

Somehow I had to wake him up. I dropped my head to the table and swept my arm underneath.

"Hey, what are you doing?"

"Feeling under this table for a microphone."

"Are they allowed to listen?"

Ah, paranoia. Suddenly—finally—I had his full attention.

"Come here!" I leaned across the table, beckoned him very close, and whispered, "I don't know if they're listening or not, but I gotta ask you something. I've got immunity because I'm working for your lawyer. Whatever you say is between us. Okay?"

"Okay."

"Whisper."

"Sorry," he whispered.

"Now answer me. I want a picture of that scene before the murder. I want to know what you saw and didn't see. So I want to know when you got there, and how."

"What do you mean?"

"Were you there the night before?"

"Why do you ask?"

"Goddammit, someone tried to torch a house. Before the rain. Were you there the night before? Just nod or shake your head."

Jeff nodded.

"What did you see?"

"Nothing."

"Paint me a picture. Do you see a truck?"

"No."

"Do you see a car?"

"No car. No truck."

"Motorcycle. Off-road four by."

"No. I didn't hear one, either."

"Did you see the bulldozer?"

"I didn't go that far up the road. I assume it was up there the night before, but I didn't see it 'cause I didn't go past the second house."

"Paint me a picture. Where is your car?"

"I didn't drive. I hiked."

"Up the road?"

"Over the hill."

"That how you got in the next day?"

"Sure."

"So the next day, you came back. "

Jeff nodded.

"What did you see?"

"The house didn't burn." He looked around the interview room and whispered so softly I could barely hear. "I did a gas and candle fuse? I guess the gas evaporated or the rain doused it. Anyhow, it just got scorched. I felt like a complete asshole."

"Who taught you the gas and candle stunt?"

Jeff gave me that I-don't-trust-anyone look. "I read it on the Internet."

Before the Internet, the Devil visited late at night in the form of a wolf or snake or a goat. I whispered, "What will you say if I discover that the person who drove that bulldozer over Billy Tiller was an Earth Liberation Front operative?"

"That's crazy. No Elfer would kill."

"How about the 'Elfer' who turned you on to the candle trick?"

"No way. I learned that years ago. On the West Coast. Besides, I never said it was an Elfer."

"You hiked in the next day, too? Or did someone give you a ride?"

"I hiked in."

With two hikes down the hill, two hikes out, plus the killer hiking out, I was amazed that I had not seen a single print. "Same trail over the hill? A deer path?"

"No."

"Why not?"

"Never use the same trail twice."

"Did you learn that on the West Coast, too?"

"No. I learned that in Michigan."

"Jeff? How committed are you to ELF?"

"Totally. Americans are killing the world. We don't need to drive SUVs that burn three times as much fuel as a vehicle needs. We don't need to build huge houses that waste energy and resources. We're destroying the planet just so we can have crap we don't even need. ELF is fighting to stop that waste. How could I not be totally committed to ELF? My only question is, how can I best serve ELF? What can I do to help the movement? How can I really make a difference?"

I was astonished and appalled. Jeff seemed to have no concept of the trouble he was in. This "serving" statement sounded as if he thought his current problem would just melt away and he'd soon be out on the street saving the environment.

I said, "Keeping in mind that it will be very difficult to make a difference from behind bars, let me ask you this: If Attorney Roth were to put you on the witness stand—I have no idea if he would, that's his decision—but if, how would you portray your total commitment to ELF? Knowing that the prosecutor would use it against you."

"Why am I committed to ELF? I just told you."

"Imagine the prosecutor asking. Imagine how you would answer on the witness stand." I wasn't sure why I had gone down this route; it wasn't my job, here, but anything to get him to volunteer more information would help, including making him aware of the danger he was in.

But all he did was dig himself in deeper. "ELF gets its point across. Do you know how unbelievably frustrating it is when something that is so important, something I believe in, is totally ignored? The environment is important. It's the source of all life. It's the only one we've got. If burning something down is the only way to get the point across, then I have no problem torching SUVs and McMansions. Greedy idiots like Billy Tiller don't even realize the fragility of what they're bulldozing to build an ugly, wasteful subdivision. I refuse to lie back and let that happen and I—"

"Okay. Okay. I believe you. Actually, I doubt Attorney Roth will put you on the stand if it comes to trial. More to the point—"

"You didn't listen," he shouted.

"Relax. I'm right here. No need to yell."

"I said that I have no problem torching SUVs or fucking McMansions. I didn't say I would kill anyone. I never could do that. Never."

"I believe you. I really do, Jeff. As bad as it looks, I believe you. Now, more to the point right now—did you hear a car or truck drive away when you went down to the bulldozer?"

He took a deep breath. "Do you really believe me?"

"Yes."

"Mr. Roth doesn't."

"I'm sure he does," I lied. I actually had no clue what the hell Ira was really thinking. "But Mr. Roth has to stay detached to serve you best. Now, did you hear a car or truck drive away when you went down to the bulldozer?"

"No."

"Could you have heard it over the noise of the bulldozer?"

"Yeah, by then it was just idling. What is all this?"

"I'm trying to figure out where the guy who killed Billy went."

"Into the woods."

"Did you see him?"

"No. I'm assuming. Or maybe he just hid in one of the cellars, and ran away later. I mean Trooper Moody didn't go looking when he had me."

I took comfort in the thought that if Jeff Kimball was guilty, it would have been easy to say that he had heard a car drive away.

"And neither time," I asked, "either the night before or the day Billy was killed, did you see a car or a truck?"

"I told you. No vehicle."

"Not even Billy's red diesel?"

"Yeah, I saw Billy's truck. How do you think Billy got there?"

Good question. And it spurred another. Did the killer come with Billy in his truck? Someone Billy knew? I felt a little "wow" tingle and the whole case got about ten times more interesting: someone he knew rode along with him, a friend, employee, a subcontractor.

But how'd he get away? To run over the hill, didn't he have to know the lay of the land? Had to be a local? Or, had methodically scouted out the terrain ahead of time. I had climbed the old wood lot hill to get a phone signal. It was dense and tangled and steep and the way down the other side toward Fred Franklin's flooded hayfield was steeper. Only an outdoor type would have chosen it for an escape route.

Like my young friend here.

I had not noticed human footprints, but I hadn't been looking as I concentrated on the cell phone. And I had to admit, my prints must have disturbed any that had been there. So much for the first rule of preserving evidence. Brilliant.

Jeff's eyes were drifting. I was losing him, again. Reliable narrator? Unreliable narrator? Passionate eco-warrior-slash-murderer? Or innocent fool? I had told him I believed he was innocent. I wanted to believe him. I hoped, but did not know if Jeff's information, such as it was, was coming from a guy who was making it up, or if he was just a frightened kid zoning out.

"Sherman Chevalley told me you had a problem turning the machine."

That caught his attention. "What do you mean?"

"That you always rotated left."

Jeff made a face. "Sherman is totally last century."

"How so?" I asked, recalling that in the previous century, Sherman had also been last century.

"He taught me on an old D4. Like Billy's. With levers and pedals and all that shit. I knew it would be the last one I ever drove. The new ones on the Federal job had joysticks. So I knew that his problem wasn't my problem."

"Sherman said you were a natural."

His whole face brightened. "Really?"

"He said that you would be really something after you learned to pivot in the direction the situation demanded."

"Yeah, well I didn't."

"Until you drove the new machines?"

Jeff Kimball reached into his jump suit to scratch. "Well that's the weird thing. Even with the joysticks, I usually rotated left. So maybe he was on to something. Funny. I never thought about that until you asked."

"So he wasn't too old-fashioned to teach you?"

"I didn't mean it that way. Sherman gave me a good start. I mean my dad was supposed to teach me, but he was too busy."

I sat up straight. "Your father was supposed to teach you?"

"He got busy. He had a big deal going down."

"I wasn't aware your father could drive a bulldozer."

"Oh, yeah. He worked his way through college. Driving them in the summers. One time he took a whole year off working on an Interstate. Federal money is really big. Union. He got in the union, he was doing fine."

"But he was too busy to teach you. And you'd seen Sherman at high school career day?"

"You should have seen him at the school. He was all snaggily toothed. Everybody was afraid of him. Even the teachers. But I liked him. He treated me like…he treated me like I wasn't shit. I felt bad when he went to jail."

"He's out on parole."

"Oh, yeah? Good. I hadn't heard. I was away."

"Mind me asking where?"

"All over. Arizona. Maryland. Pennsylvania."

"I spoke with Jennifer."

I caught the sidelong flash in his eye again. I trust nobody. "Yeah, she told me she was going to see you."

"She thinks you're innocent."

"I am, for God's sake."

"Unfortunately she couldn't offer anything to prove that."

"How could she?" Jeff asked. "She wasn't here."

"What happened to your eye?"

"Some asshole slugged me."

"You want me to try to get you transferred or put into protective?"

"He won't do it again."

"You sure?"

Jeff raised his left hand, which he had been holding under the table. A row of cuts across his big knuckles suggested the slugger would leave the jail with fewer teeth than he had entered. "I'm sure."

I left, troubled. The kid could defend himself with his fists. Until the cops hauled in some hard case who'd stick him with a shank.

⟨⟩⟨⟩⟨⟩

Across the street from the jail, the Court House Diner was frequented by jail guards, lawyers, judicial marshals, Plainfield cops, and state troopers from the barracks. I ordered their memorable tuna salad sandwich, no fries, and black coffee. Earlier, passing through the courthouse on my way to the jail, I had seen a familiar face on the witness stand. I dialed her cell.

"I saw you telling the truth, the whole truth, and nothing but the truth. Got time for lunch at the diner?"

Detective-Sergeant Marian Boyce and I had bachelorhood in common. She was trying to change her situation—mainly, I knew, for the sake of having a full-time man around for her little boy—and had been seeing a pleasant Pratt and Whitney engineer for a while.

"Already ate."

"Coffee?"

"I can't if it's social. I promised myself I'd behave myself."

"I want to pick your brain."

While I was waiting for her, the jail guard who had given me a hard time the last time I'd visited Jeff came in. He started to scowl. I stuck my hand out and said, "I'm sorry if I leaned on you the other day. I'm just worried about that kid."

The guard did the right thing. "No problem."

"Can I buy you a cup of coffee?"

"I'm just getting take out."

"So I'll buy you a take out. It's on the lawyer. Have a dougnut, too." I ordered from the counterman.

"I hear they're making you do overtime."

"Yeah, laying off some and working the rest of us harder. You want to get a day in the woods and instead they call you in last minute."

"The indoors is the tough part, isn't it? I'm a real estate agent. The thing I like most is getting outside."

"I'd give anything to do a job like that."

"Take a course for the license. It's the kind of thing a lot of people work on the side to get started."

His container came. We shook and he left.

Marian Boyce walked in wearing her trial outfit: a calf-length skirt, low heels, white blouse, and a blue blazer cut large under the left arm for her shoulder holster. The fact she was wearing a skirt meant that her ankle gun had migrated north to reside in a nylon thigh holster. The hands-off look in her gray eyes signaled loud and clear, "I fully intend to 'behave,' so don't ask if it's the red one you gave me Valentine's Day."

Among her excellent qualities was directness. "I'm glad you want to pick my brain. That way I can see your face and keep my word."

"Your hair looks great."

"Too busy to cut it. You look great, too."

"Really?"

"Actually, no. You're looking a little ragged."

"Thanks."

"Don't you work out anymore?"

"Not so much, lately. How's law school?"

A big grin broadened her face and lit her eyes. She tossed her head and her hair, a little longer than usual, fanned prettily. "Top of my class. Of course it's only night school. But, still number one." Sergeant Marian's long-range plan, after she retired from the State Police, was to get elected governor of Connecticut. Just like Vicky McLachlan. I was the other thing they had in common. Or used to.

She accepted coffee and let me talk her into a cranberry scone. "What's up? You're on the bulldozer kid?"

"The only crime in Newbury this year."

"Who hired you?"

By all that was right and decent, the person buying the coffee was supposed to ask the questions, but Marian was a cop, and a cop's daughter, and could not help herself.

"Ira Roth."

"Not the kid's father?"

"The kid's father hired Ira." Why, I wondered. Why are you asking? You must know all this already.

"And you hope you'll find enough mitigating factors to gain the kid parole after he serves his first one hundred years?"

"Not funny. The kid didn't do it."

She gave me a look and said, "Kid on bulldozer on victim?"

"He was sitting on the bulldozer and the bulldozer was sitting on Billy Tiller. Question is, in what order they got there."

Marian laughed.

I said, "I don't believe he did it."

"Whatever you say. It's not my case, anyhow."

"I know. Clinton and Brady have it."

"You realize, of course, that I can't talk about that investigation."

"Of course not."

"So what are you picking my brain for?"

"Old case. No longer active."

Marian touched her lips to her coffee and probed me with her lovely eyes. It took her two seconds to decide, "Last year's crime. The Main Street shooting."

"Am I right in assuming that with the victim dead of new causes, last year's shooting is old news?"

"Technically, no. But I'm comfortable chatting in general on that subject."

"Who did it?"

"If I knew he'd be locked up."

"Who do you think did it?"

"If I thought I knew who did it I'd be on him like paint."

"Who did you speculate did it?"

"Speculating can get a girl in trouble."

"It was your case. Yours and Arnie's." Detective-Sergeant Arnie Bender was her partner, a small, weaselly fellow she did not like that much. Except that she knew he was almost as smart as she was—and as brave—which made him an asset.

"Was the kid a suspect?"

"One of several."

"So now with the new charges you're assuming it was him then, too?"

"No. Jeff Kimball stopped being a suspect when we discovered that he had been arrested the same afternoon as the shooting."

"How far away?"

"On top of a redwood tree in Oregon."

"I didn't know that."

"Maybe he and his big shot father thought it wouldn't help his defense. All this ELF stuff has the state's attorney dreaming U.S. Senate."

"I heard."

"The redwood arrest cinched it. He's tracking ELF arrests in ten states and looking forward to TV every day of the trial."

"You might put out the word that the kid getting shanked in that jail across the street would not help the state's attorney's campaign."

"It's not a shanking kind of jail. It's a glorified holding pen."

"The kid is something of a stubborn hothead. And since he can handle himself fairly well, it's only a matter of time until a fellow holdee sharpens something."

"I'll mention it. Thanks. Any more questions?"

"Who was on your shooting list?"

"I can't tell you names of suspects."

"Can you tell me the motivations you uncovered?"

Marian thought about that a moment and grinned. "Sly. Very sly, Ben. Sure. Let's see, we had an unpaid subcontractor, an aggrieved landowner, an aggrieved neighbor, an aggrieved truck driver, an aggrieved former employee, a jealous husband, and a cheated drug dealer—Ben, you look surprised."

It didn't take a mirror to know that my jaw was hanging slackly.

"Okay," I said. "I've talked to subcontractors, landowners, neighbors, truck drivers, customers, and employees. But a jealous husband? And a drug dealer? Both are off the charts."

Marian grinned again. "Maybe you're looking at the wrong charts—by the way, there was one other suspect."

"An aggrieved what?"

"Real estate agent."

"Really? What was his motivation?"

"He had written a lot of angry letters to the local newspaper complaining about Billy Tiller's projects. And spoke out against them at zoning hearings. Seemed to have a real thing about Mr. Tiller."

"Very funny."

Marian raised a cautioning hand. "We didn't think it was funny at all. Statements like, 'We must find some way to rid our town of the developers destroying it.' And, 'Face it, the developer is the enemy. His profit is based on our loss.' Pithy, Ben. Almost witty. But statements like that made this real estate agent a prime suspect."

"Except that I was standing next to Billy Tiller at the time of the shooting and was fortunate I didn't get shot myself. Did the drug dealer indicate his beef with Billy?"

"May I ask you something, Ben? Do you know how to run a bulldozer?"

"What?"

"Maybe you were not the shooter last year. Although, there was a theory among some of the investigators that you could have been talking to Mr. Tiller to make him a stationary target for a hired shooter."

"That is insane."

"Do you know how to run a bulldozer?"

"No." I hate lying. Even for self-preservation.

"Where were you last Sunday afternoon?"

"Home."

"Alone?"

"Reading."

"Not showing houses? Isn't Sunday a big house day?"

"It was raining. I had one appointment in the morning and I was alone the rest of the day."

Marian nodded. "Yeah, it was raining. But with all the things you learned from your backwoods Chevalley cousins—hunting, shooting, poaching, logging—you never learned how to drive a bulldozer?"

"Never." Of course they taught me to run a bulldozer. Chevalleys were born on machines. But she had not read me any rights and I owed her no truth if she insisted on playing this game. "By the way, if I did the crime, why am I trying to get the kid they arrested off?"

"You're a romantic. You'd rather see a genuine bad guy do your time. Not some poor, innocent kid."

"Did the drug dealer indicate his beef with Billy?" I asked again.

She smiled, shrugged, and sat silently a while. I could not for the life of me read to what extent she was busting my chops or to what extent she thought she was on to something. It made me uncomfortable enough to repeat the question a third time.

She said, finally, "We heard rumors about a drug dealer claiming he had not been paid."

"What kind of drugs?"

"Enough. You've had your freebie, and then some."

"Thank you. One more question."

"Try me."

"Nobody was charged. But did any of these suspects stand out?"

"Oh yes."

"Which one?"

"I told you. No names."

I sat there shaking my head. "The drug dealer makes absolutely no sense. I have never heard a single world about drugs and Billy. He was never the type to risk a drug deal. Unless, of course, he was desperately broke and going under and needed the money.

"Like the car guy who got stung trying to save the company with a cocaine deal?"

"His name was DeLorean. But I see nothing in Billy that was that broke."

Marian nodded affably and saved me a bunch of wasted time. "That was the conclusion I came to."

"Of course, the government was on him for withholding taxes."

Marian stopped grinning and said, seriously, "I was told that tax case sucked. The government was barking up the wrong tree. As for his other government problems, money would not have helped."

"So that leaves a jealous husband."

"Right up your alley, Ben."

"What's that supposed to mean?"

"Look for a grieving wife who hasn't been widowed."

Chapter Fifteen

The clatter of diner dishes and the murmur of nearby conversations seemed to fade as if Marian had drawn a lead curtain around our booth. "I am amazed," I said in all honesty. "I never would have thought of any husband being jealous of that fat slob of a builder."

Marian said, "I love having you in my debt."

Stupid as I have been about women, I'm always surprised to discover that they can be stupid, too. Love, Marian was telling me, had made a blustering, bullying, sixty-pounds-overweight, land-raping developer with the social skills of a wildebeest appear attractive to some married woman who should have known better.

"Wait a minute! If that husband is the prime suspect, why are you telling me?"

"The boys running this investigation don't believe he did this murder. Neither does the state's attorney."

"Why not?"

"Because the jealous husband was not found sitting on the bulldozer on top of the murder victim."

"So why are you telling me?"

"I have nothing to lose."

"I'm flattered."

"Why?"

"You're suggesting you have me to gain."

Marian laughed and stood up from the booth. "I can have you any time I want."

"Lording that fact over me is beneath you."

She laid a strong hand on the back of mine for a moment. "You're right. I apologize. Thanks for the coffee. Great to see you."

"Thanks for the tip. Love, not money. Love, not a rip-off."

"I don't see what you're thanking me for. It doesn't do anything for you. None of last year's shooter suspects were the person Trooper Moody arrested driving the murder weapon when he was discovered on top of the victim. That person was your client."

"You're all so locked into that image. None of you can see past it."

"We don't have to see past it. The guy who did it was caught doing it."

"I know it looks that way, but—"

She interrupted me by touching my hand, again, and saying with a smile, "I think this whole attempt to get useless information out of me was a sneaky, underhanded ploy to talk me into misbehaving with you."

I grabbed her hand. "One more question."

"No, I won't sleep with you. You had your chance. You let it drift away." Her eyes had gone dark.

"We were having a great time."

"Joyous," she said. "But there comes a moment when you have to open your eyes and ask where is this going."

"You could have asked."

"No way."

"Why not?"

"The one with the child can't ask, Ben. She has to be asked. Or she'll never know if there's room for both of them."

I closed my eyes for a moment. That was as definitive as a car wreck, completely irreversible. I wished I had asked.

She knew what I was thinking. She said, "Forget it. The timing wasn't right. I have a six-year-old. He fills a lot of spaces.

You've got a twelve-year-old in your barn and a ninety-year-old across the street filling your spaces."

"It's not the same."

"Of course it's not the same. But it's not nothing, either."

"It wasn't about your child."

"I know that. You did the same stupid thing with Vicky McLachlan and she didn't have kids."

"I don't see a comparison."

"Screw you. I ran into her in Hartford. We had some wine."

I tried to crack a joke. "I don't know what you two could have talked about that would do me any good."

Marian replied very seriously. "If you're ever going to connect, you'll have to open your eyes to the moment when it's time."

"I'll keep it in mind."

"And act when it's time."

"I'll try to remember."

"Goodbye, Ben."

My face must have ratted out my heart, because she blurted, "Hey, I don't meant goodbye, goodbye. Call anytime. It's always nice to talk. But only talk. Bruce is a decent guy. He's good to me and good to my child. I can't betray him anymore. But it's always nice to talk."

"Thank you. Let me ask you something."

She looked wary. "What?"

"Not about us."

She looked relieved. Even grateful. "What?"

"Were you putting me on about do I know how to run a bulldozer?"

Marian said, "Motivation and no alibi? Was I kidding? Are you kidding?"

"That's not an answer."

"It's all the answer you're getting."

"Here's another question. Does the jealous husband know he was a suspect?"

"I don't know. We never had enough to lean on him. He was just one of many we interviewed."

I masked a spasm of delight with a wistful expression as she strode out. I upgraded it into a wistful leer when she turned in the doorway to wave goodbye. Neither expression took much effort, as they were genuine. Everything she had said was true. I had blown a great chance with her. She was lovely to look at, lovely to make love with, and she was one of the very few people I knew in whose presence I never felt bored or lonely. So I was honestly wistful. And honestly sad. But I was also deeply pleased. She had accidentally dropped a huge clue.

While investigating the Main Street shooting, she and Arnie Bender would have leaned hard as hell on suspects like the drug dealer and the truck driver. But they hadn't leaned on the jealous husband. Which meant that he was higher up the Newbury food chain. Not some poor working slob. Whoever Billy had been cheating with was married to a Newbury mover and shaker.

I threw money on the tabletop, bolted out the door. Marian was standing on the sidewalk, on her cell. She winked. I winked back and ran faster.

A great clue, to go with a generous gift. What a gift! Somewhere in Newbury was a sad-eyed woman with inside information. A woman who knew things about Billy that no one else knew. Trying to imagine them trysting in a motel or hayfield, I came up with no palatable visuals. But might not pillow talk have touched upon Billy's latest scams? Didn't lovers confide their fondest hopes? Their darkest fears? Had he whispered the name of someone—other than her husband—who wanted to kill him? Or did she know in her heart that there was no one else? Did she wonder or fear or know that her husband had killed Billy with the bulldozer?

I drove pedal-to-the-metal back to Newbury, to meet her at the funeral.

<>‹›<>

The Newbury Funeral Home occupied the old Taylor House, an eighteenth-century Colonial on Main that the last Taylor sold in 1927 to a mortician whose family has been burying Newburians ever since.

Billy's coffin looked fabulously expensive. It was made of bronze and brushed bronze fittings and was closed tighter than the time-locked vault at Newbury Savings and Loan. Closed or open hardly mattered, as I was the only person there other than six hired pallbearers lined up to carry him out to the hearse.

A single flower lay on the casket, a peony of an old, single variety with yellow petals pale as ghosts and a thick cluster of gold stamens in the center. Whoever had left it had not signed the visitors' book. No one had, except for me.

Don Brooks, a tranquil gray-haired man, whose father had buried my father and whose grandfather had buried my grandfather, walked in, shook my hand and called to the pallbearers, "Shall we go, Señors?"

Until recently, there was never a shortage of pallbearers in Newbury. Most people, but for the very, very old, could count on their church congregation or friends from high school if they hadn't enough family left to hoist their casket into the hearse and up the slope of the cemetery. With so many new and unconnected people in town, it wasn't always possible to raise a quorum of pallbearers, so Don Brooks, who was not the sort to install mechanical devices, drove down to Kohl's for the spring sale and bought blue suits for six strong immigrant Guatemalan landscapers who routinely worked seven days a week and were glad to pick up extra cash to send home. Being country people and devout they brought dignity to the task, got the heavy bronze container loaded with the quiet efficiency of a team used to working together, and piled into a van behind the hearse. Don Brooks drove the short distance to the cemetery, which climbed the hill behind the Ram Pasture.

I followed and parked a distance from the raw earth that Sherman had dug out of the ground with Donny Butler, who was sneaking a smoke behind the MacKay family mausoleum, which jutted from the hillside like a misplaced walk-in closet. I looked everywhere for a grieving woman, but no one else had come. My gaze drifted down the hill toward the old part, which was heavily sprinkled with weathered Abbott headstones, and my father's grave.

As the blue-suited Guatemalans pulled the casket out of the hearse, I was surprised to feel an immense sadness. My thoughts jumbled about as I inquired of myself what was going on in my head.

Certainly I didn't mourn Billy Tiller. Of course, all deaths are sad. And some, as Georgie Stephanopoulos said so passionately, were terrible. But there was no denying that Billy's lifted a black cloud from the town's future; new houses would still be built, but not so many, and not so ugly, and not spreading destruction as far. So I was not mourning Billy. This was not like my father's funeral, when everyone crowding around the grave knew that Newbury had lost its champion. Yet the sadness was real, and when I finally grasped the cause, I knew that only action would ease the sting. I stepped forward and spoke to the lead pallbearer.

"Excuse me, may I take this end?"

Don Brooks nodded permission, and I grabbed the sturdy swing handle closest to the front. The sun went behind a cloud and the breeze that followed it threatened the peony, which had stayed in place through the loading and short drive. The man whose place I had taken crouched down, picked up a stone, and placed it gently over the stem so it wouldn't blow away.

We lifted on Mr. Brooks' quiet count to *tres*. It felt as light as Sherman Chevalley had predicted. Maybe it was because the small men lifting with me were unusually strong, but I flashed, of course, on the D4 spinning mad circles on top of Billy, and thought again of the "no-blooded" hands on the controls.

Just then a medium-size Lexus came crunching up the gravel. The door flew open and E. Eddie Edwards ran from it, hauling on his jacket, straightening his necktie, and calling, "Hang on! Sorry I'm late—Ben? What the hell are you doing here?"

"Too many strangers," I said.

Edwards brusquely shouldered aside the man gripping the handle opposite, and we started for the grave. A tall man, he looked down at me over the coffin and muttered, "I always figured you were sentimental."

"Why do you think I complained about his cheesy developments?"

"My great-grandmother used to say, 'We reap what we sow.'" The fabled Samantha. I thought he was talking about Billy, but I wasn't sure. I left it at that. It seemed enough conversation over a man's coffin. Edwards was not through, however. "By that, I mean," he added, "that if we alienate enough people we will die alone."

A grotesque thought wormed into my head: Murdered people never die alone.

E. Eddie Edwards seemed on the verge of another pronouncement. I decided to tell him to shut the hell up. But when I glanced toward him to do that, I saw his face working, and it struck me, belatedly, that while I may have hoisted a corner of Billy's casket on a vague principle that a man ought to have some acquaintance at his burial, Eddie Edwards might actually have cared for his former boss. How many years had he worked for him? How many years had Billy and his trusty "Evil Engineer" scammed the town? How many wins had they notched together at P&Z?

Edwards said, "At least they caught the jerk who did it. There's a certain relief in that."

"Where's the minister?"

"Billy told me he didn't want clergy."

"When did he tell you that?"

"When his mother died."

We reached the hole in the ground, rested the casket on three strong straps laid out on the grass, and used them to lower it into the hole. I looked around the cemetery again. Still no grieving woman.

With neither the minister nor the priest in attendance there followed an awkward silence and some foot-shuffling confusion. Then Eddie Edwards rose to the occasion, addressing the Guatemalan gardeners, Mortician Brooks, and me like commissioners of an extraordinary Planning and Zoning session.

"I worked for Billy Tiller for many years. I watched him grow from an inexperienced kid, accustomed only to being an employee, into a savvy businessman. No one ever said he didn't work hard. And he leaves behind a legacy that Newbury will always cherish."

Every muscle in my back stiffened.

Edwards sensed a volcano starting beside him and he shifted gears smoothly. Instead of naming oversized, shoddily built McMansions as Billy's legacy, he said, "Billy Tiller leaves a legacy of open spaces donated to Newbury in perpetuity."

True, though we both knew that in every case those were open spaces that Planning and Zoning and appeals courts had already ruled off-limits to building anything larger than a breadbox.

Walking back to the cars, Edwards said to me, "One thing Billy really understood. You can't stop progress."

"Sounds like another great-grandmother saying."

"She was right."

I said, "I wonder who left that peony on the casket."

"That was a fairly rare botanical species," Edwards answered. "*Paeonia mlokosewitschii.* Kind you'd find in your great aunt's garden. Maybe somebody reached over her fence and stole it for Billy."

"Did Billy have any girlfriends?"

"None that I heard about."

"Was he dating anybody?"

"No one he told me about."

"Would he have told you?"

"I don't think so. He was pretty much a loner. I mean you just saw at the cemetery."

"No woman at all?"

"Not since his wife divorced him."

"That's a while back, isn't it?"

"Six-seven years."

"Was he gay?"

"Gay? Billy? I don't think so. Just alone. I mean he's not the only guy alone. Are you gay, Ben?"

"No. Just alone."

"So what's so odd about Billy being alone?"

Women of Aunt Connie's generation used to say of bachelors that a man unmarried in his forties never would marry because he would never change. This was sometimes an unspoken reference to sexual orientation, too. I was not gay, but I had an awful feeling that if I was I would still end up in the same fix, a single unlikely to hook up.

I said to Edwards, "If someone asked you about me, asked was I dating anyone or did I have a girlfriend, the answer would be, 'I've seen him with women. I've seen him having dinner at the Drover or drinks or going for a walk in the woods or a bike ride or a picnic on a rock in the river.'"

"Not so much since Tim Hall and Vicky McLachlan hooked up," Edwards observed with an unpleasant smile.

I wondered if he was being nasty for a reason or was just built that way. "You knew Billy as well as anyone. Did Billy suffer a similar disappointment, shall we say? Did Billy screw up a relationship and then find it hard to hook up again?"

Edwards shrugged. "Who knows?"

"You would know better than anybody, spending time with the guy."

"Working time."

"So did he?"

"Did he what?" Edwards didn't quite snap at me, but the engineer was getting irritable. Tough. I wasn't the one who started talking across coffins.

"Screw up a relationship and find it hard to hook up again?"

"No one he told me about."

"Did he ever act like a guy with a broken heart?"

"Not around me." By then we had reached his Lexus. Edwards climbed in without offering his hand or saying goodbye, started it up, backed and filled, and drove away. Leaving me to ask, if someone ran me down with a bulldozer, would Vicky drop a flower on my grave?

Of course she would. Bouquets, with Tim following along with armloads more. Friendship had survived love. But the point was, we had never had anything to hide. Neither of us had been married. Neither of us had had an angry spouse shooting our lover on Main Street.

I had to find that grieving wife.

◇◇◇

I checked out Connie's garden from the sidewalk by leaning in over the low, ornamental wrought iron fence that her grandfather had erected after the Civil War. Eddie Edwards was right. In the dappled shade under a flowering cherry, within a step of the fence, Connie had a clump of single-petal yellow peonies, or as Edwards named it formally (and correctly, I checked out later on Google), *paeonia mlokosewitschii.*

I swung one leg over the fence for a closer look. Damn. Just as Edwards had suggested, one flower had been plucked. The stem was barely dried, as if the thievery had occurred this morning.

I heard my name called in a strong voice known to make small boys wish they had not been caught. "Benjamin Abbott! Why are you lurking in my garden?"

"Just checking out a peony, Connie."

She was standing at her front door, erect, arms crossed. "Surely it's not necessary to vault my fence. People will think you're not welcome here. Someone might even telephone Trooper Moody."

I got untangled from her fence and hurried up her front walk. "May I come in?"

"Wipe your feet."

I followed her into her foyer and there muttered a quiet but heartfelt, "Damn!"

"Now you are swearing in my front hall. What is going on with you, today, Ben Abbott?"

"Sorry." I was staring at a flower in a slender glass vase. "Is that *paeonia mlokosewitschii?*"

Connie beamed. "Good for you! I know perfectly capable gardeners who would not recognize it."

"You picked it this morning?"

"They last longer if you pick them when it's cool. You know that."

"Of course."

"Is that what you were looking for in my garden?"

"There was one like it on Billy Tiller's coffin."

"Sheila Gordon probably left it, in lieu of dancing on his grave."

"I didn't see any peonies at the Gordons'."

"She had a few struggling up through mud when I was there. Herbaceous, though. And certainly not flowering, buried so deep."

"Who else grows these?"

"Scads of people."

"Connie. It's a pretty rare flower. Name three."

"I could name eight."

"Eight?"

"I gave seeds to eight people last summer. Those who planted early in autumn and kept them watered have flowers this spring."

"Who?"

She started to answer. Abruptly her face closed up. She looked away. Her voice faltered. "I'm getting so bad with names. They were on the tip of my tongue."

"Would any of them have been a married woman between let's say twenty-five and forty-five?"

"Several."

"Do you recall whom?"

"Who."

"Do you recall who?"

"From the garden club."

"Maybe if I got a list of the members, we could go through them."

"No."

"Could we try?"

"We don't have to. They'll be in my diary."

She kept a garden diary. In fact she had a library shelf lined with them going back to the nineteen-thirties. She pulled out last year's and we thumbed through to June. It had been a rainy month. *Primula japonica,* Dutch iris, *Pseudacorus,* and peonies were in bloom, as was *Camassia.* Evergreens needed pruning, she had noted, but it was too wet. In July Connie had harvested, among others, *paeonia* seeds. In August she hosted cocktails for the garden club and gave out packets of seeds. She had written that her guests were grateful for cocktails instead of tea because cocktails started later, which meant they could work longer in their gardens.

"Here," I said. "Here's when you gave them."

She read the names. Three were widows who admitted to their late seventies. Sheila Gordon was married and slightly younger, but highly unlikely to have been conducting an affair with anyone, particularly a builder who had won a zoning change in her neighborhood. There was one lady in her thirties, but she was a happily coupled lesbian. Scooter's wife was another seed recipient, but by all evidence my next-door neighbors adored each other. Georgia Bowland was a possibility, on the other hand: attractive, independent, and miserably unhappy. But Connie put the kibosh on that when she observed, "Of course, Georgia was too busy last summer to plant them. You know her, starting another of her new careers."

"Who is Caroline E.?" I asked.

"Now there is a gardener."

"What is her last name?"

"Edwards, of course. Caroline Edwards. The engineer's wife."

Chapter Sixteen

"Oh," I said.

Maybe that was how he knew the name of the flower.

Well, well, well.

A Newbury mover and shaker. A suspect too high up the food chain, too smart, and too sure of himself for state police investigators to lean on without solid cause. Not a man to be bullied.

"What is Mrs. Edwards like?" I asked.

"Sturdy woman. Hearty."

"Do you know her well?"

"Not really. Just through the club. Lovely girl. A bit lonely when she moved here. Perhaps spends more time in the garden and less with people than she should."

"Is she…" How to put it to Connie? How to—

"Promiscuous? I would think not."

"Connie why would you choose the word promiscuous?"

Aunt Connie rolled her startlingly blue eyes toward her ornate ceiling. "You are looking for a woman who left a single blossom on a dead man's casket but did not attend his funeral."

"Well I didn't want to put words in your mouth."

"Benjamin, as difficult as it may be for you to grasp, try to understand that back in the Pleistocene some of the people with whom I shared the epoch ran around on their spouses. Obviously, you're looking for a gardener who might have had an illicit affair with the murder victim."

"I think I found her."

"Well, she certainly doesn't seem like the type. Although, God knows what is the type."

"What would she see in someone like Billy Tiller?"

"Considering the couples I observe, that is unanswerable."

"Okay. What would he see in her?"

"Equally unanswerable. Although, if he was half as bad as I have heard he was, he might have enjoyed cheating his employee. But perhaps he just saw someone he liked who liked him. I don't know much about men, but I have long suspected that for men, merely being noticed is a powerful aphrodisiac."

"Connie, would you do me a favor?"

"Of course."

"Do you have some special plant you could dig up for Caroline Edwards?"

"I suppose."

"It's got to be something special that you would really want to give her. One master gardener to another."

"Why?"

"I'd like to bring it to her."

◇◇◇

We dug one of the *Primula japonica* from the shady wet spot in the back of her yard and laid it on a flattened plastic bag. Its wide, pale leaves were spreading vigorously and in their center soared a candelabra supporting six rings of blossoms.

"I can't seem to be worming my way into their house. You're sure she doesn't have one of these already?"

"No one grows this shade of white," Connie promised with a jihadist's certainty. "It gleams like an egret. I should have given Caroline Edwards one of these years ago."

Mrs. Edwards ceased to breathe for a long moment.

Had I asked if she was the lady who had placed a rare peony on Billy Tiller's casket, her reaction would have confirmed I had found the grieving wife who hadn't been widowed.

Unfortunately, it was only the sight of Connie's egret-white *Primula*, that rushed the air out of her lungs.

When the air finally returned, accompanied by a lively flush to her round cheek, she said, "I have coveted this plant since the first time I saw it. What possessed her—Oh, come in, come in." I was standing on her front step, cradling the plastic bag in my arms, the two of us bending over the plant like a pair of politicians vying to kiss a newborn constituent.

Connie had called her "hearty" and "sturdy." She was also wonderfully jolly, the kind of person seemingly prepared to celebrate. I liked her immediately and wondered, more than ever, what she would have seen in Billy Tiller. She was quite attractive, full-boned, big-bodied, with a flashing eye and smile that said, Isn't everything wonderful, and if it's not, won't it be soon? I can't say she seemed in mourning.

"Come in," she said, again. "Come inside."

"Should we maybe put this down outside?"

"No. Let's take it in the kitchen. I'll put it in the sink. I want to gloat over it a while." We walked through a house furnished with nice old pieces, mostly antiques, nothing "museum quality," just the kind of furniture that multiple well-fixed grandparents passed down. The carpets had been walked on a long time, showing lines of white warp, and there was a pleasant smell of wax in the air. The kitchen looked recently re-built, but despite the latest high-end appliances, it did not shriek "gourmet granite." In fact there was no granite at all. The counters were butcher block, an indication that they actually used the room for cooking. I lowered the *Primula* into the big porcelain sink that she used to pot plants.

"Would you like tea?" she asked. "Or coffee?"

"Tea, please, if you're having it."

I was surprised by the Evil Engineer's wife, and equally surprised by his lair. I had never given any thought to his home life. I knew him only as the remote and arrogant public figure I had observed dominating P&Z hearings, but had I been asked I would have guessed that he was married to a brittle blonde and lived in a McMansion furnished in a stark and dreary modern loft style with large televisions in every room. Instead, his was a home like others I admired in Newbury—the Gordons' cottage, Al and Babs Bells' estate house up on Morris Mountain, Aunt Connie's and Scooter's on Main—that formed an archipelago of understated, old-fashioned comfort scattered in a desolate sea of new development. There are fewer each year as the old die off or join their offspring who have moved to less crowded areas in hopes of replicating the space and serenity of their childhood.

Caroline Edwards was anything but brittle. Her hair was chestnut, and wisps of it played on her check as she filled a kettle. I could not imagine her with Billy Tiller. Nor, for that matter, could I imagine her with her unpleasant husband.

"You know," she called over her shoulder, "your aunt was my first friend in Newbury. I joined the garden club and Connie just scooped me under her wing." She put the water on the stove, lit the gas, and turned to me with a smile. "Sometimes I sort of think of her as my own aunt."

"Where did you come from?"

"Easton. I hated leaving my garden, but Eddie thought it was getting too crowded down there."

I looked closely for irony, but saw none in her expression, nor heard any in her tone. "Things are getting built up here, too," I ventured.

"It probably seems that way to you, but to me it's still empty by comparison."

She laid napkins and a plate of shortbread on a maple work table in the center of the room. We sat across from each other on stools, discussing the weather, which had been gyrating for weeks between wet and cold and warm and dry, until the water boiled. She made tea in a pot, the way Connie did, warming the pot with hot water and pouring it into the mugs to warm them before brewing the tea.

"Are you close with your aunt?"

"Connie had been my friend since I learned to speak complete sentences. She had no children and I was born right across the street. My parents were older—not as old as Connie, of course—she's my great aunt, my father's aunt—and my father was always busy. Connie kind of took me everywhere and showed me everything."

Caroline Edwards looked at me with a smile and asked, "Was your mother busy, too?" so openly that it seemed to be the most natural thing in the world to admit to this woman I had just met, "My mother sometimes had trouble getting through the day."

She poured half and half cream in a short pitcher, placed it and a matching sugar bowl on the table, brought the tea pot, and emptied the warmed mugs into a watering can. "I had a mother like that. I couldn't wait to go to school just to get out of the house." She looked around her kitchen and smiled. "To me, to be able to stay home is the greatest luxury. I love any day I don't have to leave the property."

She poured the tea. We sipped in silence a while and watched the birds swarming the feeder hung outside the window. A squirrel was staring at it from a perch on a tree, but he could not reach it because it hung from a long, long wire suspended from a tree branch thirty feet off the ground.

"Edward did that. Drives the squirrels insane. I pray he'll conjure up something as clever for the voles."

"How did he get it up there?"

"He went right up the trunk like a monkey, with climbing spikes."

I was surprised. I had figured E. Eddie Edwards for a desk guy.

Eventually, Caroline looked at the sink.

"I should get it in the ground."

"I'll carry it out."

"Would you like more tea?"

"No, I'm fine. I'll carry, you dig."

Out to her garden we went. It was huge and beautiful, enclosed between hundred-foot-long stone walls that connected the old house and a multi-level red barn. There were handsome wooden gates in the walls, broad grass paths, and stone steps where the ground sloped. The plants were in a blue phase. Blue bells, Virginia and Spanish; bluish Mountain Pinks, lilac, dark and light blue *Camassia, Aquilegia, Corydalis, Allium,* Jacob's ladder, *Baptisia* about to pop. Even her chives were studded with bristly little knots of purple blue.

She noticed I had veered from the path to inspect her peonies, which were about the only flowers that weren't blue. *"Paeonia mlokosewitschii,"* she said, cupping ghostly petals in her rough hand. "Your aunt gave me seeds."

I counted ten stems that had been cut. In a vase in her living room had stood nine.

We were approaching a dark wet spot where *Japonica* had hoisted magenta candelabras, when I heard the hee-haw noise of a wood saw coming from the other side of the barn. "Edward," she explained. "Cutting down a tree."

"By hand?"

"Manly man," she said with a smile. Mocking her husband? I wondered. But it wasn't necessarily mocking. It could just as easily have been an affectionate "boys will be boys" remark. I was utterly unable to picture her relationship with Billy Tiller.

Caroline turned a wedge out of the wet ground with a narrow garden spade. She softened the exposed earth with a few quick strokes of the blade, dropped to her knees, and fit Connie's clump of root into its new home as neatly as a piston.

Suddenly I hard a loud crack, a rush of something heavy parting the air, and a shouted, "Oh, shit!"

A shadow loomed from the sky. A tree was falling at us. I grabbed Caroline's hand and pulled her hard. The tree stopped falling, propped in the branches of a neighbor at an angle over the low part of the barn. I was still releasing her hand when E. Eddie Edwards ran around the barn with a multi-toothed tree saw that was curved like a scimitar.

"What the hell are you doing here?"

"Right this minute," I said, "I'm dodging trees."

"Are you all right?" Caroline asked.

"Yeah, yeah, fine. I just really screwed up. Damned tree fell the wrong way. I screwed up the wedge cut."

"Can I give you a hand?" I asked.

"Wha'd you have in mind?" He jammed his saw into a sheath hanging from his belt and glared up at the tangle of branches where the two trees met.

"I've got a come-along in the car. We could crank from the other direction, pull it out of that tree and maybe get it to fall where you want it."

"I have my own come-along," he said sullenly, and I could see that he was embarrassed that I had seen him screw up a "manly" job and probably kicking himself for not securing the tree with his come-along to start with.

"Even better," I said. "It'll be much easier to control with two."

"I vote for that," said Caroline. "If that tree slips, we'll need a new barn."

"It's not going to fall on the barn," Edwards grumbled, but I could see him calculating the angles. He started around the barn. His wife and I followed and we all looked at the tall, skinny tree, which had slipped off its stump and now leaned precariously over the barn in the fragile arms of a soft red maple. He pointed at a slot of open ground between two hemlocks. "That's where it was supposed to drop."

"I've done the exact same thing. It's amazing how unforgiving a wedge cut is if you get it just wrong."

"Well, if you've got the time, Ben, I'd appreciate it."

"Let's do it."

They walked me to my car to help carry the stuff. I passed him a hundred-foot coil of two-ton wire cable. Caroline grabbed the heavy chain, which was in a strong bucket. I took the come-along—or winch-puller—a cumbersome, six-foot-long web of pulleys, ratchets, wire rope, grab hooks, and clove pins all connected to a finger-threatening lever.

"You usually travel with a winch-puller?"

"I took down a dead tree for my mom. She lives by herself out in Frenchtown and the place is a handful."

"House thy name is entropy," said Edwards. "I'm taking the rest of this week off just to try and catch up."

"Speaking of which," said Caroline, "if you gentlemen can handle this, I've got things going inside."

We manly men assured her we could.

We got a ladder from the barn, and Edwards' come-along and wire and chain. He climbed up and looped both wire cables around the tree about twenty feet off the ground. Then we walked the cables at forty-five degree angles to the direction we wanted the tree to fall, hooked them to the come-alongs, and hooked the come-alongs to chains we looped around strong trees. It took a while. And it took a while longer to get the slack out by adjusting the chains. Edwards reminded me to make sure I had an escape route if the tree fell toward me.

When we had the cables stretched as taut as we could between the errant tree and the come-alongs, we cranked the levers, calling to each other to ease off and then pull again, to keep it balanced. The tree tipped up from the red maple that had caught it. It was swaying and it didn't take Paul Bunyan to realize it would have gone out of control if we had only had one cable. We kept cranking. The come-alongs had only a six-foot fetch, and the question was what happened if they reached their limit before the tree fell where it should. Nothing good. But just before we ran out of pull, the tree began to lean, gathered speed, and fell between the two hemlocks with a thump that shook the ground.

"Appreciate the help," Edwards said, after we had gathered our gear and loaded mine into my car.

"Beats sitting in the office waiting for the phone to ring."

"You didn't say what you were doing here."

"Delivering a plant from my Aunt Connie."

"She usually comes out herself."

"She's not feeling that well, today."

Caroline came out. "Edward, it's time to get dressed. I'm sorry, Ben, we've plans, or we'd ask you in for a drink."

"Just leaving. Thanks again for the tea. I'll tell Connie I can personally vouch the plant is in the ground."

I headed home, fairly sure that Caroline Edwards was the woman who had put the peony on Billy Tiller's casket, but not at all sure why. She certainly hid her grief well, if grief she felt. Edwards, on the other hand, was still only marginally civil even after a couple of hours' work and problem solving of the sort that usually gave a couple of men some sort of bond they hadn't shared before. Either he was congenitally unpleasant, or he was a very jealous husband. The look he had shot at me when he saw me releasing Caroline's hand had cut no slack.

◇◇◇

When I got home, Alison was waiting in my office, quite excited about something.

"Do you see who wrote you?" She had brought in the mail and put it on my desk.

"All I see is bills and junk mail."

"This is not junk mail," she said, extending a UPS Next Day Air envelope. "This is from Joey Girl."

She tapped a fairly clean finger on the return address.

I asked, "What is Joey Girl?"

"Are you serious? You're joking. You're always joking." She looked at me askance, tilting her head as if peering into sun glare. "You've never heard about Joey Girl?"

"Now that you mention it, I've seen the name on all that garbage they put on the e-mail screen."

"You should get out more. Can I open the letter?"

"It is 'May I,' and, yes, you may."

"May I?" She grabbed the plastic stiletto I used for a letter opener, slit it open reverentially, and drew out a square envelope made of heavy stock. "See!" she said, tapping a company logo of cat whiskers.

"Open it."

She slit the square envelope and opened the contents. Her big eyes got bigger. "Oh God. Ohmigod. You are invited to a Joey Girl Party. Ohmigod, ohmigod."

"I still don't know what Joey Girl is."

Joey Girl, she explained, was a hot hip hop clothing label prized by fashionable wagamamas.

"Wagamamas? What are 'wagamamas'?"

Nine- to-thirteen-year-olds, Alison told me. "It's Japanese for 'naughty little girls.'"

I wondered, not for the first time, how long before I would be dealing with gentleman callers on motorcycles.

"You're so lucky—how do you rate?"

The mystery of that absurdity was solved by a note scrawled on the bottom of the invitation. Joey Girl was owned by Jeff Kimball's straight-arrow businessman father. He hoped I could come to his "First Annual Watercress Picking Party," to be held at his Fairfield County Estate. (His capital 'E,' not mine.) But why? If he wanted to talk about Jeff's case all he had to do was telephone, or instruct Ira to send me down to New York.

"Bring a friend," he wrote, apologizing for short notice.

"I'm your friend," said Alison.

"You are twelve."

"It doesn't say what age."

Alison watched, barely breathing, as I dialed the RSVP number. I didn't particularly want to go, as I would have to juggle Saturday house-showing appointments. But I very much wanted to ask—face to face—why Kimball had neglected to mention that he knew how to drive bulldozers.

A polite secretary answered.

"This is Benjamin Abbott. I'll be delighted to attend Mr. Kimball's Watercress Picking Party at one o'clock on Saturday. Would a twelve-year-old young lady be welcome as my guest?"

I held the phone so Alison could hear. "I'm sorry, Mr. Abbott. The party will be child-free."

I mouthed, "Sorry."

"You tried," she mouthed back, and I said to the nice lady on the phone, "Understood. In that case I'll bring someone age appropriate. Miss Constance Abbott. That's Miss, not Ms., M-I-S-S."

"Mr. Kimball looks forward to seeing you, Mr. Abbott, with Miss Abbott."

After we had traded goodbyes, Alison said, "Maybe Connie's a little too old to go to that party?"

"I think she'll enjoy it."

"You should take Vicky."

"I'm sure Vicky wants to spend her Saturday with Tim."

"Tim's doing a seminar in Hartford. He won't mind."

"I think I'm better off taking Connie."

"You're just afraid to be alone with Vicky." Alison loved Vicky McLachlan as only a little girl could love an exciting big sister sort who let her watch her put on makeup and showed her things to do to her hair on the occasions she drifted out of Tomboy mode.

"I am in no position to ask her out."

"Yeah, but if Connie doesn't feel up to it, Saturday, you have to take Vicky."

"I'm asking Connie right this minute. Catch you later."

◇◇◇

I found her dozing in her rose garden. She blinked awake when my shadow crossed her face. "Well?"

"Well what?"

"What happened at the Edwards'?"

"Caroline loved your plant. Her husband loved my come-along."

"Come-along? You mean come-on?"

"No, he would not have liked me coming on to his wife. He struck me as jealous. No, I helped him cut down a tree. I had the come-along in the car."

"Working side by side is a good way to get to know someone. What did you think of him?"

"Methodical, precise, a little dull, someone you could count on to keep a level head in a pinch. Brusque, if not downright unpleasant."

"What did you think of her?"

"I liked her. Liked her a lot."

"I hoped you would."

"Why? She is married."

"Well of course she's married and I don't mean it quite that way, but it is good for you to appreciate other types of women—types different than you usually fall for. It suggests a budding maturity."

"Why do I think you are not complimenting me?"

"I'm sorry. I'm teasing you, Ben. But she's a lovely woman, isn't she?"

"Very. Very self-contained."

"Did you learn what you hoped to learn?"

"Not yet. Meeting her, I found it even harder to imagine Billy Tiller seducing her. But I did see ten peonies cut and only nine in her vase."

"Odd numbers usually look better in a vase."

"So unless she dropped one on the lawn, it was the one I saw on Billy's casket."

"When are you going back?"

"First thing tomorrow."

"Do you want another plant?"

"No, I'll just barge in. He's working at home tomorrow. Listen, I came over to invite to you a party down in Newtown on Saturday. Jeff Kimball's father. A hip hop mogul. It ought to be a scene."

"Are you sure you wouldn't rather take a date?"

"I tried to take Alison, but they said the party is 'child free.' Would you like to come? They're calling it a watercress picking party."

"We'll bring our Wellies."

‹›‹›‹›

I drove in the Edwards' driveway right after breakfast and parked by the barn. I heard Edwards sawing branches off the tree we had dropped and walked to him. He slid the saw into its sheath.

"You know we had a phone installed," he said. "It's handy for calling ahead to see if we feel like visitors."

"I'm not visiting. I came to show you something."

"What?"

"It's in your wife's garden."

"My wife? What are you talking about?"

"Right this way." I walked quickly around the barn. He followed. I pushed through a gate, hurried along a path, and pointed at the peonies. "Let's talk."

"About what?"

I did not want to be the one to say that his wife had had an affair with Billy Tiller. I wanted him to tell me. "Well, why don't we start with the lies you told about being with Billy when you weren't."

"What lies?"

"Your word against Jeff Kimball's. Your word against school bus driver Jimmy Butler. Two against one."

"I don't know what you're talking about."

"Six or seven years ago you told Trooper Moody the kid attacked you and Billy with an axe."

Edwards shook his head slowly left and right and left again.

"Last year you told Trooper Moody that Jimmy Butler asked if he could stash a truck in Billy's barn."

He kept shaking his head.

"That's two," I said. "Want to hear some more?" I didn't have any more.

He kept shaking his head, slowly, emphatically. Then he said the last thing in the world I would have predicted: "You want to take a sauna?"

"What?"

"I built a sauna out in the woods. I fired it up at dawn. It'll be plenty hot by now. Come on, it'll do us both good." His lips moved in a semi-smile. "Cool you down. Ironically."

I hesitated, thinking, Okay, we go out to the sauna and when I turn my back he crushes my skull with a hot stone and buries me in the woods. On the other hand, he was not that much bigger than I, and I could probably take him if I had to. "Okay. Let's have a sauna."

We walked into his woods, on a path of wood chips. His house and barn and Caroline's gardens faded behind us. Ahead the trees grew dense.

"How many acres do you have here?"

"Eleven. But it's mostly surrounded by Northeast Utility land and some nature preserve."

Which meant that he was sitting pretty. His eleven acres, and his sauna, were considerably more remote than your average eleven acres, and he had bought a lot of beautiful privacy with the money he earned helping carpet the town with new houses.

"Northeast log it?" I asked.

"They cull about every ten years. Keeps the woods open. The nature preserve is badly overgrown—I worry about fire during Red Flag alerts—but they can't afford to thin it."

The sauna appeared through the trees, and it was a beautifully proportioned little log house, with a wisp of thin white smoke rising from a stovepipe. "A real wood-fired sauna," I said.

"Got it on line from Norway. Stove, rocks, and all."

"Nice-looking structure. You built it yourself?"

"I like building stuff. Good way to unwind."

He had piped water out from his house and rigged an outdoor shower for cooling off. Inside was a little change room, brightly lit by a skylight, with a bench with room three or four people to sit and take off their shoes, which we did, and ornate brass hooks for hanging our clothes.

For nearly fifty years, no one who ever saw *Psycho* could close their eyes in a shower without recalling Janet Leigh's slaughter in the water. Now, thanks to *Brokeback Mountain* it will be another fifty years before two guys can take their clothes off in the locker room without wondering, Did he see that movie, too? Edwards didn't seem to care. In fact, he looked me over, deliberately, before he finally offered me a towel. It was a severe inspection and I regretted some recent thickening around my waist that I had been meaning to do something about. He was heavily muscled, workout-machine bulked. Or maybe, I thought, he popped steroids, which would explain his prickly manner.

We went through a thick door into nostril searing dry heat. The benches were tiered. I took a cooler one at the bottom. Edwards climbed up behind me. I propped my back casually against the hot wooden wall to observe any move to pluck a hot rock from the rack in the cast-iron stove.

"What shall we talk about?"

"Plenty," Edwards said, "now that I know you're not wearing a wire."

"A wire?"

"A recording wire. Don't be dense."

"Why would I wear a wire?"

"Because you suspect me of something."

"Is what we're here to talk about?"

"Have you any idea how often I had to haul Billy's ass out of trouble?"

"All I know is your name keeps coming up. And not in a good way. People say you lied to help Billy."

"Do they?" He shook his head. Smiled. "Do they say why?"

"Because you worked for him."

"He wasn't the only builder I worked for."

"That's what I said. People—the people I've talked to—figured you had no choice."

"Anybody figure why?"

"I'm hoping that the reason we're sitting here sweating is so you can tell me why."

"Working with Billy was like working with a wild animal. And not a particularly bright one. A stupid one, like a deer or a cow. He did what he wanted, when he wanted. He had a moral compass that always pointed north, and he was north. Which meant that he never thought he was wrong. On top of that, he was impulsive. If he wanted something, he wanted it right now."

He stopped talking, quite suddenly. I waited a while. Then I said, "I've heard from some people who knew him that he was actually very intelligent."

"A cow is bright enough to recognize edibles."

"And yet Billy had a gift for success, didn't he? A lot things he touched turned to gold."

Edwards smiled. "He was something of an idiot savant. He could look at a piece of land and see the dollar signs."

"That's just greed."

"No, I don't mean that. I mean he could see the slopes, water, where the roads would go and the driveways, curtain drains, septics."

"He built floods, for crissakes."

"Only on the neighbors' land."

"He knew they would flood? Those weren't accidents?"

"Like I said, he was the lodestone of his moral compass."

"Which means," I said, getting angry when I should have been listening coolly, "that you lied on the plans you drew up."

"I would warn him when I saw a potential problem. If he wanted to bull ahead, anyway, it was his project, his money. If he wanted to save money doing it on the cheap, he was the boss."

"Why did you lie for him about the punch up with Jeff Kimball?"

The engineer hesitated only a millisecond. "That was back when Billy was just getting started. Last thing he needed was a court case, or even a bad rep, for getting in a fight with a teenager. He was forming relationships with the banks. It would have screwed up everything."

"What about Jimmy Butler?"

"Oh, God was that a mess." Edwards closed his eyes and threw his head back and baked a while. Finally, he sat up and opened his eyes. "When the Jimmy Butler thing happened, I had one second to make up my mind and I thought, I'm the only one who can save Billy from this. The banks would have shut every project down if Billy was convicted of stealing that machine. Felons do not get construction loans."

"Did he actually steal the machine?"

"Let's just say it kind of fell in his lap and he felt he deserved to keep it."

"Jimmy Butler said the same thing, sort of."

"One of those stupid things, Ben. Just one of those stupid things."

"Pretty much destroyed Jimmy's life."

"I did it, Ben."

"Did what?"

"You know what."

"Tell me."

"I did it. I shot Billy."

Chapter Seventeen

First thought through my mind? That's why Billy couldn't outrun the bulldozer. He'd been shot and wounded. And, that's why the killer ground him to pieces under the bulldozer. So the medical examiner wouldn't see that he had been shot. Evil Engineer wasn't a no-blooded psycho. He was just being careful.

Edwards stared back at me, holding my eye so effortlessly that I wondered if I had heard wrong.

"When?" I asked.

"When? What are you talking about? When was he shot."

"You tell me, when."

"Last year on Main Street."

"What?"

"Sorry I almost hit you, too."

"Wait, wait, wait. You're telling me you shot Billy Tiller last year?"

"I'm telling you, here and now, for the one and only time. I will not repeat it to anyone and if you say anything I will swear you are making it up."

"Your word against mine?"

"You got it."

"Why are you telling me?"

"So you stop wasting time trying to connect two unconnected events and concentrate on who killed him."

"Concentrate on Jeff Kimball?"

"I don't know if Kimball did it. It certainly sounds like he did. But if you have reason to believe he didn't, go out and find who did."

"Your lawyer Woodward asked me not to. He threatened to sue me or turn me in to the cops or something or other."

"All Woodward meant was please stop fucking up our future with Billy's past. If you truly believe that kid is innocent of course you have to find out who did it."

"Where did you shoot him from?"

"The Meeting House belfry."

"They didn't find any shell casings."

Edwards looked away. He got up, poured a bucket of water on the hot rocks, and stood swathed in steam. "I'm not stupid, Ben."

"How'd you happen to miss?"

"I didn't miss. I shot him right in the leg where I meant to."

"Hell of a shot right between the bones."

"In that sense I did miss. I would have preferred to break a bone."

"Why?"

"It didn't take genius to figure that out. You did come calling on my wife within hours of seeing that fucking flower on the coffin. If you want me to spell it out for you, I will. I shot Billy to warn him not to steal my wife."

"Did it work?"

"They broke it off."

I had a bracing cold shower and drove home, back to zero.

⟨⟩⟨⟩⟨⟩

Saturday, Connie and I drove down to Kimball's watercress party in my mother's 1979 Fiat Spyder, a gift from my father, which she had driven rarely. It was an extraordinarily beautiful little roadster, British Racing Green, and there was something friendly about its flowing lines that made people smile and wave. My mother, who was fundamentally (if not pathologically) shy, had flinched from the attention. When my father died, she gave it to me, along with the Main Street house, and retreated to the remote and swampy farm she'd been born on in Frenchtown. Connie asked, as always, whether had I visited her lately and I said I had been out the weekend before last, repaired a fence and took down a tree for her.

It was warm and Connie demanded we put the top down. She was having one of her great days where you'd swear she wasn't a day over eighty-five. I bundled her in a lap robe and drove slowly so as not to blow off her hat.

Down in Newtown, we found Kimball's brand-new megamansion in a neighborhood of former estates chopped up by recent construction. Connie gave it a long, slow look and announced, "It appears they ran out of ideas before they ran out of money."

It was built of stone and stucco, with a fake slate roof, an attached five-car garage, cliché turrets at either end, and clerestory windows meant to light a chapel. All this was crammed onto a three-acre lot that dropped steeply to a stream. The bit of lawn not covered by house, swimming pool, and tennis court had been planted too closely with specimen trees that would smother each other next summer. Outdoor speakers blared Joey Girl recordings, and I found it remarkable that Kimball's neighbors, huddled in McMansions that looked almost modest in comparison, were not replying with shotguns.

There was valet parking, a rarity in our neck of the woods. The car ahead of ours was a BMW 800 series with New York license plate that read GONADS. The car behind us was a Ferrari. The fat guy driving looked happy to be arriving with two girls, labels I use advisedly.

"Child-free?" asked Connie.

Barely. Middle-aged and older men, who wore pink and white shirts flowing over their bellies, were squiring thin wives and girlfriends who looked like they would still be in high school if only they were smart enough. Many of the ladies were pregnant. Those not wore ready smiles. After I established that the kid parking cars knew the purpose of a clutch, I gave Connie my arm and we went looking for our host.

It was a generous party, food and fine wine everywhere, waiters passing champagne and small delights. No one was swimming in the swimming pool, which had a dark blue-gray bottom and a trompe l'oeil disappearing waterfall of the clever sort that for some reason very quickly became trite. A volleyball net hung between two trees. No one was playing. A pro in whites waited forlornly on the empty tennis court. A condensed croquet lawn was unoccupied. Twenty guests were watching tennis on a television on the patio, while inside the house others clumped around wide screens showing movies. No one seemed to know each other or why they were all invited. Nor did any I asked know where our host was.

We finally found Kimball in the kitchen with a dark-eyed girl (advisedly, again). She was wearing enough blush, eye shadow, mascara, lip liner, and lipstick to sing an Italian opera, and an apron with appliquéd tomatoes on her breasts and a tomato leaf for her crotch. Although there was plenty of hired help around—Central American kitchen maids in tee shirts and blue jeans, and sprightly gay waiters wearing dress shirts and black bow ties—she and Kimball were cooking up a storm, heaping plates with hot hors d'oeuvres, which servants galloped off with, and swigging red wine from huge goblets.

"Hey, Abbott. You made it." In polo shirt and tennis shorts he looked considerably less stiff than I remembered. But behind the act, his eyes were as busy as they had been at the Yale Club, and twice as opaque. Although, waving spatula and tongs, he seemed to be having fun. Proudly, he introduced his helpmate, Amanda.

I introduced Aunt Connie. Until we'd found the kitchen she'd been walking around with lips pursed tighter and tighter, but something about Kimball's pleasure at the stove (or, God knows, Amanda's apron) appealed to her and she melted them both with her most gracious smile. She even accepted, and pronounced splendid, a Pernod-drenched shrimp. It was the first time I had ever seen her eat finger food without plate, fork, and napkin.

"I have to ask," said Amanda. "Where did you find that vintage Lilly Daché hat?"

"In my closet," said Connie.

"Bruce," said Amanda, "let's knock that off. I could sell the sh—the hell out of it."

"Amanda is our merchandising consultant," said Kimball. "She's nailed our market with the wannabees."

"Wagamamas! Not wannabees."

"Where," Connie asked, "is the watercress?"

"Huh? Oh, down by the stream. I sent people down to get some."

"We'll help," said Connie.

"It's kind of yucky mucky down there," said Amanda.

"Nonsense. We came armed to participate as your invitation proposed. We have boots in the car. Come, Ben. Walk me down to the stream."

"Good Lord," she muttered when we got out of the house.

"I think we can pass on the boots. It didn't sound like his pickers were guests."

Connie held her silver-headed cane on one side and my arm on the other and we ventured down the sloping lawn. "Fascinating," she said. "These new kind of new rich. That man hasn't a self-conscious bone in his body."

"He doesn't seem worried about his kid in jail, either."

"The lively Amanda diverts. Such a pretty smile."

"I couldn't see it through the makeup."

"Ben."

"What?"

"The world is changing, Ben. Do you ever worry that you fight too hard not to change with it? Principles and standards are good and necessary, but when you are young you can make yourself very lonely by resisting the way things are."

"I'm not worried."

"You're in danger of turning into a curmudgeonly bachelor."

Fast as lightning, I changed the subject to, "The fair Amanda was actually pretty sharp, for her years." It didn't work and we were on to a theme that Connie never used to bug me about, but had become important to her, recently.

"Men should marry, Ben. If only to get a second point of view in the house."

"You never married. You seem fine."

"I am not, nor have ever been, a man. Women do just fine, unmarried. Men haven't the imagination to go it alone. They wither. If you lack an example, look at your unmarried Chevalley cousins."

"I've always thought that for every unmarried Chevalley there's a lucky woman who got away."

Connie laughed, and got off my case for the moment.

We walked slowly down the slope, found the stream where we expected to, and spied four burly guys in muscle shirts picking greenery. None looked happy to be standing in water over their Guccis.

"Ben," Connie whispered. "Those gentlemen are enormous."

"Those gentlemen are bodyguards," I explained. One had a shaved head, two wore ponytails, the fourth had a buzz cut. What they had in common, beyond the arms and chests swelling black tee shirts, was their fastidious neatness, not a hair out of place. (Though the bald guy wore a trim mustache.)

"Whom are they guarding? I've never considered Newtown that dangerous a place."

"Our host made his fortune in hip hop music."

"Clearly, Mr. Kimball is not one to overestimate the taste of the American public. But I don't see the connection to bodyguards."

"Most hip hop performers are African-American. Do you see any African-Americans at this party?"

"I see fat white businessmen and six-foot girls who weigh a hundred pounds."

"For that matter, do you see any musicians or singers or performers and anyone of any color who could be called 'the talent'?"

"I don't know that I could discern a talent for hip hop."

"Is it possible that the bodyguards are here to discourage disgruntled talent from gate crashing?"

"You have always been cursed with a villainous imagination, Ben. I think that it is far more likely that Mr. Kimball invited his New York City employees up for a day in the country."

More to the point, why I was invited? "You guys need some help?"

A fellow who looked like he would really rather be administering chin checks to the unruly in a Chelsea dance club hefted a nearly full trug of greens and said, "Thanks, buddy, we're almost done."

"That is not watercress," Connie called.

"Say what?"

"You've picked forget-me-nots. See the little blue flower?"

"Taste any different?"

"It tastes terrible. And I would imagine it's poisonous."

All four looked in their trugs. "Jesus H!—Sorry, lady."

"Man, what are we going to do? Mr. Kimball said go down and pick it. Who's going to tell him it's poison?"

"He might have been referring to that," said Connie, indicating a patch of darker green vegetation twenty yards down stream.

They started wading toward it. Connie cried, "Stop!"

"What?"

"Climb out of the water."

They exchanged looks and shrugged and obeyed docilely.

Connie said, "Approach the watercress from downstream. That way you won't muddy the water. Good, that's it. Walk down there. Good. Now dump the forget-me-nots back in the water. Don't worry, they'll take root again."

I didn't think any of them looked worried. Though I did notice one or two eyeing Connie with an expression of almost aching loneliness, as if wanting to connect with a human, never knowing how and now suddenly sensing the opportunity.

"Take your scissors and shear the watercress just at the surface. You'll be so glad you did. It will be much easier to clean."

From the back of the four I heard a muttered, "We gotta clean this crap, too?"

If Connie heard she pretended not to.

◇〉◇

"Took you long enough," Kimball grumped to the bodyguards shuffling into the kitchen at Aunt Connie's slow pace.

"Ralph, Edward, Charles, and Henry were kind enough to help me up the hill," said Connie, relinquishing the anvil arm that had been gallantly offered by the biggest, Henry. "And they've picked you a fine crop—Amanda, dear, would you have another apron?"

Amanda helped her into one with strategically placed lemons. "Would you like a stool, Miss Abbott?"

Connie allowed that she would—she was pale from the climb—and settled gratefully at the zinc table, where she instructed the hulking four in the fine points of watercress grooming. Kimball motioned for me to join him outside. He paused at the bar beside the barbeque, which was inside the house, presumably for the pleasure of those who liked their cookouts indoors. "Champagne?"

"Perrier. I'm driving."

"Sure?"

I would have liked a glass or four very much, but there was something going on here I didn't want to miss.

"Your aunt is a character."

"I'm glad I could bring her along. On a day like today when she's feeling well, she really enjoys getting out."

"How old is she?"

"She remembers when her mother first got the vote."

"Wow. So how's it going for the kid?"

It occurred to me that I had never heard him refer to Jeff as his son. It was always the kid. Not even my kid. "Well, he's convinced one person he didn't kill Billy Tiller."

"Who?"

"Me. Trouble is, I don't get to vote in the jury room."

Kimball's mouth tightened thin as piano wire. "Jury? I don't want this going to trial."

"Neither do I, but again, no one's asking my permission."

"What convinced you?"

"For one thing, his bulldozer teacher convinced me that Jeff couldn't have done it the way it was done. For another, an amazing number of people who disliked the murder victim know how to drive bulldozers. Unfortunately they were all pretty up front about it. The only person who hid the fact that he knows how to drive a bulldozer was you."

"What the hell is that supposed to mean?"

"You told me you were at the crime scene. You never mentioned you knew how to drive a machine."

"You could find that on Google."

"Actually, no. There's no mention of you driving bulldozers."

"So dump your Google stock. What do you want from me?"

"It seems a funny thing to leave out. You told me you were at the crime scene."

"Afterward. Not when it happened. What is this?"

"You told me sow doubt."

Kimball covered his face with his hands. He rubbed his eyes. He lowered his hands and turned and looked at me. "So you're demonstrating how lame a strategy it is."

"It's a standard criminal defense strategy, but in this case…"

"You're telling me to get used to the idea that the kid is going to prison."

"Not if I can help it."

"You have anything to go on?"

"Yes I do," I said, watching for his reaction. "Somebody shot at Billy Tiller last year. Wounded him."

Kimball made a face. "Everybody knows that. You know some connection?"

"No," I lied, really uncomfortable with him not telling me about driving bulldozers. "But as big a chiseling unprincipled jerk as Billy Tiller was, I'm having a hard time believing that two different people actually would try to murder him."

"So find the shooter." Did he look relieved, that I was looking elsewhere?

"Terrific idea. Unfortunately the combined efforts of the Connecticut State Police Major Crime Squad and our resident trooper did not turn up the shooter."

"Don't you have your own sources?"

"They don't know who did it, either."

"Weren't there any suspects?"

"Half a dozen. Including your son," I added, to get him off the shooter topic.

"What?"

"Stemming back to the ruckus he had with Tiller."

"That was years ago."

"Don't worry. He had an iron-clad alibi."

"How iron clad?"

"The day of the shooting, Jeff was in Oregon. In custody."

"For what?"

"Chaining himself to the top of a redwood he was trying to protect."

"Jesus H, the kid is a nut."

"You could say that. Or you could say he's passionate in his beliefs."

Kimball practically shouted, "Don't say that. You'll make him a prosecutor's wet dream."

Several tall, thin women were watching curiously.

Kimball lowered his voice and looked me in the eye. We stared at each other in silence. He was probably hoping I wouldn't say aloud that Jeff was already the prosecutor's wet dream. I was hoping that he wasn't letting his son stand trial for a crime he himself had committed for some reason I knew nothing about. I knew it sounded crazy. But he had not admitted to me that he knew how to drive a bulldozer. Maybe it was nothing, but it seemed to me that it should have come up. Maybe I would never had considered it if he just once referred to his son by name. Maybe I was clutching at straws thinner than he was.

"Can you tell me where you were last Sunday afternoon?"

"What?"

"I think you heard me, Mr. Kimball."

He barked a bitter laugh. "You are a piece of work. You want an alibi from me?"

"Can you give me one?"

"I was here."

"Was Amanda with you?"

"Amanda was in St. Louis."

"Servants?"

"No."

"Friends?"

"No one."

"All alone in this big house?"

Kimball glanced back at the kitchen door. "Not quite."

I looked at him, and barked my own laugh. It was either a brilliant lie or he was having more fun than anyone who looked like him deserved to.

"You get it? Capish?"

"Sure. But if I felt I really had to speak to the, uhm, young person? Would that be possible?"

"If absolutely necessary, that could be arranged."

"All right."

"Jesus, were you off base."

"Don't expect an apology."

"Why the hell not?"

"Because, essentially, I am working for the kid who's in jail."

"Is there any hope?" he said, finally. "Have you learned anything that can help?"

"Not in the doubt department."

"Anything else?"

I considered laying out my theory that Billy's killer rode to the murder scene with Billy in Billy's truck and left on foot. I considered explaining exactly why Sherman Chevalley was so positive that Jeff couldn't have killed Billy. I even toyed with telling Kimball that I had found the grieving wife who wasn't widowed. And had a sauna with her husband.

"Nothing worth saying out loud, yet."

Suddenly, Kimball waved across the lawn. "Hey, Judge," he called, "you made it."

To me he said, "There's somebody here I want you to meet. Don't say you're working for me."

"I'm not. I'm working for Ira Roth."

"Whatever you do, don't say you're working for my lawyer."

"It's a party. It won't come up in social conversation."

"That's right. It's a party. So just say hello."

"Why?"

"I want your take on him."

I looked at Kimball. This was plain weird. A hotshot rich businessman connected politically in New York did not need my take on anybody. "What is this?"

"Maybe another way to skin a cat."

He gripped my arm, and I let him walk me in the direction of a man who looked like most of the males at the party—overweight, underdressed, and in possession of a young woman probably not his daughter. This one had a Chihuahua under her arm and, for reasons that escaped me, considering the lug-nut diamond on her finger, a pout on her very pretty face.

Kimball shook hands with the guy, leaned over the dog to kiss the daughter, wife, or girlfriend on the cheek, asked how was the drive up and had they found anything to eat yet. Then he introduced me as Ben Abbott from Newbury. I was already reaching for the man's hand when Kimball said, "Ben, meet Judge Clarke from Stamford."

I performed a lightning fast face lock, an instant before my expression betrayed my desire to punch His Honor in the face.

This was Judge Clarke from Stamford—Judge Gary Clarke—whose edicts from his far-off Stamford bench had bulldozed the Town of Newbury's P&Z Board's attempts to rein in Billy Tiller's worse developments, including the flood-spawning Tiller Heights. Why, in my opinion, was no mystery. While Connecticut's judiciary maintained a high standard of honesty—pure as the driven snow compared to numerous corrupt mayors, Hartford lobbyists, and an infamous governor—Judge Clarke was, in my humble opinion, an exception who hadn't been caught, yet.

I had no proof that the judge was a crook. But why else would he intervene in zoning battles half a state away? Certainly, he hadn't bought the girl's diamond on a judge's salary. I once asked a federal prosecutor why public servants risked their careers and incarceration by spending bribe money like drunken sailors. Because they think they deserve to, was the answer. And why risk everything for what were so often relatively small bribes? Cash. So their wives wouldn't find evidence of girlfriends on their credit card receipts.

Perhaps Judge Clarke had inherited money. Perhaps he had invested wisely. Or perhaps Billy Tiller cut him in on a land deal. Or simply bribed him with a FedEx envelope full of twenties and fifties. At two or three hundred thousand dollars extra profit on every additional house Billy could squeeze into a subdivision, he could easily afford a judge.

I managed to say hello without shaking his hand, and sent a polite smile in the direction of the lady and dog in case they were innocents. Judge Clarke asked, "Newbury? That's to hell and gone. What do you do up there, Ben?"

"He's a real estate broker," Kimball answered for me.

"Who are you with?"

"I'm independent."

"Must be the last one in the state."

"There are a few of us still standing."

"How do you compete with the big boys?"

"We have different standards," I said, and I swear the Chihuahua winked at me. "You're a long way from home, too, judge. How'd you come up?"

"Back way. 106, 107."

We discussed roads for a moment or two, as newly met folk will at a country party, and the lovely weather. His consort finally spoke. "We saw a fox," she said. "Rachel chased it."

Rachel was the dog. The judge explained they had stopped the car so the dog could relieve itself and it ran after the fox. I said that the fox must have been in a particularly benign mood considering the Chihuahua had returned intact.

"I was afraid she'd catch Lyme disease," said the girl.

"Rabies," said the judge. "Rabies is from foxes. Lyme disease from deer."

"Whatever."

"Rachel is safe here," said Kimball. "They spray the place every Friday, right before I get here."

Imagining the weekly pesticide dose draining into his stream, I resolved not to give Kimball my take on Judge Clarke until he told me why he wanted to know. I would not be surprised to learn that Kimball was working a scam to get Jeff's trial moved from Plainview to Stamford. He must have known the judge very well to think they could pull that off.

"I gotta get back to the kitchen," said Kimball. "Ben, see if you can find the judge a drink."

With waiters flitting everywhere that was not hard. Clarke ordered cosmopolitans for himself and his lady, who suddenly shrieked recognition and ran to a woman who looked much like her, minus the dog. Judge Clarke and I watched them kiss the air around each other's faces. "The ladies," said Clarke. "Where would we be without them?"

I said, "I recall you sat on a case involving one of our zoning applications."

"I sit on a lot of cases."

"I remember wondering how you got involved up in Newbury."

"I hear cases from all over the state. We're rotated regularly."

"I remember wondering how difficult it must have been to rule on a case that involved land you were not familiar with."

Clarke turned hard-eyed attention to me and I was kind of glad I was bugging him at a party and not in his courtroom. "I rule on law, not land."

"I remember wondering—"

I expected him to turn on his heel and walk away. Instead, he seemed to decide that I was not a threat. He smiled and said, "I am sure that you understand that I don't discuss cases—Oh, there are our cosmos. Over here, fellow," he beckoned the waiter. "Cheers, Ben, nice talking to you." With that he led the waiter to the girl and her dog.

I wandered back to the kitchen, thinking that it was not surprising that the judge was so affable despite my provoking him. Whatever evil he and Billy Tiller had floated over the Newbury dam in the past, was in the past forever.

Connie was still perched on a stool, holding court for the bodyguards, who were grouped around her like adoring bears. Amanda kept pressing small bits of food on her and I was delighted to see her eat more than she would ordinarily in a week. Somebody gave me a fresh Pellegrino and Kimball steered me toward a plate of beautifully grilled scallops.

"So what do you think?" he asked quietly.

"Why do you want to know?"

"I think you can guess that."

"I'm impressed."

Kimball looked astonished. "By Judge Clarke?"

"By the fact that you are so determined to save your son that you would risk getting in bed with the kind of sleaze-bag public servant who will sooner or later end up betraying his friends to plea bargain his way out of a prison sentence."

"What is that supposed to mean?"

"It means I'm impressed. I didn't realize how much you cared about Jeff."

"Abbott, how the fuck would you feel if you had a kid going to prison?"

"Desperate."

"So?" He spoke so intensely that Amanda looked over anxiously.

"Bribing a judge won't help. It will only make it worse."

"The trick is not to get caught. I would never put myself in a place where the judge can set me up for a fall."

"Wrong," I said.

"It's just a matter of getting the details right."

"It is wrong to subvert the legal system."

"What? What? Don't get holier than thou with me." Amanda looked over again and started our way. Kimball waved her off.

"It is wrong to subvert the legal system."

"The legal system is grinding up my kid."

"Beat the system. Don't beat it down. You've got the best lawyer in the state and you've got my word I will do my best to help get him off."

"Big help."

"Weird coincidence."

"What do you mean?"

"Did you know that Judge Clarke intervened in some zoning cases on Billy Tiller's behalf?"

"No I didn't. That is weird." He studied the judge, who was across the lawn with an arm around the lady with the dog. "Actually, now that you mention it, I think I saw Tiller once, at a party at Clarke's house."

"You met Billy? You knew him?"

"No. No. I never spoke to him. I would have remembered it right away, if I had. Somebody pointed him out as Clarke's builder. He'd done some work on the place."

"Probably for free in exchange for screwing Newbury."

"Weird coincidence—him, my kid." Kimball gave a flat laugh. "Goes to show you, there are damned few crooked judges in Connecticut."

"He implied that he happened to be rotated through our district when Billy connected. How'd you hook up with him?"

"Nothing to do with Billy Tiller. One of our performers got in a dispute on I-95."

"You're kidding."

"No I'm not. It was a serious situation. Very serious. My consultants explained that the way it usually works is you let the performer go to prison. Use the opportunity to pump publicity going in. Another big push when they try to burn some tracks inside. Then a big release when they get out with new material. But this one was just launching a clothing line and he had to appear at openings. Our store orders were phenomenal."

"Zip hoodies?" I'd checked the Joey Girl collections on line and I assumed he was describing one of their adolescent male counterparts like Rawkus Joe.

"No. A baller collection. Suits. Like they make the basketball players wear now. It's unbelievable, but our thug customers are dressing like attorneys. Amanda saw it coming and the line was very sharply placed. So, there was no way we could let him—you know—go to jail. So we cut a probation deal."

"With Judge Clarke?"

"He made it, shall we say, possible. No jail time. It all worked out. The line is selling. Not as good as we hoped, but still selling."

"How much did you pay him?"

"I don't answer stupid questions. I don't even hear them."

"Stupid is the operative word. We're facing a chief state's attorney who sees the road to the United States Senate paved with your son's conviction. He would like nothing more than to appeal a thrown trial and send all three of you to prison: you, the judge, and your son. I'm amazed. I would have thought you were too smart to try bribing a judge in a capital case, for crissake."

"I'll do anything I have to."

"It won't work. Forget it."

His jaw set hard, just like Jeff's, and I knew he regretted confiding in me.

I said, "Just back off. I will prove that your son didn't kill Billy Tiller."

"How?"

"I'm working several angles."

"Like what?"

"I'm not ready to talk about them."

"I'm supposed to just trust you?"

"I'm on your side. I know your kid didn't do it."

Kimball looked away, across his lawn and empty pool. "Then you know more than I do."

Chapter Eighteen

In the car, as we started down the driveway, Connie asked, "Benjamin? What were you talking to Mr. Kimball about?"

"Corruption, cynicism, and the collapse of civilization."

"Look out, Ben! Stop the car!"

I saw him too. One of the bodyguards was racing across the lawn to cut us off at the end of the driveway. He skidded to stop beside us. "Thank God I caught you. Miss Connie, you forgot your watercress. Everybody gets a bag to take home. He held out a sealed plastic bag tied with a yellow ribbon.

"Thank you, Edward. I am very pleased to have met you."

"Same here, Miss Connie. Drive careful, fella."

I promised I would. As soon as we got rolling, Connie said, "Mr. Kimball seemed very upset."

"He's worried."

"Will his son go to prison?"

"At this moment it looks that way."

"But you don't think he should?"

"I just don't think he killed Billy Tiller."

"Air guitar."

"What?" I glanced over at her. She was biting her lip. "I beg pardon, Connie?"

"Air guitar. I keep thinking about air guitar and I don't know why."

"It's been a long day. You're a little tired."

She looked down at her hands, which had begun twisting in her lap. "I am tired. But I keep on thinking air guitar. It keeps racing through my head."

"You want to close your eyes, catch a little sleep?"

"When I was a girl every department store sold sheet music… We'd look for new songs, run home and learn them, and play for each other."

I glanced from the wheel again. She had never been big on reminiscing—though she had always been a font of history if you asked her. She sounded wistful. She kept working her hands and her eyes were bright, miles from sleep, so I asked, "Did you have a good time at the party?"

"Oh yes. Don't you prefer parties where there's something to do?…The bodyguards were such proper young men. Did you notice?"

"I didn't talk with them much."

"Oh, you should have. They were just brimful of knowledge."

"Like what?" I asked, glad to be off air guitar.

"Nothing about their employer. They were discreet."

"Then what," I asked, disappointed. I would have liked to learn a little more about Kimball and his relationship with Judge Clarke.

"Henry wants to be a musician. He's studying the harmonica. With a man who plays classical music on it. Ralph was in the Army. I gathered he served in Iraq, though he did not want to discuss it. But he loved the Army and he said he missed it. Charles was in prison. For something he didn't do."

I could relate to that. Though in my case I had believed in my heart that I deserved to be there anyhow. "Was he bitter?"

"He seemed quite philosophical about it. And he was grateful for the opportunity to improve his physique. Lifting weights."

Connie began working her hands again and I nudged her back to the moment, asking, "What about the other one. Who was he?"

"Edward. Edward was not very talkative. But he did tell me he had a child, whom he doesn't see much of."

"How did that come up?"

"He was observing how children would love Mr. Kimball's house with the grass and pool and all that. As I said, they were quite forthcoming, but discreet. Though Edward did mention that Mr. Kimball keeps a bowling alley under his pool house."

"They seemed to like you."

"They were grateful to be noticed…I learned that at parties long ago."

Her hands were working faster. She was tearing at her fingers. Her skin was paper thin and I feared she would cut herself with her own fingernail.

"Learned what?"

"People are so grateful to be noticed."

Desperation made me brave. I tried a different tack, straight at it. "Tell me about air guitar."

"I don't know, Ben. I just don't know…Oh, Lord, I hate this."

"Close your eyes," I said. "Take a nap. I'm okay driving…No, I didn't drink. Not a drop."

I got her home and settled with a glass of warm milk and a promise that she would at least try to eat the thin cheddar cheese sandwich I made. Then I went across the street and poured vodka free hand.

I had touched the glass to my lips before I realized I wasn't alone. Alison was seated on the floor, propped in a dark corner of the living room. The big tom cat was sitting up on her lap, yellow eyes fixed on me with deep skepticism.

"Hey, sweetie, I didn't see you there. How you doing?"

"Guess what?"

"What?"

"The guy my mother went out with?"

"Did you meet him?"

"It's my father."

I put down the glass. The last time I had seen Tom Mealy I had put him on a bus to Massachusetts, having banned him from the property until he got sober—an event unlikely to ever happen. This had followed a knock-down-drag-out fight that had started when I interrupted him beating up Alison's mother. He was a large and fearless bar room brawler and I had won, barely, because he had been too drunk to throw a straight punch. The thing I remembered most vividly about the fight was afterwards, after I had finally had him down on the floor. Alison clung to my leg, begging me not to hurt him.

"How is he?" I asked.

"Okay."

"Did you talk?"

"A little…I showed him Redman."

"Did he like him?"

"Oh, yeah. He thought Redman was great."

"Is he at your mother's now?"

"No. But he said he wants to talk to you."

I took my glass and carefully poured the vodka back into the bottle, spilling very little.

"Are you going to talk to him?"

"Anytime he wants. He knows where to find me."

"He said he'll come back, tomorrow."

"Then I'll talk to him, tomorrow."

The phone rang. I picked up, wondering who was calling on what was—even this early—already a weird Saturday night. Vicky having decided to leave Tim? Marian having decided to dump her kind engineer? Alison's father looking for a rematch? Billy Tiller's murderer asking me to introduce him to Trooper Moody?

"Hey, Ben?"

"Pink?" Cousin Pinkerton.

"Hey, buddy. Can you do me a favor?"

"Name it." I couldn't think of a time he had ever asked for a favor.

"You want to go drinking?"

"Sure. Where?"

"I don't know. Where do you think?"

The penny dropped. I said, "What do you say we hit the White Birch. Say hi to Wide Greg."

"You think?"

"I am sure I can get Wide Greg to listen to reason." Code for, commute Pink's one-week ban to time served.

"I'll pick you up."

"That's okay. I'll meet you in the parking lot." It was always fun driving with Pink—a dirt-track race champ throughout New England with an infallible sixth sense for radar traps in general and Trooper Moody's in particular—but I preferred to be my own designated driver. I knew from experience that if I could persuade Wide Greg to give my cousin a break, Pinkerton Chevalley would be just getting started when a person of normal capacity approached the early stages of alcohol poisoning.

Chapter Nineteen

Wide Greg was busy separating rival gangs when Pink and I hooked up in the White Birch parking lot, and not in a forgiving mood. "Maybe I'll go in and give Greg a hand," said Pink.

"Greg doesn't want a hand."

"Yeah, but then next time I get in trouble, maybe he won't bar me."

"I don't think it works that way."

Pink looked longingly at the bar, where the sound of breaking glass was getting louder. "Wouldn't mind getting into that."

"Until they unlimber firearms. Why don't we drive up to the Hitching Post?"

But the Hitching Post, Pink informed me, had still not recovered from a disgruntled woody from Norfolk chainsawing its bar in an attempt to get served after hours.

"Lorenzo's?"

"Not on a weekend." Lorenzo's Pizza Palace had gone upscale in a successful attempt to attract the new McMansion crowd. Weekends, the whiskey-drenched regulars fled squalling toddlers and ill-bred eight-year-olds.

I wasn't about to suggest the Yankee Drover, which Pink regarded as an uptight bastion of Main Street privilege on the scale of the Ritz of London. But I knew that if I didn't get him out of here very soon he would wade into whatever was unfolding in the White Birch.

"Boat launch?" The warm night would see a crowd drinking beer until Trooper Moody interrupted the party.

"Mosquitoes," said Pink. "Besides, it's just kids."

"How about the River End?"

"All right!"

The River End Bar was managed by Matthew Jervis, a yet-to-be convicted member of the felonious Jervis clan. It was on a dirt road, deep in the Jervis woods, not far from the Indian reservation. Any McMansion dwellers who somehow stumbled upon it would assume, judging by the vehicles in its parking lot and the plywood walls without windows, that the patrons roasted unruly children on spits.

We drove north, Pink in his truck, I in my overpowered Olds. Just before we hit the dirt roads, he signaled me to pass on a straightaway, and when we arrived at the River End, his was the (borrowed) vehicle caked with dust.

The crowd drinking and dancing quieted noticeably, as crowds tended to when Pink darkened a door. The noise picked up again when he exchanged civil hellos with Matthew, the owner. We ordered Screech for Pink and a Rhode Island Red, the house beer, for me. Screech, the private stock rum, was imported from Newfoundland by snowmobile, speed boat, ATV, and beneath-the-radar aircraft. Or so it was said.

"Fine-looking trucks outside," Pink said to Matthew, who replied, "Folks are doing all right," and left it at that. A new prosperity was evident indoors, too: a wide plasma TV, encased in wire mesh in case someone threw a bottle, diamond nose studs, even some platinum teeth bling.

I remarked on the kitchen Matthew had added, with a cook and a teenage Jervis waitress passing plates of decent-looking burgers and remarkably crisp French fries. In the past, a patron who wanted solids with his beer or Screech had purchased them from a dusty rack of beef jerky or carried in take-out. "What's next, Matthew? Windows?"

"Not likely."

Two beers and four Screeches later, Sherman Chevalley wandered in, looking aggrieved, and I thought, Oh hell, here we go again. Pink braced him right off. "What the hell are you doing here?"

"Wide Greg kicked me out."

"Wha'd you do?"

"Nothin'."

Pink shook his head at the injustice and bought Sherman a Screech. Soon they were gazing peacefully up at the TV on which was playing a DVD of "American Chopper."

Half an hour and several Screeches later, Pink nudged me.

"Thought Little Rick was still inside."

"Early parole," I said. "Good behavior."

Little Rick was a son of my long-time friend Gwen Jervis, daughter of old Herman Jervis, clan leader emeritus, who had recently celebrated the retirement of the third generation of state police that failed to pin convictable charges on him. Gwen's brother Bill now ran day-to-day operations with a firm hand and was, by most accounts, only murderous when he had to be. Little Rick looked up to his uncle.

Pink, unusually talkative tonight, said, "Makes you wonder what his cell mate was like."

A while later, in walked Gwen Jervis, and her daughter Josie, home on leave from the Army, which had included Iraq this year. Josie had enlisted as a chubby little eighteen-year-old. Every time she came home she arrived a little taller and leaner. It was possible that she was developing a kind of beauty that one day might rival her mother's.

Josie sat with her brother.

Gwen spotted me at the bar and swayed over smiling. She appeared to have started drinking earlier, back around the time Connie and I had arrived at Kimball's watercress party.

"Hey, Pink." She punched him on the arm, said, "Hi, Ben, slumming?" and gave me a warm, rum flavored kiss on the mouth. She was a tightly strung redhead, missing a front tooth.

As Old Herman's daughter, she was as close to royalty as you'd find in the River End Bar.

I kissed her back and bought her a Screech and basked in an unexpected glow of well-being. I had admired Gwen since I was eight years old and she was twelve. When I reached twelve I had begun to realize why. At fourteen, I was given an introduction and a six-pack by Pink, which had led to a night that was incandescent. Over the years we had stayed friendly. Now and then we managed to do each other a favor. She had been having a love affair with my cousin Renny when he was murdered, and sadness lingered.

"Josie looks great."

Gwen was hugely proud of her daughter, the first of the clan to complete high school, though Gwen herself had come close.

"You know she made sergeant?"

"Read it in the *Clarion*." I had leaned on Scooter MacKay to do the right thing and reprint the Army press release even though Jervis territory wasn't officially in Newbury and Jervises lay beneath Scooter's social radar. "Is she going back?" I asked, meaning Iraq.

"I hope not. Hey, there's poor Jimmy Butler. I've never seen him here. He looks scared stiff."

He would not be the first, upon first entering the River End. Jimmy lunked in the doorway, ducking his head like a turtle. I could just see Billy Tiller sizing up the sucker to drive a hot truck. Just when I thought he would bolt out the door, he broke into a relieved grin and hurried over to Sherman Chevalley, who had drifted down bar from us. Sherman greeted him with a skeleton-rattling clap on the back and let Jimmy buy him a Screech.

"What are you doing here?" I heard Sherman growl.

"Humongous fight at the White Birch. Troopers brought a Corrections bus and a flatbed for the bikes."

"How'd you get away?"

"Got there late."

"Guess I got lucky, too, getting kicked out, early. Greg okay?"

Wide Greg was boarding up windows, Jimmy reported, and their conversation moved on to the merits of multi-position V-plows. Gwen reeled across the room to say something to Josie. I turned to Pink, who was arm-wrestling two truck drivers from Vermont. "You want another Screech?"

"I'll need a straw."

I got him a Screech with a straw.

"What the hell is that?" Pink and the truck drivers cocked ears toward the open door. Something huge was clanking and rumbling up the road.

"Sounds like a tank."

Everyone exchanged looks. What were the Jervises into now?

The cement floor was trembling.

I got to the door first and stepped out for a look. Guided by blazing headlamps, an absolutely enormous machine trundled into the parking lot and stopped just short of demolishing my Oldsmobile. Bearded, long-haired men and close-cropped women began jumping down from the bucket and the rear deck.

"That's a goddamned D-7R," somebody said behind me. "Look at that sucker. Brand new."

Someone asked, "Where the hell did that come from?"

A third voice answered, "It's from the Fed job."

"What Fed job?" I asked.

"EPA doing the Jervis dump."

The bulldozer crew bunched tentatively beside the machine, as if unsure of their welcome. Most of the men were skinny and bespectacled. Most of the women were round and bespectacled. And all had the sun-burned glow of academics released from the academy to romp outdoors. A tall figure shut down the lights and the motor. And who should climb down and lead her colleagues toward the bar but Ms. Jennifer Giraffe?

She stopped when she recognized me. She was wearing blue jeans and a hoodie. The hood was sprayed over her shoulders, framing her angular face like a cowl. Her hair was shorter than I'd seen three days ago. "Hey! Ben Abbott, how you doing?"

"I wasn't aware you knew how to drive a bulldozer."

"Remember, I told you, I'm doing the Northwest Connecticut Landfill Reclamation project? The site characterization study?"

"And you picked up bulldozing this week?"

"No," she said, as serious as ever, despite a new exuberance. "I took courses in school."

"She's fantastic," said a graduate student.

"First rate," said an older fellow who was clearly the professor.

"And you brought the machine here to characterize the site of the River End Bar?"

"My van wouldn't start. We wanted some wine. No one else's car was big enough for all of us."

That made a kind of sense, though I did wonder whether they had considered the environmental impact of the gallons of diesel the monster would burn on a pub crawl. On the other hand, a single vehicle represented a kind of carpooling.

The academics got a lot of looks on the way to the bar, and I could see various Jervis reprobates preparing to separate the college girls from the college boys by the simple expedient of pounding the boys through the floor. An eager fellow lurched at the women, grabbing his crotch to present it like a bouquet. Gwen Jervis gave a nod toward the parking lot. Numerous less drunk Jervises led him away, opening the door with his head.

"Welcome," said Gwen. "Matthew, buy our Audubon friends a drink." To me she muttered, "I love these kids. The Feds are paying us a fortune to let 'em work the dump." That was the source of the new wealth. Well, why not? As long as they didn't use it to replace their house trailers with McMansions.

Matthew splashed blood red wine from a gallon jug into a row of highball glasses.

Jennifer passed them around, then took a sip. "Oh, that's great. I really was thirsty. You know what we're doing, it is so cool. We're going to return that dump to marshland!"

"Have you seen Jeff?" I asked.

"I saw him yesterday after work and I went down again today. We had a long talk."

"How is he?"

"Haven't you seen him?"

"I'll try to get over there Monday. How is he?"

"He's seems to be doing a lot of thinking."

"About what?"

"How he wants to live his life."

"Is that what your long talk was about?"

"We talked about lots of stuff." She glanced away from me. "You know, just talk." Suddenly, her face grew pretty with a smile. "Hey, Georgie! Georgie. Hey, how are you? Later, Ben." She crossed the room with long-legged alacrity and threw an arm over the low, narrow shoulders of George Stefanopoulos, who looked happy to be out of his Home Depot apron and glad to be hugged.

I got a fresh beer and stayed at the bar conversing with any who stumbled near.

I had to marvel at how many Billy Tiller victims I had interviewed had made their way to the River End on this same night. Jimmy Butler. Sherman Chevalley. George from Home Depot. Okay, the cops had closed the White Birch. The McMansion dwellers had taken over Lorenzo's. The Hitching Post was dark. But still, this was practically a Billy Tiller memorial, waiting only for the Gordons, Andrew Sammis, and the couple with the McMansion-quaking Jacuzzi to begin.

I imagined the lawyer who threatened to sue me or disbar me or something if I didn't stop smearing the present with Billy's past would conduct the service. Evil Engineer Edwards would march to the podium with Total Landscape's blueprints to turn the Jervis Woods into a Billy Memorial Shopping Mall tucked under one arm and his sturdy, lovely Caroline on the other. Judge Clarke would gavel for order, while Jervises homed in like bats on his girlfriend's diamond. Any Kimballs? Not likely, with father wrapping up his watercress party down in Newtown, Mom watching TV in her kitchen, and Jeff in his cell.

I talked to Sherman. I talked to Jimmy Butler. I talked to George when he came to the bar to buy another wine for Jennifer. I learned nothing new from any of them. Josie came over to say hi. She seemed happy, which she deserved to be. Later, when the crowd had begun to thin and I was thinking of calling it a night, Gwen reeled up to me. "I'm shit faced. Would you drive me home? Josie's staying."

"Sure."

I got her into the Olds and buckled her seatbelt for her. Then I walked across the parking lot, planting each step immediately after the other, toe to heel.

"What the hell are you doing?"

I stood on my left foot and timed sixty seconds on my watch. Then I balanced on my right foot for sixty seconds.

"What the hell are you doing?"

"Making sure I can pass a DUI checkpoint."

"Jesus Christ, it's easier to outrun them."

I got in the car. "Hold your finger in front of my nose. Okay, now move it way to the left. Hold it there. Is my eyeball shaking?"

"Why the hell would it be?"

"There's a kind of astigmatic reaction you can't control when you're high. Is it shaking?"

"No."

"All right. We're outta here."

Gwen closed her eyes. I maneuvered the car around Jennifer's bulldozer and headed down a dark road into the woods. Gwen woke up after a while and asked, "Are you going to try to take advantage of me drunk?"

"Could I have a rain check?"

"What for?"

"I'd much more enjoy taking advantage of you sober."

She slumped down in her seat. I thought she fell asleep again, but she was watching the side mirror. "Wonder who's following us?"

Their lights were higher than a car, lower than a truck. "I was thinking your husband."

"Buddy's out with the boys." That could range from poaching deer to delivering sidearms to customers too busy to linger for an instant background check. Although, to be fair, Buddy was often legitimately employed as an offshore oilrig roustabout, working months on and months off. One thing for sure, Gwen's husband hadn't been caught up in the White Birch fracas back in Frenchtown. Jervises did not waste their energy on police-attracting activities that didn't put food on the table or cash in the mattress.

It was slow going to her trailer, with the Olds scraping the crowns of the dark, dirt roads. Halfway there, she said, "Still following."

"Probably looking for a place to pull over and make out."

"I wonder if they're after you or me?"

"Who would have the balls to follow you into the Jervis woods?"

"So I guess they're after you."

"Or lost. "

"Maybe you better stay the night, just to be on the safe side."

Tempting. Very. Although a prime example of polar opposites would be "safe side" and Buddy Jervis concluding his night's business early. "When's Buddy heading back to the Gulf?"

"He promised me he'd stay home a while." She glanced at me and the dashboard lights glinted green in her eyes. "It's gotten so I miss the son of a bitch. I like having him around. We're getting old, Ben."

"You're not old. Neither am I. Neither is Buddy. Well I guess he is, actually. What is he, fifteen years older than you?"

"They're turning off."

"I see."

"I'll lend you a sawed off. In case they're waiting for you."

Wouldn't that would make Trooper Moody's night if he pulled me over back in Newbury with an illegal weapon in my car? Still, I was debating Gwen's offer when I saw in my mirrors red tail and white backup lights where the headlights had disappeared. Brake lights flashed and off. Then tail lights disappeared as whoever had been behind us turned around and pulled away in the direction from which we had come. "Thanks. I'll be fine."

A half mile on, her trailer came in view, one of a dozen whose lights speckled the woods. I pulled up beside the wooden steps, kissed her good night longer than Buddy would have liked, and helped her climb the steps. "Wait a second," she said. I heard her rummaging in the dark. She returned with a shotgun that had been hack-sawed down to sixteen inches of barrel and pistol stock.

"Safety's on. Stick it under your seat." She was holding it in a dishrag. I stretched my sweater cuff over my fingers, kissed her cheek and said, "Thanks."

Her door shut behind her, I waved in the general direction of the other trailers, nipping clan gossip in the bud, and drove away. Surrounded by cousins, nephews, uncles, and aunts, Gwen would sleep as safe as a general in the Green Zone.

I drove for a half mile and lowered the windows to see better as I neared the point where the car behind me had turned around. Apparently it had kept going. Nonetheless, I drove with my high beams high and watched carefully at every indent in the road where someone could be waiting. I was not surprised to make it to the River End still intact.

The bar was closed, the parking lot empty. Even Jennifer's bulldozer was gone.

I kept going. Then, after another mile or so of curving dark road, I topped a little rise which sent my headlights farther than normal. In the distance I saw the gleam of a car. It didn't seem to be moving. Closer, I saw it had stopped in the middle of the road, blocking it. I drew within a hundred yards and slowed, liking the situation less and less. I couldn't see the marker plate or tell what it was, except it looked like one of the smaller kinds of SUV.

I checked my mirrors, half-expecting a vehicle to come up behind me. Nothing. Or at least nothing with lights on. I stopped the car. Part of me wanted to pick up the gun under my seat. Part of me did not because once it filled my hand up went the potential for a misunderstanding turning deadly.

I shut the engine, doused my lights, and listened for someone coming up on foot or leaping from the woods. It was near silent, too early in the year for bugs to sing. I heard a barred owl bark. Then all I heard was the ticking of my engine cooling down. My eyes adjusted to the dark. But there was still nothing to see except the car ahead, the empty road behind, and the trees to my left and right.

I felt for the switch to deactivate the interior lights when I opened the door.

Suddenly the vehicle sprang to life. Headlights on, engine roaring, it raced away. I cranked the Olds and floored it. A couple making out would receive my apologies for interrupting, but I wanted to know who the hell was in that vehicle.

It was immediately obvious that I would never catch them. I had the speed, but not the clearance. The Olds was too low slung for the ruts and high crown of a dirt road. The red lights ahead dwindled and soon had disappeared. Just as well. Probably just a couple, or scared kids smoking dope. Still, I watched carefully until the dirt road finally returned me to the smooth macadam of a hilly, winding road which would connect me to Route 7 and home to Newbury.

It was past midnight. The road was empty. The speed limit was 45. I held to 50, with just enough beer on my breath not to want to be pulled over for speeding. I passed the occasional farmhouse, dark or with a single light on, but the land was mostly overgrown fields and dense woods. Where the tree canopy didn't cover the road I caught glimpses of stars in a black, moonless sky and once, where it opened by a farm field, a bright swath of Milky Way meandering south like a river.

I was back under the trees, entering a sharp curve, when I was stunned by a loud explosion and a dazzling flash—searing, stark and penetrating as a million bolts of lightning. I saw the trees leap before my eyes, bright as icicles. Blinded, I stomped the brakes. The car screeched into a skid. I tried to steer away from the trees I could not see.

Chapter Twenty

Not a tree died, thanks to a stone wall, which the Olds mounted at a terrible angle.

The impact threw me hard against the five-point competition seat belt that Pink had salvaged from a race car he had cracked up. Air bags would have been nice, too, but the Olds pre-dated them. I banged my head on the steering wheel, but the belt kept me inside the car as it rolled over and over and over shedding doors and windshield and sliding a ways on its roof. When metal finally stopped shrieking, the stink of spilled gasoline roused me to pop the belt and crawl out a jagged hole. I rolled away, scrambling for distance between me and an explosion, tried to stand, stumbled a few steps, and slowly collapsed in the road as if my body was saying, Enough, already, we're just going to lie down right here and have a little nap.

I heard a bell. Not a bell. A dragging clanking metallic noise. Like I was dragging old Marley's chains, I thought. Except it wasn't Christmas and I wasn't dead. I was alive and suddenly so sharp and aware I could hear another sound, some rustling in the woods, the snap of a branch. Then the bell started, again, resonating, clank, clank, clank.

I opened my eyes. I could see, for which I was deeply grateful. I could see my car, or what was left of it, wheels in the air. One of its headlights was still burning, pointed straight at me. The bell sounded near my ear. I raised my cheek from the cool road and read by the light of the headlamp—in capital letters, six inches from my face—the words, COMBINED TACTICAL SYSTEMS FLASH-BANG 7290.

Before I could register their meaning, they started moving. And as they moved, the bells started up again. The words were printed on a metal container the size and shape of a large beer can. But it wasn't a beer can because it was perforated with numerous holes. It moved past my face.

I reached out—vaguely aware that my limbs still worked—and grabbed it.

It had a string attached to an eye bolt. A string which I traced across the road and into the woods. Someone in the woods was pulling the other end of the string. And it occurred to me that the string was a lanyard for retrieving this metal can. Considering the light that had blinded me, the explosion, and the words FLASH-BANG, it dawned on me that my automobile accident was no accident. I had been blinded by a flash grenade—like the cops used to disorient criminals to keep them from shooting back when they raided their hideout. Cousin Sherman had mentioned them at the White Birch while asking Wide Greg about a purveyor of illegal weapons named Angel. Latino dude from Waterbury.

Right now I needed an angel. I looked at my car, wondering if I could get to the shotgun fast enough to get the drop on the son of a bitch tugging the string. I gathered my legs, but before I could rise, I was blinded, again, by bright headlights. A car had come along. The FLASH-BANG got away, clanged across the road, and disappeared into the woods.

Several million red, white, and blue lights started flashing, all at once.

I felt a painful nudge in my ribs and looked up to see Newbury's resident Connecticut State Police Trooper Oliver Moody gazing down at me with an expression more curious than sympathetic. "You okay?"

"I think so."

"License and registration."

"Ollie! Somebody just tried to kill me with a flash grenade."

Trooper Moody crouched down and shined his Maglite in my face.

"You smell like you've been drinking."

"I had a beer. Before somebody tried to kill me with a flash grenade. If you move quick, you can catch him in those woods, over there."

"How many beers?"

"Breathalyze me for crissake. If you don't believe me."

He didn't believe me. He did breathalyze me, after calling an ambulance. When I passed, he wrote me a ticket for making a restricted turn.

I convinced the Newbury volunteer ambulance crew that all I needed was some Band-Aids for a cut on my left palm I got crawling out of the car, some ice for a bump on the forehead, and a ride home. Sally Butler, the crew chief, kept shining her flashlight in my eyes. I demonstrated that my arms and legs were working. I didn't even limp. Sally finally decided that I was relatively undamaged. We agreed I would be sore in the morning.

But before Ollie allowed them to drive me home, he motioned me over to the Chevalley wrecker he had radioed to pick up the pieces. My cousins Albert and Dennis had hoisted the remains onto its flat bed and were standing by, curious as hogs on a truffle hunt. Ollie shined his light through the hole where the driver's door had been.

"What's this?"

"What's what?"

"That. Under the driver's seat."

"Looks like a sawed-off shotgun," chorused my cousins.

Ollie said, "You two get in the cab and sit there 'til I tell you otherwise."

Albert and Dennis lumbered away. Ollie asked me, "What's a sawed-off shotgun doing in your car?"

"It's not mine."

"Yeah? How did it get there?"

"Probably some crazy biker at the White Birch stashed it when you guys raided the joint."

"Better not have your prints on it."

At last, a reason to smile. "I would be surprised."

‹›‹›‹›

Next morning, Sunday morning, while I was waiting in my office for Alison's father to pay a call, nursing a headache and numerous body aches, and wondering who had done that to me last night, Pink telephoned to report mournfully, "She's a goner, Ben. Frame's bent. Motor came right off the mounts, tore up the tranny something awful."

"Son of a bitch."

"Sorry, man."

"I just bought new tires."

"Yeah, I see they came in yesterday. "

"What would it cost to fix it?"

"She'd never be the same, Ben."

A big shadow filled the door and knocked on the glass. I stifled the groan it took to remove my feet from my desk and called, "It's open. Come in."

But it wasn't Alison's father. It was Trooper Moody. Six foot five from boots to hat, he looked way too large to be indoors. "Got a minute?" he asked in a tone that suggested he would get a warrant if I didn't.

"Sure. Sit down."

He filled the clients' couch. "I checked out the site in the daylight. Found indications someone had been in the woods by the road."

"Find the flash grenade?"

"Nope. But I saw where the lanyard mighta got hung up in a spice bush. Looked like the guy broke some branches yanking it loose."

"Now that I'm a believable crime victim will you take back that ticket for making a restricted turn?" It was sitting on my desk, folded into a paper airplane. I sailed it in his direction.

Ollie snatched it from the air without once removing his eyes from my face.

"Any idea who did it?" he asked.

"If I did I'd give you his phone number."

"You been poking around trying to poke holes in the Kimball case. So I'm wondering who you pissed off."

"Why not wonder who the killer is who thinks I'm getting close to proving Jeff Kimball didn't do it?"

"Because I arrested Kimball sitting on the bulldozer that squashed Billy Tiller."

"I'm questioning the order they got there."

Ollie emitted a blast-furnace sigh of disbelief. "Ben. I was there. The kid thought fast and made up a story about coming on the scene after it happened. But I caught him red-handed."

"All I'm asking is, what if he didn't make it up? What if he's telling the truth?"

"Let me ask you something. Something you should have asked yourself when Roth hired you. Would you have climbed onto a bulldozer that was sitting on top of Billy Tiller?"

"No."

"Why not?" Ollie asked triumphantly. "That's what the kid did."

"There's a crucial difference between me and the kid."

"Yeah, he's a murderer, you're not."

"That's not the difference I'm talking about."

"What is?"

"I don't know how to run a bulldozer."

For some reason, Ollie looked even more triumphant.

"Besides," I said, "Jeff Kimball is not a murderer."

"Sure about that?"

I did not answer right away. Instead, I reviewed once more in my mind all the reasons I was sure that Jeff was innocent. His habit of turning the machine left. My belief that Billy's killer had arrived with him in his truck. True, I would have been happier if Evil Engineer Edwards hadn't admitted saving his marriage by shooting Billy last year, effectively eliminating a mysterious shooter as a suspect this year. Countering that was a powerful gut feeling that Jeff could not crush the life out of a fellow human being. And, of course, Jeff was not, by far, the only citizen of Newbury with reason to hate Billy Tiller. Besides, whoever exploded a flash grenade in my face last night thought I was getting too close for comfort. Someone in the River End Bar. Or hiding in the woods, watching my car.

"I'm absolutely positive Jeff Kimball is not a murderer."

My declaration ignited the biggest grin I had ever seen on Ollie's face. "Then how come," he asked, "Jeff Kimball just confessed?"

Chapter Twenty-one

I don't recall my answer. It was something bright like, "What?"

"The kid started rattling his bars this morning and when the guards came he told them he killed Billy Tiller with a bulldozer." Ollie laughed. "State's attorney is really pissed. There goes his TV trial."

"I cannot believe—Wait a minute, Ollie, if the guilty party was already locked up, last night, who exploded a flash grenade in my face?"

"You been screwing any wives lately?"

"I'll check my diary and get back to you."

Ollie unfolded my airplane and spread it on my desk. "Better do it before the answer date on this ticket."

He left. I lifted my shoes onto my desk and stared at them.

Mindblown, to say the least, I picked up the phone and called Ira Roth. I got his voice mail, left my name, and immediately dialed his cell. This did not seem possible. Why in hell would Jeff Kimball confess? And if he really did do the murder, then who tried to kill me last night? Who and why? Ira picked up, after checking his caller ID. "I can't talk, now, Ben. I'm with a client."

"Did Jeff confess?"

"That's who I'm with. I'll get back to you when I can."

"What can I do?"

"Nothing." He hung up. I looked up. Tom Mealy filled my door.

If this weekend had not already become my worst in memory, it was about to. Alison's father was almost as big as Oliver Moody and had more scars on his face because Trooper Moody fought his fights sober while Tom brawled when feeling no pain.

He rapped on the glass.

I returned my feet to the floor the better to move rapidly. "Come in."

He opened the door and promptly stumbled over the sill.

"Hello, Tom. How are you doing?"

He came at me fast, crossing my office in a single bound, and thrust out a big hand with scarred knuckles. "I want to apologize, Ben. I behaved like a real jerk in the past and I promise you I won't do it again."

Almost as mindblown as by Jeff's confession, but more inclined to smile, I stood up and took his hand. It was trembling and a little damp. He was very nervous.

"Great to see you, Tom. Sit down. Sit down."

Nervous, but clear-eyed. His skin was smooth and he looked ten years younger than when I'd seen him last. I guessed he hadn't had a drink or a cigarette in months.

"I was just going to make some coffee. Want some?"

"Coffee would be great. Thanks."

He lumbered after me, through the house, into the kitchen, and stood by, shifting foot to foot as I assembled the coffee. "How've you been?" I asked.

"Well, next week, I celebrate a year sober."

"Congratulations."

"I gotta thank you for what you've done for my family."

"I will tell you in all honesty, Tom, it's a pleasure having them here. Alison is a fine little girl."

"Man, I can't believe how much she grew."

I sensed her presence and looked at the screen door. She was scrunched up on the granite slab that formed the low step, watching and listening. When our eyes met, she put a finger to her lips.

"Where are you living?" I asked Tom.

"I just rented a place down in Frenchtown. With an option to buy."

"Excellent," I said, wondering how. The high point of his employment record had been a brief stint plowing snow for the town, a job he lost for drinking and stealing. However he had pulled it off, I knew deep in my heart that I was going to lose my backyard neighbors. Had to happen some time, I thought. Right? Kids grow up, go to college, move to a city. Besides, Frenchtown wasn't that far away. Close enough to bicycle up the hill to ride Redman.

"It's a little ranch," he said. "But it's got a barn I can fix up and some land. Two bedrooms and a nice kitchen designed by Home Depot. When I showed Janet that kitchen she cried."

"That's great," I said, pretending I could not imagine a rusted pickup backing a second-hand horse trailer into Scooter's barn. "You're lucky to find it. Prices are going nuts and builders are buying little places just to tear them down." I was surprised I hadn't seen it listed. I'm always looking for a such a property for the grown children of many people I know who were dying to find a place like that so they can afford to stay in Newbury.

"Man, I know I'm lucky. I'm renting from the man I've been working for. He wants me to stay with the store, so he made it easy. I think he'll give me a mortgage if it keeps working out. Wants to make me manager so he can open up another one."

"What kind of store?"

"Liquor store."

I looked up from the coffee pot. "Isn't that tough on you?"

"Everybody asks that. But my sponsor—you know, I joined AA."

"Figured."

"My sponsor, he's worked in a bar fifteen years. He said for him the only way he could stay sober was face it every day. He said when he sees all them bottles, he knows damned well he's not going to get in trouble skipping a meeting. That's what I'm doing and it's working out."

"Good luck."

"Thing is, Ben, I'm hoping to make a home. You know. For my wife. For my little girl. That's making it easier, too."

"I'll bet."

Chapter Twenty-two

I drove the Fiat to Plainfield. A block from the courthouse, I got nearly run off the road by a jerk in a Cadillac. I only realized as he disappeared in my rearview mirror that it was Ira Roth, speeding home to spend the rest of Sunday with his horses. I presented myself at the jail. The guard checking ID said, "You're off the list."

"I'm Kimball's attorney's investigator."

"Attorney Roth just left. He said you're off the list."

"What?"

"Sorry, man."

I went outside and found a private spot across the street in the pretty Plainfield green, which had some healthy old elms and views of handsome Greek Revival mansions, to phone Ira's cell.

"What, Ben?" I could hear tires squeal as he bulled the big car through a sharp bend.

"What's going on, Ira? Jail says I'm off the list to see Jeff."

"You got your wish, Ben."

"What wish?"

"You're off the case. I don't need you anymore."

"Did he really confess?"

"We're negotiating that."

"What 'we'? You and Jeff or you and the state's attorney?"

"I don't need your services anymore."

"Mind me asking why he did it?"

Ira barked a bitter laugh. "He says he did it for the environment."

"Not revenge?"

"Revenge would be too easy. Hot-headed. Madness of the moment. Trauma revisited. Best case, I could knock an argument that got out of hand down to manslaughter. But 'for the environment' sounds way-in-advance premeditated. As in first degree murder."

"Did you tell Jeff that?"

"Oh, yes. But he's a very principled young man. He would never hurt a fly for revenge."

I said, "I don't get it. He told me over and over that ELFers don't kill."

"I never met an anarchist yet who plays by the rules."

"What are you going to do?"

"The way he's acting, maybe I can pull off an insanity plea," Ira said with little hope.

"You mind if I talk to him?"

"I don't need you muddying the waters."

"I won't muddy anything. Let me talk to him. This whole thing sounds way off kilter."

"No. This is tricky stuff right now. Let me remind you, we still have the death penalty in this state."

"Did you remind Jeff of that?"

"Oh, he knows. The little bastard knows that he'll get his trial. Even if the judge accepts his guilty plea, he'll get a death penalty hearing where he can spout his commitment to greenery. And again in the mandatory appeal. He's got himself a forum right up to the moment they slide the needle in his arm."

"Let me talk to him."

"Stay out of it. I don't need you on this case anymore. I don't want you in this case anymore."

"Horse paid in full?"

"Not quite."

"Then I'll keep looking."

"No you won't. You're off the case."

"Only if the horse is paid in full."

"Ben, why are you so goddamned contrary?"

"Is the horse paid in full?" I gave him plenty of time to say yes before I hung up on him. But we both knew he was too greedy to allow that.

I had to laugh. If it was Billy's actual killer who tried to kill me last night, he should have waited a day for Jeff to confess. A Honda with NYP press plates pulled up to the jail and out jumped a guy with a camera and a woman scribbling notes on a pad, and I had to laugh again.

No wonder Ira had been driving like a maniac. The attorney who pleaded a Manhattan mover-and-shaker's son guilty of first degree murder was not the image he wanted splashed around New York City. Becoming known as the lawyer who won life in prison instead of the death penalty would not be much better.

Right behind the NYP Honda came a Saturn with Connecticut plates. It decanted a reporter I recognized from the Hartford *Courant,* the state's leading daily. And here came a TV crew in a satellite truck, which meant that a disappointed chief state's attorney must be lurking in the courthouse. Run, Ira, run. And weep, prosecutor, weep. No Senate race for convicting an eco-terrorist who has already confessed. The only good news today was a death penalty hearing would cost the taxpayers less than a long trial.

I got home in time to keep my Sunday appointments.

First I took a pair of house hunters out to see the old Richardson place—a treasure of an old-fashioned weekend mansion that I had been trying to sell for years and was now even harder to sell since Billy Tiller had plunked a pair of McMansions across the road. Next was a couple that had been priced out of Manhattan. They wanted to convert a Connecticut tobacco barn into a loft-like artist's studio and home. Or, they wanted buy an authentic saltbox. Or, maybe something ultra-modern like they'd seen last week in the Hamptons. They were pretty much going to kill the rest of the day, I thought. But at five, when it was time to call it a day, Patrick said to Brenda, "You're not happy, are you?"

Brenda said, "I was hoping to get thrilled."

"Ben?" Patrick turned to me with little hope. He had the glazed eyes and furrowed brow of a man who had seen too many properties in one weekend. "Can you thrill us?"

I was wishing I had a third arrow in my quiver—open heart surgery or portrait painting—as I was the batting the same zero real-estate-wise that I'd been batting detective-wise. Well, if I couldn't thrill them, I could at least entertain them so they'd come back smiling next weekend.

"There is a house that just came on the market. It's unusual."

Brenda perked up. "Can we see it?"

"Unusual as in about to fall down?" asked Patrick.

"No. It's in perfect, move-in condition. Except the garden needs work."

"What's wrong with the garden?"

"Needs a major weeding. It's unusual, too. Kind of a walled garden. Very unusual."

"Come on, Pat. Let's look at it."

"Let me find out." I dialed Fred Gleason. "Sorry to call you so late, Fred. I've got a charming young couple here looking to be thrilled and I thought of the builder's house you just listed. Is it still available?"

Fred knew that I would be angling the cell, surreptitiously, toward the charming young couple, and he answered to the effect that some people who had looked this morning had told Sherry Carter that they were considering coming back for another look the middle of the week and that Sherry had a feeling they would put down a deposit.

I said, "Well, my clients saw a contemporary they loved in the Hamptons, but they want to give Connecticut a shot, before they commit."

I tilted the phone again so they could hear Fred say, "I'd rather spend the summer in Abu Ghraib than fight that Hamptons traffic."

"Thanks Fred. Talk to you later."

"Builder's house?" asked Patrick.

"His own home. Built to his standards."

"Why's he selling?"

"He passed away recently."

"Oh. But's it's new. Modern?"

"Postmodern. Ish. Though more Wright than Gehry."

"Pat. Come on, let's see it."

By now, Pat looked like a man in need of a cocktail. I said, "Let me make a suggestion. If we can give it a quick look, now, we'll be just in time for drinks at the Yankee Drover." I led the way in the Fiat. They glided after me, slick and silent in an electric hybrid.

"Wow," they said when we climbed out of the cars. Then Patrick said, "It's kind of bright, isn't it?"

"The brick is glazed," I answered. "I would imagine it's impervious to weather."

I unlocked the front door as fast as I could get the key out of the lock box, but not fast enough for Brenda, who said, "I hate this door."

I said, "I would replace it with a nice solid piece of oak."

"This is the ugliest door I've ever seen in my life."

"I would stain the oak a tobacco shade to play off the brick."

I got the damned thing open and they chorused, "Oh my God."

I kept my trap shut.

They stood in the foyer a while, repeating, "Oh my God."

Then they started through the rooms. I remained in the foyer, tracking their progress by swellings and decrescendos of Oh my Gods.

What, I wondered, had it been like for Billy Tiller to come home at night to this monstrosity. He had built it as his dream house. But his wife had filed for divorce while it was still under construction. Within a year she had remarried and moved to Arizona. I hadn't seen anywhere in the house to cosy up on a winter evening. Maybe he sat in a closet.

At least he'd been lucky in divorce. Somehow he'd gotten the house. And the business. A lot luckier than most guys I knew.

Though not all. Bruce Kimball had made out like a bandit, too. Despite what he had told me at the Yale Club, somehow I didn't believe that all of his new riches miraculously materialized the day after his divorce was official.

Patrick and Brenda returned, laughing. "What's that fireplace made of?"

"Some kind of art material."

"I told you, Pat."

Pat said, "Where's this walled garden?"

I led them into the master bedroom suite and hit the curtain switch.

"Oh my God."

My thought exactly. For a different reason.

"I don't see any weeds," said Brenda.

They were gone. Weeded.

"Some of those plants are kind of scraggly."

Scraggly—leggy—because they'd been fighting the weeds for sun. But they had survived and were even lightly speckled with blossoms. Like the tentative laughter of suddenly freed prisoners. Camassia, blue bells, aquilegia, corydalis, allium, Jacob's ladder.

"Ben, do you know about flowers?"

"A bit."

"What are those dark blue clusters?"

"Baptisia."

The weeds had hidden a reflecting pool.

"This so cool. Pat, how would you like to see this when we wake up in the morning?"

"It is so peaceful."

Brenda said, "I'd spend the whole day in bed."

Pat perked up. "Sounds good to me. Ben, have you ever seen a garden like this?"

"Only once."

Chapter Twenty-three

I called Fred from the car. "Ten bucks says they'll buy it."

"You're kidding."

"They want to sleep on it."

"Uh oh."

"Yeah, but they're going sleep here, at the Drover."

"Can we get Anne Marie to give them the Orgasm Suite?"

"Already done. I'll take them over again in the morning."

"Excellent."

"Another ten bucks says, the only thing they're going to change in the whole house is the front door."

"God bless you, Ben. If I live to be a hundred I will never understand this business."

My machine was blinking when I got home in a celebratory mood. The first message was from Aunt Connie, her voice thin and agitated. "Ben. It's Connie. I just wanted to say, air guitar."

The second message said, "It's Bruce Kimball. I appreciate the work you tried to do for Jeff. The negotiations are at a very delicate stage, so I know that you will do nothing to upset them. When they are completed, I'm sure that Attorney Roth will tell you the outcome." As in, "Butt out."

The third message said, "Ben, air guitar."

The fourth and fifth and sixth said, "Air guitar."

The seventh said, "Oh God, where are you, Ben?"

I ran across the street and found her thawing soup she had frozen in single portion containers. "Are you all right?"

"Perfectly fine. How are you?"

She looked absolutely normal. "I thought maybe you had telephoned."

"No."

"There was a hang-up on the machine. I thought maybe it was you?"

"No. Would you like some soup?"

"No thanks. You're sure you're okay?"

"Perfectly fine."

"Call me if you need anything."

"Thank you, Ben."

I walked back across Main Street. Tom was sitting under the kitchen table, staring at his dish. I fed him. Then I went back to the barn to invite Alison and her mother to grill pork chops on the fire, but they were just leaving to go over to their Tom's house for supper, so I opened some wine and went on line, bounced around the websites of the *New York Times*, the *Washington Post*, the *Guardian*, the *New York Observer*, Late-Night Political Jokes, and National Weather Service. It beat television, but not by a lot. It didn't matter. I was marching in place, wondering what would be the point of approaching Caroline Edwards.

◇◇◇◇

In the morning, I walked over to the Drover, found my potential buyers smiling over breakfast and anxious to see Billy's house again. We drove out in their Prius. As we pulled up and the slanted morning sun revealed just how yellow the brick was, I fully expected them to scream, "What were we thinking?"

They clamored to be let in and they ran room to room, exclaiming. I stayed out of their way by wandering room to room, from cellar to attic. In the master bedroom, I opened the curtain. I had a stronger than ever impression that Caroline Edwards had spent days weeding a garden she had originally helped Billy Tiller plant.

"Ben?"

There was a problem in the living room. Pat hated the fireplace. Brenda agreed it was ugly, but respected the concept of an art material surround. They wanted me to mediate. Reluctantly, and very gingerly, I observed that on one hand an artistic fireplace was a fine thing to have, but on the other hand, certain art was not the kind of art you wanted to look at every day.

"I'd feel funny jack hammering it off."

"We don't want to be Rockefellers destroying Diego Rivera murals."

I opted for silence until they chorused, beseechingly, "Ben?"

"I would say this. If you do want to replace it, do it before you move in your furniture. Messy job."

That was a mistake. Their faces clouded up.

"But a quick job. One afternoon, no more."

"Hey," said Pat. "I wonder if we could get any more of that brick. Like the outside."

"Oh, cool. Reprise the theme. Ben, do you know where the builder bought the brick?"

"I gather it was a one-of-a-kind run. It would be impossible to ever buy such brick again." They looked devastated. "But," I said, "let me show you something."

I led them down to the enormous cellar. One thing about builders. They build great cellars. I pointed out that Billy's was dry, and a full nine feet deep. Massive I-beams carried the upstairs. Lovingly stacked against the furnace room wall was a fireplace worth of extra hideous yellow brick.

We drove back to my office, discussing a bid in the car. They asked my advice. I suggested they estimate what it could cost to replace the front door and the art material fireplace and make an offer accordingly. They came up with a shrewd number. I called Fred with it and he said, instantly, "Done!" which, as I had suspected, meant Fred had already informed Total Land Rape that he had a couple of live ones who should be encouraged to close a deal before their keeper escorted them back to the asylum and took away their checkbook.

We went through the paperwork. It was a lot simpler than I was used to, with no need to enumerate worries like removing buried oil tanks, wet cellars, dubious wells, weary septic systems, termites, mold, and rot.

We signed the agreement contingent on them getting a mortgage and the house passing inspection, neither of which would be a problem as they were pre-approved and Billy had done a fine job of building his own house. Pat and Brenda hugged and kissed. Then they hugged me, thanked me profusely, and galloped back to the Orgasm Suite.

I walked their binder check over to the bank.

When I got back, Bruce Kimball was parked outside my house in a white Hummer. Amanda was perched beside him, head tilted into her cell phone. Kimball was drumming the wheel with busy fingers.

I stepped into the street and rapped on his window. "If you drove up here to tell me to butt out, I already got your message."

"I need a favor."

"What?"

His mouth worked, like he was re-chewing a piece of garlic that had gotten caught in his teeth. He stared straight ahead and drummed the wheel harder. "Go on," Amanda whispered. "Ask him."

"Ben?" I heard Aunt Connie call. "Ben Abbott."

Outfitted for gardening in a cotton dress and a simple string of pearls, Connie barreled down her front walk, banged open her gate and crossed Main Street waving her cane at the cars she stepped in front of. "Ben! I saw you there—Oh, good morning, Amanda. Good morning, Mr. Kimball. Mr. Kimball, you should be ashamed of yourself driving such an extravagant vehicle."

"I need it for business."

"The nature of your business permits you to set an example. Neither our environment nor our national security can abide spewing pollutants into the atmosphere and wasting precious fossil fuels—Ben, when you have a moment, please come see me." She lowered her voice. "I finally remembered air guitar. Don't worry, I wrote it down, this time."

I walked her safely back across Main and told her I'd be over as soon as I got done with Mr. Kimball who needed my help. I returned to Kimball and asked, "What do you need?"

"Could you possibly talk my son into letting me visit?"

He still wouldn't look at me. I looked past him at Amanda, who mouthed, "Please."

"Jeff still won't talk to you?"

"No."

"I can try. But I'm not on the visitor list."

"I already had Roth fix that. Hop in."

I glanced across the street. Air guitar could wait a few hours.

Many gallons of gas later, we pulled into Plainfield. I'd been in more uncomfortable vehicles, but I could not remember when. Kimball and Amanda, who had spent the journey repeating over and over that they could not believe that Jeff had confessed when he had such a good lawyer, waited in the Hummer.

"Ben Abbott," I said to the duty guard. "I'm back on the Kimball list."

"Just got the call."

He escorted me to the interview room and came back in a few minutes with Jeff.

"What the hell did you confess for?" I asked, the minute we were alone.

"Because I did it."

"Could have fooled me—Actually, you did fool me."

"Sorry, Ben. It wasn't personal. I just was kind of confused and now I'm not."

"Well, I wish you luck."

Jeff Kimball's face fell. He got a haunted look in his eyes. I thought for a second he would cry, but he got past that and said, "Thank you, Ben. You know, it was always cool talking to you."

"Will you do me a favor?"

He looked around the room and gave the heavy mesh that protected the small window in the door a thin smile. "Sure. If I can."

"You can. And if you would, I would feel a little better about everything."

"What do you have to feel bad about?"

"Lost hope, my friend. Will you do me this one favor?"

"What?"

"Your father desperately wants to talk to you."

"Fuck him."

"Jeff, please. He's been on your side all along. He's done everything he could think of to help."

"Throwing his money around? Big fucking deal."

I motioned him close, pointed at the table where there could be a mike and whispered, "He was ready to risk his own freedom to bribe a judge."

"Bribe? He would bribe—that's disgusting."

"I know it's disgusting. I told him in no uncertain terms that it was both wrong and stupid. I'm only telling you because as misguided as he was, that's how much he cared, that's how much he would risk to help you. Talk to him."

"What good will it do?"

"None at all. Just let the man see your face."

‹›‹›‹›

Kimball said, "Wait here, Amanda."

I walked him back inside and introduced him to the duty guard, who remembered him from earlier attempts to see Jeff. I was heading outside to sit with Amanda, when I ran into the guard I had talked to in the diner. Prison guards, who had loomed large in my days at Leavenworth, were not my favorite people, but this man's lament about overtime keeping him from a day in the woods had struck a chord.

"Hey, buddy. Are you taking that real estate course?"

"Matter of fact, yeah. Went over to UConn. Signed up for a night class, starting in July."

"All right!"

"I'm scared stupid. I haven't learned something new since high school."

"Good luck with it."

"I feel lucky just doing it. So your kid confessed."

"I couldn't believe it."

"You couldn't believe. You should have seen the state's attorney. Came in Sunday morning, tearing his hair like a winter cat stripping down for summer."

"Were you surprised?"

"What do you mean?"

"When Kimball confessed?"

"Well, I would have been, except for one thing."

"What was that."

"I been here so long nothing surprises me."

"Why would you have been surprised if you hadn't been here so long?"

"I don't know. Just talking. But you get so many people like him in here. Young ones, mostly. They think they're invisible. Like they get their license suspended for DUI, right? And their vehicle impounded. Right? So what happens, the troopers pull over a guy doing sixty miles an hour in a thirty zone and who is it? The guy with the license suspended who's somehow got his paws on another vehicle that he puts old plates on without a current marker. And he's doing sixty in a thirty. They haul him in here for driving under suspension, with no insurance, while transporting on the seat beside him six ounces of something that probably isn't oregano and he goes, 'What lousy luck, the troopers busted me. Man, I can't get a break.' Why's he doing sixty in a thirty?"

"You tell me."

"He thinks he's invisible. Or he's dumber than a tree stump. Same thing with this kid. Kid is telling everyone who'll listen, 'Soon as I get outta here, I'm going save the environment. I'm going to serve Earth Liberation Front.' Outta here? He's facing murder charges. He's got no clue. He thinks he's just going to walk out the door, like he's invisible?"

"So why did he confess?"

"I don't know. I think he's a little screwy. Saturday night he's bawling his eyes out. Sunday morning he's saying he did the deed."

"What set off the crying?"

"I don't know. Girlfriend, maybe. When she left he just fell apart."

"The tall, skinny girl?"

"Jennifer. Man, I thought if I was only twenty years younger and three feet taller."

I said, very casually and very carefully, "I thought they were just friends."

"You're probably right about that," said the guard. "They acted more like brother and sister, except he's not tall enough. But she made a lot of visits for just a friend. Here every day."

"Did you let them meet in the interview room?"

"No! Course. Not. There was glass between them."

"What did they talk about?"

"No idea. But man was she intense. You could feel it coming over her like electricity. He'd hunker up to argue and she'd just bore into him like a laser."

Chapter Twenty-four

Kimball was very quiet driving back to Newbury. Amanda, apparently blessed with wisdom beyond her few years, kept quiet, too. But I found myself wondering crazy thoughts. What if for some crazy reason Jeff had confessed even though he didn't do it. What if, as I had wondered—with no basis for any connection between Bruce Kimball and Billy Tiller—his father had killed Billy. For some reason. Which made no sense at all, except the thought kept running through my head. But if—then what weight of guilt was Bruce Kimball carrying? In reality, though, it had to be devastating to see his only child in prison garb. My mother claimed that it had killed my father.

Swaying and bouncing in the back seat, getting queasy, I waited for Kimball to open up, assuming it would be easier for him to talk to a stranger than his girlfriend. But when I caught his eye in the rearview mirror, he looked right through me, and we made it all the way to Newbury without a word. Only when I got out in front of my house did he say, "Thank you, Ben. I owe you a big one."

"Did it help?"

"It helped me. I don't think it helped Jeff. But it helped me."

"Any chance he'll withdraw that guilty plea?"

"None."

"What would you say if I said I still don't believe he's guilty."

Kimball snorted a sad, dry laugh. "That's not what he says. Stubborn little bastard. I felt like he was still punishing me for the divorce."

"That was nine fucking years ago," said Amanda.

"He just told me that I ripped off his mother."

"What did you say?"

"What was I going to say? Goodbye, Ben. You want some advice. Don't get married. And if you do, get your tubes tied."

Amanda flinched.

⟨⟩⟨⟩⟨⟩

I changed out of my shoes into my wood chopping boots— Raichle climbers I had long ago bought for a junk bond seminar in Aspen—backed the Fiat out of the barn and drove to Chevalley Enterprises. I borrowed a big four-wheel-drive pickup from Pink and headed north, up 7, and onto the county road where the Oldsmobile had met its end. Broken glass glittered in the sunshine at the curve I missed. I turned off onto the dirt roads that led, eventually, to the joint Audubon-EPA Federal Marshland Restoration Project formerly known as the Jervis Dump.

The yellow D-7R I had last seen in the River End's parking lot was snorting up an immense hill of detritus that did not bear thinking about. I drove past a trailer that housed a field office, waved to the professors and grad students gathered around a trough in which they seemed to be sorting things, and kept driving as if I belonged there. At the foot of the hill, I got out and waved to Jennifer, who was descending toward me at a pretty good clip.

I backed away, fearing I would have to return Pink's truck in a sack. She veered aside at the last moment and clanked to a dusty stop. "Don't worry," she yelled. "I wouldn't run you over."

"I was less concerned by your intention than your ability. Getting pretty good at it, aren't you?"

"It's easy with the joystick." She jumped down from the machine and sauntered to me. "What's up? What are you doing here?"

"I saw Jeff. You heard he confessed?"

Her smile went out. "I know."

"I was shocked."

"I wasn't. I knew he would do it."

"Do what? Kill a man?"

"I didn't mean that. I meant confess."

"The poor kid is going to spend the rest of his life in prison."

"But look what he's doing."

"What's that?"

"He's standing up for truly important ideas, Ben."

"Is that what he meant when he kept asking how could he serve?"

"He will use the trial to convince everyone to join the movement."

"And then he'll go to prison. Or maybe get executed."

"But he will do so much good."

"Easy for you to say. You're not going to prison."

"Maybe I am."

"What are you talking about?"

"I think I'm going to turn myself in."

"For what?"

"The SUV fire. We'll have two trials."

"Oh, good God," I said. She sounded as benighted as the prisoners of my Plainfield jailer friend who acted as if they were invisible.

"People need heroes. We'll stand trial together. Every reporter in the world will come to Connecticut to publicize our trials."

"They're not going to try you together."

"No. Two separate trials will draw more attention."

"Jennifer, did you actually set that fire?"

"Can I trust you?"

"No. You can't. You can't trust anybody when you talk crazy. It'll come back at you. But do me a favor and try to think about the consequences of what you're doing. No one was hurt at that fire. But if you confess, you're going to prison for a long time.

They'll get you on Federal charges. They'll get you on terrorism charges."

"Everyone will see."

"The trial will be old news before you know it. Ask yourself what the hell can you do to change things when you're in a cage."

"Jeff's in a cage."

"Did you put him there?"

She looked suddenly very, very young.

"You did, didn't you? You talked him into confessing so he can stand on a soap box at his sentencing. How long do you think that soap box will last?"

"With blogs and the internet, it will last forever."

"I don't doubt the blogs will last forever. But who will read them, in a year? Other than Jeff in his cell. And you in yours. If they allow you access to computers."

"Every movement needs martyrs."

"Name one since Jesus Christ who's made a difference."

I could have named a few. She could not, and it clearly made her uncomfortable.

"'Martyr' is Jeff's word. He says if no one listens at his trial, at least he'll be a martyr."

"Oh good. A fallback position for a fall guy."

"Jeff's not a fall guy," she said, fiercely. "He believes. He's committed. He's a hero, Ben. He'll be a hero."

"His word or yours?"

Her chin came up. "Mine. I gave it to him when he needed strength."

"What are you going to give him a year from now?"

"Who knows where we'll be a year from now."

"If he stands by that fucking confession, he'll be in prison. If you confess, you'll be in prison, too. That is where you will be a year from now."

"Then I'll be a hero, too."

"Jennifer." I grabbed her hand and did not let her pull away. "I believe that both of you are heroes in your own hearts. I believe you are brave. I believe you are committed. But I do not believe for an instant that either of you has any idea of what you're getting into. Or what the cost will be."

"The earth is burning up. Now is no time to count the cost."

It was as dismal as talking to a suicide bomber who had somehow managed to step so far out of her own body that she couldn't imagine ceasing to live and breathe. Virgins awaited virgins.

"Let me quote Jeff's lawyer on the subject of a reduced sentence of 'only' fifteen years in prison. Fifteen years: 'The heart and soul of a young's man's life.'"

Ira, God bless him, had a way with words. They made her weep.

"You can change the gender if that's not personal enough."

She cried harder, shaking her head. "You're ruining everything."

"Do me one favor."

"Why?"

"So you can thank me a year from now. Will you do me that favor?"

"What?"

"Do nothing until next week. No confessions. No statements. No graffiti. No blogs. No fires. Just keep on restoring this marsh and stay out of the picture."

"While you try to change Jeff's mind?" she asked bitterly.

"I promise you that I won't waste one minute of my time trying to change Jeff's mind."

⟨⟩⟨⟩⟨⟩

Billy Tiller had constructed a slab-sided commercial building on Church Hill Road, painted it "colonial yellow," and installed in it a branch of an out-of-town bank, a massage therapist, a CPA, my friend Mike's Allstate insurance office, a tanning salon, and a lawyer—Attorney Owen Woodward. A chandelier hung in the lobby to distract the visitor from the creaking stairs and the Luan plywood doors. I opened Attorney Woodward's and told his receptionist, a woman I had never seen before, that I would like to speak to him. She went into the inner office, while I examined Woodward's splendid collection of vintage U.S. Marine recruiting posters. Two were excellent digital reproductions. One, from the 1930s, was the real deal, expertly mounted.

The woman returned. "He's tied up, Mr. Abbott. Why don't you come back tomorrow afternoon. He might have some time then."

I stepped around her, pushed through the interior door, closed it, leaned against it to keep her out, and said to Woodward, who rose from his desk in a defensive crouch, "Billy had no relatives. No one to complain when you stole his company."

Chapter Twenty-five

Thanks to Jeff's father and thanks to Defense Attorney Roth, I had wasted my time trying to raise doubt by looking for Billy's enemies. Employed to throw sand in the face of the charging bull, I had caught an eyeful myself. I should have looked for his friends.

First stop, Total Landscape's lawyer, Owen Woodward.

"Stole?" he echoed indignantly. "Stole Mr. Tiller's company? Where did you get that idea?"

"Total Landscape is a Connecticut corporation. Connecticut corporations are required to register their principals with the Secretary of State. It's in the public record. Before you moved to Newbury, Billy Tiller was the sole principal. After you moved to town, you added your name."

"So what? Mr. Tiller asked me aboard and I came. Between you and me, it was mostly for tax purposes."

"But a couple of months later you removed Billy's name and replaced it with Caroline Edwards'."

"Look, Abbott. It's no secret that Mr. Tiller had potential liabilities owing to certain—overzealous—state investigations into his business practices. Ultimately, he would have prevailed, but we made a decision to limit our exposure."

It was my turn to echo and I did, astonished. "Exposure? Billy was the one exposed. He suddenly owned nothing. What if you and Mrs. Edwards decided to take the company south?"

Woodward smiled. "I suspect that Mr. Edwards would have objected."

"Was it your idea to put his house in the company name?"

"I think we've had enough conversation on this subject."

"That left him with absolutely nothing. Not even his own home."

"Nothing he had his name on, true. That was the idea, for the reasons I stated."

"Did you pay him?"

Woodward smiled again, but this time like a man on high ground. "Of course we paid him. Had we not, and had the state of Connecticut prevailed and sought monetary restitution, it could have been judged a fraudulent transfer of assets."

"With what? Based on the house alone that's a ton of money."

"None of your business."

"Where did the money go?"

"Where Mr. Tiller put the money would have been between Mr. Tiller and the State of Connecticut. In the unlikely event those investigations went against him."

"I was told that those investigations were no longer a threat."

"Then your informant knows something—" He stopped, about to say, I was sure, "Something I don't know." Instead he amended it to, "something that would have made Mr. Tiller happy, had he not been murdered by the lunatic who confessed the crime."

"Did he start complaining?"

"Complaining about what?"

"Losing control of his company?"

"Not to me."

"Or about being forced to rent like a tenant in his dream house."

"He lived rent free. A perk of his terms of employment."

"So he was back to being an employee? He must have hated that. That must have really gnawed at him. Is that why he had to be killed?"

"Jesus, Abbott, you are certifiable."

"No, Billy was certifiable to let you do this to him."

Woodward picked up his telephone. "If you don't leave I will call the State Police."

"His name is Trooper Moody. We've known each other forever."

One friend down. Four to go.

◇◇◇

For self-preservation, lawyers keep close track of judges' habits, attitudes, and reputation. I could ask my pal Tim Hall about Judge Clarke. Or I could ask prickly old Ira Roth, who had been practicing since Connecticut's penal code was chiseled from stone. I chose Ira.

"What can you tell me about Judge Clarke?"

"Which Judge Clarke?"

"Superior Court. How many Judge Clarkes are there?"

"One judge, two robes. Back in the late nineties he was in family court. Returned to private life. Then came back and ended up in Superior Court. What do you want to know?"

"Does he know how to drive a bulldozer?"

Ira laughed. "For crissake, Ben, let it go."

"Just dotting i's, Ira. Does Judge Clarke know how to drive a bulldozer?"

"I doubt he ever got his hands dirty. Working, that is. He was a seminary student who switched to law."

"Ever hear anything about him being bent?"

Ira swiveled a hand in the air. "You've heard the same rumors I have."

"True?"

"Could be. Or the Land Conservancy mob could be sore losers. Fact is, I've heard of no complaint addressed by the Judicial Review Council. And none has ever gone to an open hearing. Just so you understand what that means, the Judicial Review Council does not fuck around."

I was half way out the door when I turned back. Ira was already hitting his speed dial. "Wait a minute, Ira. Doesn't Family Court hear divorce cases?"

⟨⟩⟨⟩⟨⟩

I telephoned Bruce Kimball in his New York office. I was told he was busy. I left my cell number. When he had not called back in a half hour, I called again. And again in fifteen. This time the secretary put me through.

I said, "You told me that you owe me. I'm calling in my marker."

"Oh yeah?"

"It could get expensive."

"How much?" he asked coldly.

"You'd know better than me."

"I don't know what that means."

I said, "Not on the telephone."

"Yeah, well, why don't you give me a call next time you're in New York?"

"I'm on the sidewalk in front of the Old Town. The bartender is guarding my beer." The stained glass and old wood joint on Eighteenth Street, half a block from Joey Girl, hadn't changed since I had worked on the Street. "Shall I come up?"

Kimball said, "I'll come down."

He walked in so fast his jacket was flying, shot a look around, spotted me down the long bar, and hurried over, saying, "I haven't been in here since I was your age."

"I haven't been here since I was Jeff's age."

The bartender ambled over. Kimball ordered a Diet Coke. "Okay," he asked, "how much?"

"Before we get to that, let me ask you something: What do Bruce Kimball and Billy Tiller have in common?"

"What are you talking about?"

"Beyond you having a son charged with killing him?"

Kimball turned around and started to walk away.

"Sweetheart divorce," I called after him.

He stopped. Turned around. Came back. "What the hell is that supposed to mean?"

"You both had your divorces adjudicated in Connecticut Family Court presided over by Judge Gary Clarke. You both came out of it with a hell of a lot more than your ex-wives."

"So what?"

"Here are two guys who each bribed the same judge. One of them gets killed. By the other guy's son? It makes no sense."

"You're right about that."

"But you both bought your settlements, which means you were both in bed with a crooked judge who might one day be spooked into flipping you."

"That's a lot of big ifs."

"Only question is, who gets flipped first."

"Abbott, you are a raving lunatic."

"You won't flip anybody, because you aren't in trouble—at least as far as I know. Billy was the one in trouble. Maybe he happened to mention to his bribee—Judge Clarke—gee I'm really in trouble, and the bribee—Judge Clarke—panicked and moaned to you, gee I'm really in trouble because Billy Tiller is in trouble. Then you could see an awful problem coming at you. Billy gets nailed for one of his developer scams. Billy tries to save himself—or reduce his jail time—by naming Judge Clarke, then Judge Clarke tries to save himself—or reduce his jail time—by naming a big shot businessman who got a sweetheart divorce."

"Statute of limitations."

"Not for bribing a public official in Connecticut. And let's not forget more recent events involving the rap star with the new career. You call me a raving lunatic. But you never told me that you already knew the judge from his family court days. And you never told me you knew how to operate a bulldozer."

"I haven't run a machine for twenty-five years."

"Even if it is not like riding a bicycle, I'm equally drawn to the fact that the gentlemen guarding your party Saturday can't be the only bouncers a man in your business knows—only the most civilized."

"I don't know what you are talking about."

"You, more than most people, have access to the kind of bulldozer operator who wouldn't mind killing Billy Tiller for a price."

"You know what I think?"

"I wish I did."

"I think you've done your homework. I think you've made some very intriguing connections that appear damaging to me and my reputation. I think you have found an excellent way to jack up your price. How fucking much?"

"I don't know. I never bribed a judge before."

He looked at me sharply. "Judge? What are you talking about? I thought you want money."

"I want you to spend your money on getting me access to that crooked judge."

"Wait a minute. What's all this about me killing Billy Tiller?"

"Did you?"

Kimball rubbed his face. "Everything you insinuate could be true."

"But?"

"Ask yourself this. Would I let my son—a kid I've already damaged, possibly beyond repair, by escaping his mother to make myself a new life—would I let that child go to prison for me? Don't answer. Think about it."

"I honestly don't know."

"Don't answer—Just tell me what the fuck do you want from Judge Clarke?"

I watched Kimball's eyes as I said, "A hour of his time and some honest answers."

Kimball actually smiled and I had to remind myself that he could turn the charm on and off like a faucet. "Honest answers? From Judge Clarke? That could get expensive."

"As I warned you it would. Can you do it?"

"Are you saying he has something to do with Jeff's situation?"

"I'm saying I don't believe Jeff. I think he's grandstanding with some warped idea to turn himself into a living soap box for ELF."

"That would be really stupid."

"But not surprising."

"No," said Kimball. "Not surprising."

"I need to interview the judge."

"Why?"

"Because he was connected to Billy Tiller. I've talked to you. I've heard your story. I should talk to him. You're not afraid of what he'll tell me, are you?"

Kimball neither shook his head nor nodded. He just said, "I'll see what I can do."

"Let me make a suggestion."

"What?"

"It would be best if he would meet me in his chambers. That way he'll know I've gone through the metal detectors. He'll know that I'm not trying to trap him with a recording wire. You should tell him that. Now that Billy's dead, the judge is probably not afraid to talk. For enough money. Which I imagine he is generally short of."

"Always," Kimball said grimly. "I'll get back to you."

<>< ><>

"I think I owe you a commission," I told Caroline Edwards when she answered her telephone.

"I'll take it. But what for?"

"Or at least a finder's fee."

"I'll take that too, but I still don't know why."

"If you would have lunch with me at the Drover, I'll explain."

There was a pause. "Are you inviting Edward, too?"

"No. But the only place more public than lunch at the Drover would be a picnic under the flagpole. Should I ask Edward for permission?"

"I'll get my own permission, thank you very much."

"One o'clock?"

One o'clock it was. At a window table in the front room. In full view of the foyer, the front desk, the bartender, two harried waitresses, a cabal of mortgage brokers guzzling wine, two under-paid officers of Newbury Savings Bank glowering enviously at them from the next table, numerous Main Street matrons—whose cheeks I stopped to kiss as I walked in in a blazer and tie—and some McMansion moms, whom I didn't know, but smiled back at.

Caroline was late. She rushed in, flustered and apologizing. "I'm so sorry. I couldn't find my other shoe."

"I beg pardon?"

"It was way in the back of the closet. We don't go out much. I mean Edward goes out, lots, on business, but I'm much happier at home. So I'm really sorry. I'm late."

"If you sit down, then I'll be able to sit down, too."

She sat and smoothed the tablecloth with her fingers. If she wasn't married, and if I didn't intend to ask some very rough questions, I would have told her that she looked absolutely lovely. Which she did, despite hair askew and a flushed cheek. She inspected the flowers on the table—roses from the Drover's ancient garden, which Anne Marie was restoring—and that seemed to calm her.

"Would you like a drink?"

"Way too early for me."

I ordered ice tea for both of us and picked up a menu.

"What's up, Ben? You were way too mysterious on the phone."

I said, "This is hard. Because I like you very much—I'm not making a pass. I know you're married. But I like you. Connie told me I would."

"I'm waiting for the but. What is hard?"

"The 'commission' I 'owe' you would be on the commission I earned for selling Billy Tiller's house."

The lady would be tough across the poker table.

"Yes," she said. "Edward told me you had sold it. Quite remarkable, on the market less than a week."

"I got lucky. A couple of very nice flakes who had no clue what they wanted fell in love with it."

"It is a unique house," said Caroline.

"So is the garden."

"Not unique, strictly speaking. It's patterned after mine."

"Yes," I said. "Though I didn't realize it at first. Only after it was weeded did I see the similarity."

"Almost a copy. Structures at either end connected by walls. Scaled down." She could have been sitting on four aces or a four flush and I hadn't a clue which, especially when she said, "So why are we having lunch?"

"The garden cinched the deal."

"Well, it's like my garden, but I don't follow."

"Not only your design. It was weeded so beautifully."

She looked me straight in the eye and said, "Not beautifully, Ben. Lovingly."

"I give up," I said. "You're an absolute master. I have no clue what was going on."

"Well, it wasn't what you thought."

"Can I ask what it was?"

"An infatuation experienced by a lonely man."

She looked out the window and watched cars go by on Main Street. I watched her eye trace the gardens across the street and settle on something. I couldn't see what unless I turned around, but I suspected it was the hints of color through Connie's fence.

"And an unfortunate kindness on my part. Which only made it worse."

She finally looked down at the table, saw the ice tea that had arrived without either of us noticing, and looked up at me.

"I was never considered attractive until I was sometime in my thirties. When the change occurred it was absolutely thrilling. It might not make up for all the adolescent years of feeling plain. But it is a kick. You walked into my house with Connie's plant and I could see in every gesture and expression that you would give anything to jump my bones."

"You should see me when I'm not subtle."

She did not hear me.

"I hadn't yet realized the change a few years ago when Billy first walked into my house. It would never have occurred to me that he would see me as anything other than Edward's plump, dowdy wife. So it never occurred to me when I befriended the poor, lonely man, that he would fall in love with me. That he would drive Edward absolutely nuts."

Nuts enough to spray Main Street with gunfire. Did she know it was him who had shot Billy? Did she know he had told me?

"Where did that leave you?"

"Destroyed by guilt and remorse."

At that she stopped talking. She looked out the window, looked back at me, looked out the window again, and I believe that if I hadn't prompted her, she would have eaten an entire lunch without another word.

"I met you the day of the funeral. You seemed…"

"Dry-eyed?"

"Unmoved." Not a woman who had lost her lover. E. Eddie Edwards was right that they had broken it off a year ago when he shot Billy.

"I'd had time to get over it. Though I was surprisingly upset the day he was killed. I sort of wanted to go to the funeral, but I knew it would kill Edward, so I brought a flower to the funeral home. Probably more for me than poor Billy."

"Are you aware that you are registered as a principal of Total Landscape Corporation."

She looked puzzled, then irritated. "Of course. I sign papers all the time."

"Did Billy know that your name was added?"

"I don't know. Probably not."

"What kind of papers do you sign?"

"Whatever Edward asks."

"Do you ever worry it could put you at risk?"

"Of course not," she said, clearly annoyed. "Edward would not do anything to hurt me. He loves me."

She told a great story. I believed her so totally that I wondered if I shouldn't. Three down? Two friends to go? I did not know.

We parted stiffly after lunch.

⟨⟩⟨⟩⟨⟩

I checked my messages. Bruce Kimball had left one on my cell. "His Honor will see you in his chambers at four o'clock." I looked at my watch, jumped in the Fiat, and raced south.

Chapter Twenty-six

Judge Clarke's clerk was waiting just inside the Court House metal detectors, looking at her watch. Something set off the machines and we had to wait while I removed my belt and my shoes. Two guards wanded me. Then they asked me to step behind a screen, where they frisked me thoroughly.

"Sorry I'm late. Long run in bad traffic."

"His Honor waited for you," was her cold reply.

"This security stop didn't help either."

"His Honor had me alert the judicial marshals about your graduation from Leavenworth."

"Well you can tell His Honor the only metal they found was in my teeth."

Once his door was shut and we were alone in his chambers, Judge Clarke said, "So what can I do for you, Ben?"

"You could start by canceling this speeding ticket I just got trying get here on time."

He laughed amiably. "I'm afraid not, Ben. One little indiscretion leads to another and soon one is careering down that water slide into the swamp."

Considering his history in Newbury, I thought he was pushing it a bit with the water analogies. Or was he was boasting how Billy Tiller's death had freed him from a bribery investigation.

"Sit down, Ben." He indicated the couch and we settled there, backs propped against the arms with a few feet of space between us. His chambers looked like a comfortable, book-lined law office, with decent state-purchased wooden furniture. Blinds were partially closed against the early evening sun, which was lighting the air pollution a rich shade of red. On Clarke's desk was a framed photograph of his girlfriend and her dog, and another of him with his arms around a twenty-something man and woman who were probably his kids from an earlier life.

"So what would you like to talk about?"

I said, "I don't believe that Jeff Kimball killed Billy Tiller."

"Despite his confession."

"Despite his confession."

"So your first question will be, 'Do you know how drive a bulldozer? Like the one that flattened Billy Tiller.'"

"We could start there."

"No," he said. "Never drove one of those. Then you'll ask whether I hired someone to flatten Billy with his bulldozer. My answer is no, though I am fully aware it is hard to prove a negative. But you'll ask anyway if I could somehow prove that. And I will answer, no. While noting that there is no evidence of a second operator on the bulldozer. Do you have any more questions?"

Bruce Kimball had assured me that he had forked over no more than a small down payment for Clarke to talk to me. "A long list," I said.

"Go right ahead. I've cleared my entire schedule. We can talk all night, if you like. Ask me anything you like. Did I kill Billy Tiller? No. Am I glad he's dead? Nothing personal against Billy, but yes, he had the potential to become a problem. When a man is as crooked as he was, he is eventually going to get caught for some crime and when he is caught he will do damage to his friends while attempting to save his own skin. So yes, my friend Mr. Kimball's son did me and any number of people a huge favor, inadvertently, when he killed Billy Tiller."

"You're home free?"

"Well, I always had the right to be, but now I have the reality as well. My fear was that Billy would name my name in return for a lighter sentence and that even though I did nothing wrong, I would be ruined."

"If you did nothing wrong, what could Billy say about you?"

"He could say I took bribes to overrule Newbury P&Z in his favor. I did overrule P&Z in his favor, but I didn't take bribes from him."

"Why did you rule for him?"

"I thought he had the better case."

"Why?"

"I don't remember the details right now. Is it that important?"

"You yourself just said there's a suspicion of bribery."

"No. There is no suspicion of bribery. The man who would have paid such bribes no longer exists. At least in bodily form. I don't speak for Heaven and Hell."

"Does the same hold for your earlier service in Family Court?"

"Same situation," the judge smiled. "Dead men don't turn state's witness."

I get up from the couch and stood with the blinds behind me. "The reason I'm late is I got lost on the way down. Overshot the Court House, ended up driving around a ritzy neighborhood on the Long Island Sound. Water views to kill for. Gorgeous old houses. Beautifully kept up. I saw one that had been completely renovated, with a replica gate house added on as a kind of a guest cottage. Up in Newbury a job like that would run half a million at least. Down here, on the Gold Coast, wow. Almost incalculable unless you had a builder in the family."

"Very fucking funny, Abbott," said Judge Clarke. He stood too, moved to the center of the room and folded his arms.

I said, "The trouble with taking cash bribes is you have to launder them. The trouble with taking service bribes is that they're hard to hide. Especially from the tax man."

"Tiller is dead. He's gone. He doesn't exist."

"Lucky, lucky you. Unless the guy you hired gets in trouble, and then you're right back where you started."

"Hired? What are you talking about? Tiller's crews did the work. I didn't hire anyone."

"I meant to drive the bulldozer."

"There was no bulldozer. Well, I guess there was a backhoe to dig the cellar. Why are you staring at me?"

"I'm referring to the bulldozer that killed Billy Tiller."

Judge Clarke laughed.

"What's funny," I asked. "We're discussing the homicide of a human being."

Judge Clarke sat down at his desk, made a tent of his hands, and smiled at the imaginary contents. "I am a far simpler person than you seem to assume. Until I was forty-seven years old I behaved myself as I was supposed to. I did well in school. I went to law school. I worked for a respectable firm. I finally made partner. Nothing spectacular, but nothing to be ashamed of, either. I was married. I had children—all doing well in their own careers, thank you for asking. When I was forty-seven I had an affair with a law clerk, a young lady just out of school, who was nowhere as attractive a woman as my own wife, but deeply passionate. If you've ever been there, you know that such an experience changes the course of your life.

"Having broken one rule—the proscription against adultery— and having discovered impoverishment, thanks to an expensive divorce, it was almost logical, shall we say, to revisit, shall we say, certain other rules—thievery, bearing false witness. But only those rules. I still attend mass. I still go to confession. I am devoted to my elderly mother. And ever since I built the guest cottage for my place on the water, I do not covet my neighbor's house or any-thing in it, including his new girlfriend, who, even if she is only the thirty-nine she claims, is still nearly double the age of mine. Having confessed simple sins, Mr. Abbott, I find it very easy to look you in the eye…" He folded his hands and looked me in the eye. "…and say to you that I could not even imagine committing murder. Much less hire some miscreant to do it for me."

"Subverting the legal system is not a simple sin."

"We are discussing murder. I am not a murderer."

"Even if murder was absolutely the only way that you could protect all these revisited pleasures?"

"I got lucky when Tiller was killed. I didn't kill him. And I don't give a damn if you believe me or not because I know that I didn't do it and therefore I have nothing to fear."

"Who do you think did?"

"Sadly, my friend Kimball's son. The boy who confessed."

I said, "Your friend is paying you a bunch of money to give me a break. In some ways you knew Billy Tiller better than anybody. Who else might have experienced a 'great favor' when Billy was killed?"

"Who else did he bribe?"

"Exactly."

Clarke hesitated. Then he answered carefully. "I have no personal knowledge. But once he boasted that he had some state EPA official in his pocket. I have no idea who. He never mentioned it again."

"A state official? Wasn't the state investigating him?"

"Not about that, to my knowledge. If so, same story. And yet another reason I am in the debt of Mr. Kimball's son."

〈〉〈〉〈〉

The next day, I finally got over to Connie's. "Sorry I took so long to get back to you. I got all tied up with Kimball. Boy, you really stuck to Kimball, the other day."

"I like Mr. Kimball."

"You like Kimball?"

"He's redeemable. As I told you, he hasn't a self-conscious bone in his body. It's better for society to have new money with new ideas rather than aping their so-called betters."

"New ideas?"

"We should observe new worlds with a clear eye, not automatically decry change because we happen to fear our youth passing away."

"Anyway, sorry I'm so late getting back to you."

"Back to me for what?"

"Air guitar."

"Oh, Ben, that silly phrase. Did I say that again?"

"You told me that you remembered air guitar."

"I don't remember."

"You said you wrote it down."

"Did I? Well let's go see."

We went to her writing desk, in the bay window of her morning room. She snatched up sheet of note paper, which lay on the blotter. "Look at this. Air guitar. All right. Sit down, Ben. Sit down."

I perched on a chair originally upholstered for a small Victorian lady. Aunt Connie sat at her desk and read her notes. "Oh, yes, of course. 'Mulch without flowers is like air guitar.' I am so relieved. It makes perfect sense."

"Could you, uhm, draw the connections for me?"

"Do you remember when air guitar started?"

"Not really. You're talking about kids pretending to play an imaginary electric guitar?"

"It is the saddest thing. A young person who has never learned a skill—never had a teacher, never practiced, never drilled, never played scales, never learned a chord—jumps about strumming the air, pretending to have skills, while others with no skills applaud. I remember, now, I was talking about Samantha's boots."

"Samantha—E. Eddie's great-grandmother. You said she wore boots, like a Polish peasant."

"It's not about the boots."

"All right," I said. "Although from where I am sitting Great-grandmother Samantha and air guitar are quite a leap."

"It's about Eddie Edwards' great-grandmother."

"That's who we were talking about the other day."

"Samantha used her peasant image to great advantage. When someone came to her to buy land, she would pretend to be an ignorant old woman. But all the while she'd be worming out of them why they wanted the land. When she saw they were assembling a parcel for development, she would buy the key lots out from under them. A very clever woman. She always took the long view. She bought on both sides of the Merritt Parkway, before it was built."

"Wow. Did she leave all that to Eddie?"

"No, she gave it to the church. The priests started coming around and before she died she gave it all to the church."

"He must have loved that."

"She did the right thing. Engineer Edwards is perfectly capable of earning his own living. I mean, you wouldn't want me to leave everything to you, would you?"

"Honestly?" Inheriting her wealth was a compelling thought that had never been on the table. "I'm fine," I said. "I'm glad you're leaving the land to Newbury Forest. Protecting open space in large chunks."

"And my house?"

"I love this house. But only an entire museum staff could keep it the way you do. So leaving it to the Historical Society is a much better idea. I can always visit."

"And my money? Such as it is."

"I don't know, Connie. I mean I wouldn't do anything different if I had more of it."

"Exactly. You've got the house your mother gave you and you're perfectly capable of paying your way. The last thing I want to leave behind is a dreary trust fund child—Did I tell you that Samantha Edwards had a clever trick when she wanted to buy land? She always had an old farmer to buy for her."

"A front."

"She kept the prices low, and her competitors off balance. They never knew where she would turn up next."

"What did she give the farmer?"

"Haying rights, I'd imagine. Enough to keep him loyal."

"I wonder if E. Eddie is a chip off the old block?"

Connie said, "He seems as clever from what I've seen. Oh, Ben, I'm so glad I remembered. I hate when thoughts disappear. It's the long view that counts."

Had Evil Engineer Edwards learned the long view at the old lady's knee? He had certainly been standing close by when Billy Tiller inherited his uncle's farm.

"Ben, would you like tea?"

"Actually I think I'm going to head over to the White Birch."

"Must you?"

"I'm feeling a sudden, powerful urge."

"One of these days those rapscallions will start a gunfight and you'll be caught in a cross fire."

"Come on, Connie. They never have gunfights this early in the afternoon."

In fact, things were starting to heat up at the White Birch. My conversation with Wide Greg was interrupted, repeatedly, by thirsty customers. Sans interruptions, it went like this:

"I guess you heard what happened to the Olds."

"Tough break. That was a fine machine." High praise from a man who did not believe in more than two wheels on any one vehicle.

"I want to meet a guy named Angel."

"Come on, Ben, you don't want to get into a revenge thing."

"I just want to do business with the man."

"Can't help you."

"Greg, I just want a chance to sit down and talk to the man."

"Well, he won't want to talk to you. The man's not responsible for how an individual chooses to use his product."

"I'm not blaming him. I just want to talk."

Greg kept shaking his head. I kept talking. Finally he said, "Look, Ben. I've known you a long time."

"A very long time. Remember the first night—"

"I've known Angel a long time, too."

"So he'll believe you when you tell him you trust me."

"No way."

"Greg, I'm up against a wall. I need the man's help. I need his advice. I promise you I won't ask him to rat anybody out."

Wide Greg sighed. He shook his head some more. Then he said, "Here's what I'll do for you. I'll go to him. I'll tell him whatever you want."

I was surprised and I said so. "I didn't know you were a go-between. That's risky for a guy who owns his own legit business."

"I'm not a go-between. I run a bar. But I respect the man and I respect you. So if I expedite something to help both of you, I'm ahead of the game."

"I don't see it generating a lot of money, Greg."

"Screw money. I'll take two men owing me favors any day."

〈〉〈〉〈〉

On my way home from the White Birch I stopped at the Newbury *Clarion*. Scooter was pounding away at the computer, with an ear cocked to the police scanner.

"Scooter? Remember that cranky letter to the editor I wrote?"

Scooter kept typing. "Which one?"

"About your Billy Tiller shooting article?"

"The personal attack on my integrity?"

"That's the one."

"Including the implication that my news-gathering skill-set, as they say, was in need of an overhaul?"

"I wasn't necessarily implying that."

"And the mocking reference to the fact that this small newspaper cannot afford to maintain a 'correspondent' in Hartford, the State Capital?"

"Light-hearted humor is a gentle, effective device to capture the reader's attention."

"Yes, I do remember that cranky letter. What about it?"

"You were actually saying something very subtle in that story, weren't you?"

Scooter finally stopped typing. He hit Save and turned to me. "It only took a year for you to figure that out? Why waste your time selling houses? You should be a detective."

"I knew it! You knew something that you couldn't write. You meant that about the investigations."

"Everybody knew about the investigations. Everybody knew they were going nowhere."

"But you had some kind of an instinct that there was something else."

"A newspaperman's instinct?" Scooter asked, absolutely deadpan.

"I wouldn't go that far—Seriously, Scooter. What did you know that you couldn't write?"

"None of your business. If I can't publish it I don't talk about it."

"This is important."

"So is integrity." He turned back to his computer and cast over his shoulder, "That vertically positioned oblong in the wall is the door."

"You caught a whiff of something."

"Out!" Wide Greg could not have sounded more convincing.

"Was it bribery? A bribery investigation?"

"Goodbye."

"Something about bribing a judge?"

Scooter stopped typing again. His eyes got big. "A judge? Are you kidding? Oh, I know what you're thinking. You think I found some great story about that jerk Judge Clarke? Sorry, Ben, the *Clarion* is a just a little weekly."

"Scooter, you own the richest weekly newspaper in New England."

"Being rich is not enough, I want a Pulitzer. But I don't have the goods on Judge Clarke. I've just got some off-the-record stuff I can't use without a lot of new information."

"Were they investigating Billy bribing Clarke?"

"Not that I found out. The stuff I caught wind of was small town as small town can get. Although, let us remember that bribery is still bribery, still a serious crime."

"Was it an EPA official he bribed?"

Scooter repeated himself word for word. "I've just got some off-the-record stuff I can't use without a lot of new information."

"Is that investigation ongoing?"

"Ongoing? The briber is dead."

⟨⟩⟨⟩⟨⟩

I had learned just about all I could learn from asking questions. It was time to stop asking questions and take a chance. There was one "friend" of Billy's I hadn't talked to. At least recently. I telephoned his office.

"I think we should have another sauna."

Chapter Twenty-seven

"I don't have time for a sauna."

"I found some stuff in Billy's computer."

"Bullshit, we cleaned everything out of the house before we let Fred show it."

"You missed the laptop Billy stashed under a pallet of yellow bricks in the cellar."

After a long while, Edwards said, "What kind of stuff?"

"Sauna stuff. Not phone."

"Did you give the computer to the police?"

"Not yet."

"Shouldn't you, if it's evidence?"

"In time."

"Is it safe?"

"It's safe. Plus I burned a CD. In fact, I burned two. One for you to peruse at your leisure."

"Let me ask you one thing?"

"What?"

"Is all this to help that kid?"

"My guess is the kid will be out vandalizing SUVs by the end of the week—Name a time, name a place."

"I'm meeting the electrician at the Newbury Common job at six thirty. Meet me in the model house at six fifteen."

"Let's make it six."

⟨⟩⟨⟩⟨⟩

At two o'clock I stashed my car in Fred Franklin's barn, climbed the hill behind his flooded hay field, and followed deer paths down through the woods. I found my way into the model house through a back door. No one saw me and I saw no one. Occasionally I heard the busy, hollow thrumming of an air compressor, so I assumed carpenters were driving staples in a house deeper in the subdivision.

By four o'clock I had visited every room from the cellar to the attic and made myself comfortable in what would be the living room. Windows were installed and the outside walls sheathed. But most of the interior walls were not yet Sheetrocked, and I could see bundles of electric wiring and computer and TV cables stretching between dense stands of two-by-six studs. More wire bunched from the unfinished ceiling. Sheetrock was stacked on the plywood subfloor, along with nail boxes, oak flooring, and the thinner steel-reinforced studs that would be used to build the pockets for the sliding doors leaning against a wall. The electricians had left their usual debris of stripped insulation, box knockouts, and scrap wire.

At five the compressor stopped and a truck drove off and things got quiet. I felt under my shirt for my father's .38, which I had holstered in the small of my back. It didn't make me feel that safe. I'm hopeless with a handgun, victim of a weirdly sidearm-specific, hand-eye uncoordination. It would have been nice if Ollie had left me Gwen's sawed-off.

I stood in the living room window, watching the woods, where shadows were falling. Something flew at my face. It happened too suddenly for me to do more than flinch. A downy woodpecker banged into the glass and fell to ground below the window. It flopped weakly, but before I could tell whether its neck broken or it would wake up soon with nothing worse than a headache, there was a second flicker of motion, far more purposeful than the first. A small falcon, a taiga merlin, swooped down, snatched up the woodpecker, and carried it to the edge of the woods. Pinning the struggling woodpecker with its talons, it began ripping out the smaller bird's feathers with its curved beak.

"What an amazing example," Eddie Edwards called from behind me, "of when your number is up, your number is up."

Chapter Twenty-eight

I asked, "Where the hell did you come from?" while I searched for his reflection in the glass. Outside, the birds were gone but for a few fluffy black feathers.

"Safe room."

"What?" I was trying to locate exactly where he was before I turned around.

"This model has a safe room in the cellar so the owner can hide his family from hostage takers. Like the stars have in Hollywood."

"What hostage takers?"

"It makes people feel like celebrities."

He was speaking with the confidence of a man holding a weapon. But once again, I had underestimated him, I discovered when I turned to face him. Two weapons. I had expected the gun in his right hand, an alarmingly heavy automatic of the caliber that doesn't leave the trauma surgeons much to work with. The surprise was the curved tree saw in his left. He was, I recalled from our day in the woods, left-handed. He was wearing gloves.

"Lift your shirt."

"I'm still not wearing a wire."

"Lift it slowly."

I did. "See. No wire."

"Turn around."

I turned around. "See, no wire."

"Using only your thumb and index finger and lifting it by the grip, remove that weapon from its holster. Slowly. Good. Now throw it over there. To your right. Behind that pile of flooring."

"What if it goes off when it lands?"

"No one will hear and the flooring will block the bullet. Throw it!"

I did. It landed with a thunk and did not discharge.

I turned around. "I wondered why a former running back couldn't outrun a bulldozer. What did you do to Billy? Gut him with your saw before you ran him down?"

"Castrated."

"What did you say?"

"Partially. He was screwing my wife."

"He was not. You're using your wife. It's a story covering something else. You didn't shoot Billy over Caroline and you didn't kill him for her, either. You killed him because he was going to rat you out to the state's attorney for bribing Judge Clarke."

"That's not true." He said it so matter-of-factly I had to wonder was Scooter right.

"What is true?"

"What would you do in my position? Here's this jerk you pull up from nothing, you put a pen in his hand and say sign here. Do this. Do that. Keep your mouth shut, I'll do the talking. You'll get rich. You'll be an important man. You'll be the biggest builder in Newbury."

"You didn't pull him quite from nothing. In fact I'll bet you never gave him the time of day until he inherited his uncle's land."

"I started years before he inherited. I mean here's this petty crook who was the only heir of a bachelor uncle in poor health?"

"The long view. So you coached him away from small time thievery, tried to make him see the long view, warned him not to get caught for small stuff."

"But he did get caught for small stuff. Billy bribed a wetlands inspector. There were so many ways around the inspector, but he stuck his hand out and Billy filled it. I tried to drum it into his head. Never, never bribe low lifes. Bribe their bosses. He wouldn't listen."

"I thought it was Judge Clarke."

"Clarke was terrified that I would flip him if Billy turned me in."

"Why didn't you kill Judge Clarke? Do the entire state a favor?"

"No need. Lucky bastard comes out of this smelling like a rose. He'll be a valuable friend in the future. Everything else stops right here."

"You're forgetting Billy's laptop."

Edwards smiled. "I am willing to bet my life there is no laptop. First of all I never saw Billy use a laptop. Second, you made a stupid mistake, Ben. Your lie was too specific. There was no laptop under those bricks. I stacked them there myself while we were cleaning out the cellar."

I heard a car door slam and wondered had I just gotten luckier than I deserved.

Edwards said, as if we were gathering to discuss the details of a new subdivision, "I asked Owen Woodward to join us."

This made no sense. But Eddie took the long view. He had set me up identifying his wife's peony so I'd believe his shooting story when I connected him through my cop connections. He had "confessed" so I would not suspect him of murder. It had been a preemptive attack.

"In here, Owen! We've got company. Look who came to visit."

Owen Woodward took one look at me and got a very unpleasant look on his face. "Mr. Certifiable. What, did you catch him trespassing, Eddie? Hey, Ben, any reason why we shouldn't beat the crap out of you before we call the cops?"

I couldn't see how he fit into this.

Woodward turned to E. Eddie Edwards. "Eddie, what is—What are you doing, Eddie?"

He didn't fit into it, but the gun was more than the lawyer could process and he got a slow start. Even if he had bolted instantly it probably wouldn't have helped. Eddie Edwards was astonishingly quick. He shot Owen Woodward in the chest, had me back under the gun in a split second, bounded across the floor to where the heavy slug had thrown Woodward, and placed the saw in the dead man's hand.

"Bad blood between you two. He braced you at Town Hall. You braced him in his office, scared the hell out of his secretary. Today he threatened to cut your balls off with a tree saw. You shot him. Self-defense. Except that he was a tough ex-Marine. Even as he was dying, he got the gun away from you and shot you in the head."

"How did he get your tree saw?"

"My saw is back at my house. He must have bought this one at a tag sale. Sorry about this, Ben. I tried everything I could to keep you out of this."

"Including a car wreck."

"Anybody else would have gotten the message."

"Some message. The only reason I'm not dead is I was wearing a five-point seat belt."

He pointed the gun at my head.

I closed my eyes. I covered my ears. I backed up and kicked a trip wire of electrical cable that I had strung from the rafters, down the wall, and across the floor. The thunderclap roared through my hands and the flash seared my eyelids. For Eddie Edwards—staring down the barrel of the gun he was holding in both hands—Angel's flash grenade was much louder and brighter.

He fired his gun anyway, jerking the trigger repeatedly. But by then I was rolling across the floor and picking up the nearest reinforced steel wall stud.

Chapter Twenty-nine

Most summers in Newbury we get a brief end-of-July chill. This one arrived August 1, riding a damp, wet, east wind, and lingered. Aunt Connie said if it got any colder the birds would start migrating. When I stopped by for our Tuesday afternoon tea, I found her bundled in a sweater that smelled of mothballs.

We carried our tray into her dining room and settled at a marble tea table in the window that, last week and next week, would be open to the sweet perfume of her rose garden. She poured and stirred and after our first several sips of welcome warmth, I showed her a sheet of paper on which I had drafted a new ad for the *Clarion* and printed a photograph of a house for sale.

"This does not look like a Benjamin Abbott Realty property."

"The word got around how I sold the Tiller 'manor.' Now Fred and the others are leaning on me to handle some of theirs. I thought maybe I should give it a whirl."

"Why?"

"For one thing, I need the money to replace my car. Also, I'm taking your advice not to end up like a curmudgeonly bachelor. You know, trying to judge the new with a clear eye, and not automatically decry change."

Connie looked dubious. "Read it to me, Ben."

It had all the words. New. Unique. Custom. Colonial. Prestigious. Stunning. I mentioned "granite" twice and ended with the reassuring, "In a neighborhood of comparable homes."

"Surrounded," Connie added, "by fellow vulgarians."

"But you said—"

"I meant accept the existence of new worlds. I didn't mean encourage them."

I scanned the ad for the fifteenth time. "I'm not sure I know what I'm doing."

Connie reached for it. "Let me see that. Hmmm." She peered at me over the rim of her reading glasses. "I'm happy to see that your heart was not entirely in it. 'Grand, yet invitingly opulent'?"

She handed it back. "I feel a chill. Shall we have a fire?"

Her wood box contained dry seasoned apple and crisp kindling. One match to my ad sent orange flames soaring up the chimney.

"Did I mention," Connie said casually, "that I called on Caroline Edwards?"

"How is she doing?"

"Holding up remarkably well. Sturdy woman."

"Give her my best when you see her again—if it seems appropriate."

"Caroline made a point of saying that she holds nothing against you. More tea, dear?"

"No thanks. I've got to go. There's something I have to do."

I paused on the sidewalk outside her gate and admired my house across the street. In the gray wet light, black shutters and white clapboards shone like the gun ports of a man-of-war. The barn was empty. The secondhand horse trailer had come and gone. Down Scooter's driveway I could see grass growing in Redman's paddock.

I started up Main and passed the Yankee Drover and the flag pole. A hundred feet above Church Hill the huge summer flag was thundering. The weather vanes on the steeples all pointed north as the wind backed, still cool, but drier.

Across the street, in front of Newbury Savings, Ira Roth was deep in conversation with the region's leading real estate appraiser. Main Street was too broad for me to read their expressions, but body language said a lot: stricken client indicted for scamming the bank with inflated appraisals; grave attorney doing an excellent job of concealing his glee. Ira had one hand concernedly on the crook's elbow, and the other resting lightly on his new Bentley.

A grateful Bruce Kimball, who had sent his son—under strict probation for reduced charges of criminal mischief and impeding justice—to study environmental engineering at Montana Tech, had paid Ira handsomely. My share? The books were clear on the horse. And if I ever needed another one, Ira promised a discount. As for Redman's mascot, Tom, who had wandered back to my place from Frenchtown: no charge.

I walked past the General Store and waved to Tim Hall, who was hurrying up the outside stairs to his office. It looked like he had just had a rare, long lunch with Vicky McLachlan. Vicky was vaulting Town Hall's steps two at a time, chestnut curls flying, summer dress clinging.

I crossed the street, dodging a muddy Range Rover driven by Scooter MacKay, who leapt from it, crouched down on one knee, and carefully aimed his camera at Newbury Volunteer Hook and Ladder Company One's folding sidewalk sign. The one that read, *Volunteer Wanted—One Good Man or Woman.*

"Breaking news?" I asked.

"I'm starting a three-part special on the volunteer problem."

"That sign could be old news."

"No way. The locals are retiring and there just aren't enough of the new people willing to come out and serve. Fire Department's suffering. Ambulance. Even church. Reverend Owen told me they toss a twenty in the collection plate on Sunday, but don't raise a hand to help all week."

"Don't say I didn't warn you."

I waited until Scooter's Range Rover had careened around the flagpole. Then I picked up the volunteer-wanted sign, carried it into the firehouse, and handed it to Jay Meadows, who was emerging from underneath an elderly pumper, covered in oil.

"What are you doing with our sign?"

"I want to join."

To receive a free catalog of Poisoned Pen Press titles, please contact us in one of the following ways:

Phone: 1-800-421-3976
Facsimile: 1-480-949-1707
Email: info@poisonedpenpress.com
Website: www.poisonedpenpress.com

Poisoned Pen Press
6962 E. First Ave. Ste. 103
Scottsdale, AZ 85251